Other books by the author:

A Jealousy for Aesop (short stories)
    Swallow's Tale Press, 1988
William Eastlake: High Desert Interlocuter (criticism)
    Borgo Press, 1993
Kenward Elmslie: A Biblographical Profile
    Bamberger Books, 1993
The Works of William Eastlake (bibliography)
    Borgo Press, 1994
*Riding Some Kind of Unusual Skull Sleigh: On the
    Arts of Don Van Vliet* (music/art criticism)
    Alap Editions, 1999

Editor:
    *Routine Disruptions: Selected Poems and Lyrics
    by Kenward Elmslie*, Coffee House, 1998

The Master Tanner Heads West

W. C. Bamberger

Livingston Press
at
The University of West Alabama

Library of Congress Control Number 2004117256

Printed on acid-free paper.

Printed in the United States of America,
Publishers Graphics

Hardcover binding by: Heckman Bindery

Typesetting and page layout: David E. Smith
Proofreading: David E. Smith, Larry Cowan,
Jennifer Brown, Chris Hawkins

Cover layout and design: Joe Taylor
Cover photo: Tricia Taylor

for Aja,
and for all the Dolleys of this world.

This is a work of fiction.
You know the rest: any resemblance
to persons living or dead is coincidental.

Livingston Press is part of The University of West Alabama,
and thereby has non-profit status.
Donations are tax-deductible:
brothers and sisters, we need 'em.
Printed and Bound by Publishers' Graphics, LLC

first edition
6 5 4 3 3 2 1

The Master Tanner Heads West

The past is a foreign country;
they do things differently there.

—L.P. Hartley, *The Go-Between*

"Remember, Junior, this is the West,
Where men are men."
"That's what she likes about me
—I'm a novelty!"

—Bob Hope, *Son of Paleface*

Chapter 1

THE body of the dead sheriff lay stretched full-length on an over-turned horse trough in the tornado room of the Royal Hotel. To insure the body against corruption the hotel's cook had packed it in crumbled sourdough loaves. In the broken bread and the soft shadows thrown by the single tallow candle the body looked like a sleeper in a blanket of flocked Manila. The sheriff's arms and legs were already cooler than the dry exposed stones and rough-adzed old timbers that shored up the earth walls around him, as they had kept some of the heat the sun had baked into the sandy ground during the day, while the body had kept none. His hips had settled into the gash that had retired the trough, and a single sandstone pearl of blood had dried in the olive notch of the corner of his eye. On his chest rested a freshly whetted knife, its blade a heavy black metal badly smelted, its edges as sharp and waved as a quizzical eyebrow.

In the well-lighted room above, the investigators were pacing: sober faced men in grey vests, each a firm advocate of lynch law; able-minded frontier jurists with silver-tipped canes and gold watches. Glowering down on them all was a portrait of Chester A. Arthur. Another man had been elected president more than nine months ago, they all knew, but a new portrait had yet to arrive. Every few minutes one of the investigators would break from his pacing and cigar-chewing to lift the trapdoor and peer down at the motionless body beneath them, as if alert for some sprouting clue. When the trapdoor was dropped again, the red dust that had blown through the crevices and attached itself to the underside of the floor would float down onto the dead man's lips, adding more red to his color. He looked more alive with each drop of the trapdoor, and the men all wanted the case closed in a hurry.

In the center of this circle of men, square on a cinnamon Persian carpet, bolt upright on a Louis XIV copy chair, sat Dolley Kenninac, mother of two, and prime suspect in the death of Sheriff Saz Temiz—though none of the men in the room was sure as yet that any crime had actually been committed. The men in their brocade vests kept close eyes on Dolley, as if expecting her to somehow ascend out of their circle and pass through the ceiling. They knocked pipe or cigar ash onto the cold firedogs, then spun around to ask another impertinent question.

The hands who had brought Dolley in, who had snatched her up in a dark alley, white-eyed as a scared colt, stood just outside the locked French doors, grinning and nodding, pleased with their deed, and with their memory—how pale her skin had been; how dark the blood on her knees; the odd garment that had barely covered her; how it had felt as thin as mattress-ticking over her curves as she kicked at them. Their hats were stoved in, but they were pleased.

Outside the hotel, ranch hands stood in knots on the board walk, uncomfortably sober and aware of how the night's chill addressed their bones. The expected Saturday night fights, some passed down from father to son in a proud tradition, had died out like unfed fires at the news of the Sheriff's death, and of how the woman had been brought in. None of them knew if she was guilty of anything, but they all wished they had been part of the arresting party. Guns hung unloaded in sandy holsters, tempers were hobbled. No hand wanted to be the first to throw a spark in the tinder of the suddenly lawless night; no one wanted to miss any chance to see Dolley if she were brought out. They surrounded the hotel, not like encircling Indians, but like tumbleweeds, there only until the wind found a new direction. They talked quietly, fingered dice in their deep pockets and waited for a verdict. They chewed the fat and kept their hat brims pulled low, making a show of respect. Then one hand made a lean-to of his body, pressed his ear against the frosted glass of a high thin window, and squeezed his eyes tight shut to tune up his ears.

"What's it sound like in there?" another hand asked him, in a whisper.

"Sound like?" the first hand repeated. "Well, like 'Don't badger her.'"

"Who's defending her!" said a third hand.

"Sounds like that gooseneck cattle lawyer."

"Him. He's a man of the future, that one. Wants to look virtuous, in case elections ever get made legal out here."

The listening man took a handful of bullets out of his pocket and popped them into his mouth, like a carpenter readying nails on a roof.

There was soft laughter then the lean-to hand said, "Now she's saying it's horse blood. Somebody's saying, 'Don't bull us.' Now, 'Stop pussyfooting around,' and 'What are you fishing for?'" His words were rubbery as he talked around the bullets in his mouth.

"Why are they all talking so funny?"

"Now, you boys know I'm translating all this. Now it's, 'Snake in the grass,' real loud. Now, 'You can't outfox us.' Now like. . . . What's that mean?"

"Who said that?"

"I did."

"What the hell?" the third hand asked.

"It was the woman talking. She says that Temiz told her if you die because you can't tell what's real from what you're dreaming, then nobody's murdered you, you've murdered yourself."

Some of the hands laughed out loud, but most shook their heads, straightened their hats, and looked away.

"Do they believe her?"

"Now she's saying something about her hair, I think. . . . I hear chairs scratching now. Sounds like they're getting ready for a long think in there." The listening man stood straight again, rubbing his ear and blinking his eyes to open them.

One hand turned his palms up in silent question, but the listening man just shrugged. Then he took his pistol out of its holster and began to load the wet bullets into its chambers. A few of the other hands loaded their guns, too. One man scratched at the frosted glass that separated them from the woman who might have coaxed their sheriff to his death, as if to create a peephole, but then his arm dropped to his side and he turned his face away, too. One hand gestured up the street to where the reflection of the fire in the knacker's yard could be seen flickering up the white clapboard sides of an alley in the weak dawn light.

"Still, it's a shame he killed a good horse against that wall he imagined hitting."

THEY agreed on this much all around. Then they moved apart, began walking slowly away in different directions, glancing back over their shoulders.

Finally there was only one tall man in a box-back coat left on the dark porch. He leaned against a wide-mouth rain-barrel, looked up at the strings of stars shining through gaps in the high clouds, and hummed "Turkey in the Straw" through a slip of tissue paper wrapped around a woman's curved tortoise-shell comb.

Chapter 2

It was two weeks earlier to the day that Dolley and her husband Jarry had first set eyes on the town of Hugo. And just the day before that, they had come upon their first bison, in a low hard pan of plain cut by the seam stitch of a railroad track. There was no way of knowing how long since the animal had been killed. They had been traveling all day and had heard no train or whistle, and echoes carried for miles across the bare desert plain, up the rocky chutes and rippled chimneys of the lost water-cut canyons. But it couldn't have been much earlier, for there were only a few carrion birds perched on the shaggy mound of the dead bison. It lay on the west side of the tracks, on the red sand at the base of the gravel slope of the rail bed. On the east side of the track lay the even larger black shape of a locomotive. It had torn a long scar in the earth as it skidded along on its right side. There was a kidney shaped stain where the split boiler had released its water into the sand. The engineer's compartment was half filled with sand and gravel, the red scree piled up and over the door to the firebox. It was deep enough to cover a man, but Jarry guessed the engineer and fireman had walked off into the desert after the crash.

He turned his attention to the bison, its huge long shape, like the swells of a new dark sea. For Jarry, it was like being a child again, walking through the Quebeçois woods with his father, axes in their hands, looking for the perfect blue fir on Christmas Eve. The bison's pelt would be perfect, would tell everyone just who he had come west to be.

Jarry tied the horses to a thick crop of brush on the locomotive side of the tracks. The horses rolled their eyes back and fought the reins. Even against the wind they had caught streamers of recent blood in the air. He would wait to boil the barks and ashes, attend to the cleaning out first. He knew he had only a little time before the stench spread its invitation across the desert and drew in the top of the scavenger line. An animal the size and weight of an overturned pianoforte would take a lot of work, he knew, and some improvisation. But he thought he had time and skill enough.

At the tailboard of the wagon he called softly in, "Dolley?"

The inside lacings of the wagon cover loosened and the face of his son appeared. "Père, are we there yet?" the boy asked.

"Not yet, André. Now, I need to talk to Mémère."

André pulled back inside the wagon and, after a moment, Dolley appeared. Though André was only six, his face was almost a copy of Jarry's own, the dark hair and long nose of the French Canadian side, and Dolley was a sharp contrast. Her hair was sand colored—not the red sand they were crossing now, but the color of the sand on the rough shores of the town of Providence they had left behind. Her pale blue eyes narrowed in the late afternoon light, and her prominent German nose cast a shadow across her long cheeks. When she spoke, her lips would purse almost to a kiss, then spread wider than seemed possible if she smiled. But Jarry hadn't seen her smile for some time now.

"I need you to get out our silver ladle," Jarry said.

"Our good silver?"

"Yes."

She looked beyond him, her eyes narrowed against the brightness of the afternoon. "Are we stopping now, Jarry? Isn't it early?"

"There's something here I have to attend to." He knew she couldn't

6

see across the tracks.

"What?"

"An opportunity," Jarry said. "Please, I need the ladle."

Dolley looked at Jarry, blankly, then her chin rose an inch. After a moment she turned back into the wagon. Jarry looked over his shoulder and saw more small black birds gathering. Then Dolley came and passed out the ladle. It had never been used, and its shine was brilliant in the afternoon sunlight.

"Shall I make a fire?" Dolley asked.

"Soon. But you might want to keep to the east side of the wagon."

"Why?" The light breezed stirred her boyishly short fine hair.

"Bison," Jarry said. "It's dead and I'm going to cut its head off."

Except for one eyebrow rising slightly, her expression didn't change. "All right," she said. "I'll keep André over here with me."

"You can let him play on the locomotive, if he's careful."

"There's a train station?"

"No, you can't buy any tickets here. You'll see when you look out the front. I'll finish as fast as I can. But it's a big job. And be ready to move when I'm done. We've got to get away before the big scavengers come."

"I'll be ready."

Jarry labored the rest of that afternoon, and on through the twilight. He heard André whooping and laughing, and clanging the train's bell, but he didn't disobey his mother, and stayed on the far side of the tracks. Jarry noticed when Dolley built a cooking fire, but he didn't cross back over for supper. His clothes and skin and even his hair were slick with thick blood, and so he kept to his side of the tracks and to his work. The fine silver ladle was dark with blood, too, but it had proven too small for the scraping to be done, its curve too tight to clean the top of the bone vault Jarry lay inside of, and he had broken a small spade loose from its handle for the job. He had been scraping for what must have been hours, by lantern and by candle, but the inside of the bony skull was still thick with pulpy streamers like the strings inside a jack-o-lantern. The smell that had seeped into

7

him was a weaving of brewer's yeast and cheese and the iron bite of blood and the clean fishy smell of the marrow inside the great neck bones he had cracked with smithing tongs. Sawing the head free had been an ordeal, and he had had to scrape the deep teeth clean again and again, stropping the saw against the nickel-bright top of the railroad rail at his back.

Jarry's arms were tired, the insides of his elbows achy, his shoulders cramped. He rolled over on his side, and the big skull that surrounded him from his middle ribs up rocked, and his shoulders were pinned by the sinewy throat of the opening. All the space inside the huge head seemed to evaporate. Jarry heard his own hard breathing and the sudden squawk of a carrion bird close by. He struggled to pull himself free and the candle tipped and hissed in the wet chips beneath him. The streamers brushed his face like cold bats flying past, and he could see nothing in the black. He twisted again, trying to find the broken spade, and the loose strips wound themselves around his face, stuck to it, cut off his breath, the head trying to take him where it had been sent. Jarry bent his knees and twisted, afraid that he would be suffocated by his own exertion, but then he managed to plant his knees and force himself up off the ground. He knelt there in the dark, the huge dead black head rising from his ribs like Ichabod Crane's headless horseman with its pumpkin. The air was beginning to taste foul, with his breath and the sweat of his fear.

He turned in the direction he thought led to the rail bed, and took a cautious step. He thought it was a clear path back to the tracks. One step, then two, and the third step didn't come down as low, and he knew he was on the railroad rise. He leaned forward, and nearly fell. Shuffling, his own head thickening as the air grew more foul, Jarry plodded up the gravel bank, a drunken Punch. The toe of his boot struck the rail, and he lifted his leg high, and stepped over. He didn't know what Dolley could do to help, but he hoped she would look up soon and see him, that he wouldn't collapse in the dark outside the limit of the firelight. The thought of it made him move too fast, and he stumbled against the other rail, and pitched down the opposite bank. He knew he had to keep his legs under him, and he ran to catch up to the tipping weight that was locked on his shoulders. He felt his knees begin to buckle, and heard a scream—high and girlish but not Dolley—and his lungs burned, trying to find oxygen where there was none, and blood-red blotches began to appear among the invisible wet streamers in the dark, and he pitched forward on his face.

The next thing Jarry knew, the night creatures had come. He was surrounded by yipping and growling and grunting barks. Coyotes, or even wolves, he heard sounds he knew were animals fighting in the dark, teeth tearing, and he heard the wind rising. It was strong enough now that the inside of the wagon smelled of dead meat, and then Jarry wondered how he came to be in the wagon. He propped himself up on his elbows and found that he was naked. His skin was red, but it was the red of the scrub brush and not blood, and he was wrapped in one of Dolley's patchwork quilts. The wagon rocked gently, and creaked, and Jarry knew they were moving. Outside, he could hear that the rising wind was carrying loads of grit, and he knew a sandstorm was rising.

He got to his knees in the dark wagon, and pulled a shirt out of his wooden box, and found pants and socks. He heard his baby daughter whimper in her sleep, and wondered where André was. Shivering now, he finally found his stockings—wet and smelling of strong soap—and pulled them on. When he pulled open the front flaps of the wagon cover Dolley and André turned to face him, their noses and mouths masked by bandannas against the blowing sand. "Père!" André shouted.

Jarry gave André a quick squeeze on the back of his neck, and then had the boy trade places with him. Then Jarry took the boy's bandanna and tied the wetted cloth across his own face. The sand was dancing in the moonlight, and slamming into his forehead and rasping across the wooden of the hitch and the leather of the harness. "Where are we, Dolley?" Jarry asked, as he took the reins.

"Across the tracks," she said, "still moving west. I took us this

9

way because the hills were closer. And because the wolves were coming in. I want to be miles away from them by the time it's full dark."

Jarry remembered what the train master had told them—that the thing to do in a storm was to dig in, not to lose your bearings by running, that a sandstorm, any sudden change in the weather, meant dig in. But Jarry could hear the wolves. "How did I get out of that bison?"

Dolley was half-standing now, turning to go back into the wagon with her children, the moonlight masking her eyes in long teardrop shadows. "I heard you scream inside that ugly head." So it had been his own voice; he hadn't recognized it inside that shaggy head. "And when I found you I just took you by the boots and I pulled. I stripped you clean and lifted you into the wagon, too," she said through her mask.

"How could you get me out? I was wedged in."

Dolley threw one leg over the back of the seat, and swung the other around, nimble and strong. "I guess when your breath passed out you got smaller . . . or maybe the buffalo just decided it didn't want to kill you after all," she said, and she disappeared inside the canvas.

The wind blew hard most of the night, rattling the kegs and the pans that hung on the sides of the wagon, bringing odd whimpering sounds from the old horses, who kept up their plodding step even in the worst of the rasping sand. Jarry slept in short fits, his body swaying with the wagon while his head hung loose on his shoulders. He looked back through the cover every time he woke, and every time he saw Dolley, her body spooned against André, the fullest part of her, where her thighs swelled and held her strength, turned against where the wind snaked in through the loose back laces.

At dawn the wind lessened, but the earth and sky were still both whorls of red, the light a dull red haze that was half daylight and half darkness, a color like the inside of an open throat. Ahead of him now were the hills Dolley had remembered seeing, moss green now through the blowing curtains of red. He urged the horses toward the nearest of those green islands, but suddenly the wagon was sinking down.

Finding their own escape from the winds, the horses had turned into the fan-shaped mouth of some lower level. Jarry thought it must be the entrance to some arroyo, and he gave them their heads, shielding his burning eyes with the edge of his hand against his forehead, his thumb on his temple. When the sand in the air thinned, the light around the wagon was red and slate-grey, and there were dark shadows passing overhead. Jarry lifted his eyes to find that they had descended into a slot canyon. The curved walls, hollowed rock that bowed out at his seat level then loomed back in overhead like waves about to break, were water-carved sandstone. Stretches of the walls were stained in icicles of rust red and curtains of slate-grey and black.

Jarry had seen small slot canyons before, some so closed off at their tops that they were almost tunnels in the desert floor, but he had never seen one this large, or even heard about one in any of the tall tale sessions that went on around the wagon train fires. As the wagon moved along the winding canyon passage the walls closed and opened, in shapes like fists or featureless heads thrust into the space, like something inanimate but living, like hard ridges of animal horn or knobs of bone. The rhythm of the widening and narrowing, the massive boniness of the jutting stone, made Jarry feel he had been shrunk and was now following his tired horses up the hollow spine of some great extinct Western creature.

Tumbleweeds, strangely colorless, as if only ghosts of live tumbleweeds, compact as sleeping cats, dotted the silt of the canyon floor. Jarry looked down every time the wagon's wheels crunched through one of the weeds, and he noticed that the sand at the bottom of the slot was deepening, that the wagon would soon be mired. The wind that had been rushing through the flute of the canyon was dying now, and the air above the lip was clearing to the buttermilk of a cloudy morning. The big wagon, and the smaller work wagon it pulled along behind, began to wag and slither in the chalky silt.

Then Jarry saw a kind of ramp of rubble, a hard slope where some of the wall had crumbled and loose sand had packed itself into

11

the fissures. Jarry steered the horses up the steep slope, cracking the frayed reins, hard. The horses slid and nickered and pulled. The wagon shivered like a tired man's muscles, but then they were out, out of the constricting spine and into the buttermilk day. The last of the sand was falling out of the curtains of wind. The green hills looked no closer now than they had, but now they didn't need shelter, only rest. Jarry drove the horses to the top of a small dome of bare rock, pulled them up and set the hand brake. He tied off the reins and slapped the sand out of his lap. Then he reached under the seat for his hat box.

Jarry had been leading his family west for nearly two months now, but he had stubbornly kept to the dark blue Canadian beret he had set out in, pulling its soft slack from one side to the other as the sun passed overhead. He had looked into the box days when the traveling was hard, looked at the crown with its crease like the top of a fresh loaf of bread, at the curled edges of its wide brim. But he hadn't wanted to claim to be anything he wasn't, and so had left the ball of tissue inside the big hat, and the hat inside its box. Now he took off his beret and threw it, watched it flatten and sail off into the scrub. He placed the batwing Stetson squarely on his head, and took a deep breath. He smiled. And felt the grit in the creases of his face.

Jarry climbed down from the wagon seat and wiped the faces of the horses with the clean side of his bandanna. The animals were too hot to water, their stomachs like tuned drums. They were too old for this, he knew, had known when he bought them. They belonged back where he had found them—walking an eternal left turn, power for an old farmer's machine that ground corn to meal.

Dolley was stirring inside the wagon, and Jarry knew he should help open the lacing so she could breathe clean air again. But he lingered with the horses, and looked out across the pale bare country. The land had looked the same for days: there was some waving and wind carving in the rock, some rising and falling at odd angles, but mostly the land was empty, sanded to a slate-board sameness. Even the cottonwoods grew only so tall before they flattened and spread out like smoke against an invisible ceiling. But those green hills just to the northwest made a change. That's where he would go next. Wise folks would have settled there, where there was real green to be found. There could be a town, an out-of-the-way place. Off the beaten track. He hoped so.

Because he was wondering again if he had out-witted himself. Sheering off from the wagon and cattle line he had told Dolley, "If we don't strike out and find some town off the beaten path, we might as well go back to Providence." And he had told her why: "On the beaten path there's bound to be somebody with an establishment." But the real reason for sheering off, the reason he hadn't given Dolley, had to do with what he had learned about the beaten path. That it stretched and shook itself like a big dog, shed its skin like a snake, and changed its spots; that it upended and scrambled everything on it, and even along its fringes. Providence, for sure, was shaking, changing. It had seemed to be on the very day he had at last stepped out of his apprentice's apron and opened his own shop that the town had suddenly crossed some time line, had whitewashed its shaken fences anew, and become a real city. And in a real city tanning was a ramshackle trade, a business backwater.

He had tried to ride it, to change as Providence changed, but nothing in what he had studied had taught him how. So he had felt himself being left behind, stuck as if his feet had roots. No, the beaten path wasn't for him; he couldn't shed his skin that fast. So he had taken his family west, hoping to meet his match. But, some days, he did wonder if it might not have been better to have meekly tagged along with the other torn-loose families, to have gone on to the long necklace of cities along the California coast. But everything he had heard about California, the gold strikes, the long growing seasons, the warm winds, made him afraid. It sounded like a territory that could break and run in any direction without notice. Jarry had even heard that the very ground quaked and changed its shape. His promised land would be one that stayed stock still under his feet. Where a man could draw up a plan and not have his careful lines cracked by a shaky earth.

"Are you all right in there?" Jarry called to the wagon.

"We are fine, Jarry," Dolley answered. "As always." Her voice had sounded tired the last two weeks, seemed to be growing thinner each day since they had left the train.

"Père?" André called from inside. "When is he going to jump out at us?"

"Any time now, son." Jarry gave the horses' faces one last wipe each, then walked to the back of the wagon. He straddled the slim ash tongue that reached from the undercarriage back to the set of twin wooden tanning tubs that rode on small cartwheels. Even after months empty, the tubs were acrid smelling from all the seared hair and scalded skin they had held, all the ash and bark that he had boiled in them, preferring them to the newer copper boilers some used. Jarry slapped the red dust from the gathered sail canvas before he untied the lacing. He stretched the hole big enough for André to push his face through. André saw his father's hat, and he struggled to make the opening bigger. Jarry reached in and lifted him to the ground, André touching the brim of the new hat as he was set down.

"Do you see those mountains ahead?" Jarry asked the boy. "The West just might be hiding behind those. You go keep a good eye on them."

With a slap on the seat of André's pants, Jarry sent him around the corner of the wagon where he would be in the shade. Then he leaned in over the wagon's tailboard. As his eyes adjusted to the dusky light inside, he made out Dolley's sandy hair moving, then saw her thin wrist rise to her forehead, and then the lines of her body in the pale rose and cinnabar dress. Then he could see his daughter, too. He watched as Dolley sponged Gertrude, heard the baby laugh at the coolness of the water as it ran over her round stomach. Gertrude was nearly six months old now. Dolley still breast fed her, always with a sad look in her pale blue eyes, eyes Gertrude had inherited.

Jarry turned away from his wife and daughter and walked around the wagon, into the shade where his son stood, his eyes on the distant green of the mountains. "Anything?" Jarry asked.

"Not yet, Père. But I know he's going to jump out, like you told me." Jarry knew the boy was trying to start up the game they had worked out over the weeks in the wagon, a remedy for the constant calls of "Are we there yet?"

"Any minute now," Jarry said. "I expect him any minute now."

"But his legs are tired, right Père?"

"Oh, well now, tired isn't the word for it! His legs are old and they're skinny like a praying mantis. He's going to come jumping out from behind those mountains, thinking he's going to surprise us, but . . ."

"But we're going to tan his hide!" André said, triumphant.

Jarry pushed his hat far back on his head, a gesture of his French-born father, who had tipped his hat back as a sign of concentration when considering anything from the next year's fur sales to the best place to spit. Jarry spat. He moved closer to André, and together they looked the mountains over. Long and rounded, with irregular trees and brush, the mountains looked like a group of turtles with moss on their backs.

"Can we let the herd out, Père?"

"First things first," Jarry said. He went around the wagon, setting the chocks, then took a deep brown crock out from under the seat of the wagon and pried off its sticky lid. He scooped out a few fingers of the lamb's oil and tallow blend, knelt down, and smeared it across the tops of his son's boots. While André was working the grease into his boots, Jarry cared for his own. He admired his own handiwork every time he cleaned his boots: a family of Ponderosa pines in gold thread that grew up and disappeared under his pant leg. He could still recall the feel of the long bowed leather needle against his tongue as he wetted it for each small stitch, his elbows braced on worn-out, hammered-off ladies' heels in the Providence workshop the week he had laid his plans to go West, the week Dolley had laid abed with the newborn Gertrude.

"I want to let the herd out!"

"André, let your father tend to the horses first." Dolley stood at the rear of the wagon, bareheaded in the weak sun, a blanket loosely folded over Gertrude's face. Jarry tried always to help her down from the wagon so her skirts wouldn't wind, but sometimes she would appear behind him without his help, without warning. There was a lot of strength in her thin German arms, he knew.

"The horses need rest more than anything, Dolley. If André will give them a little water—just a little, mind you—I'll let him take the herd out."

When the boy ran around the wagon to fetch the water, Jarry told Dolley, "This will be a good chance to shake everything out clean before we go any farther."

She nodded. "It is time," she said. Then, "Do you know where we are going yet, Jarry?"

"Still west, Dolley. But I thought those green mountains looked promising." He pointed, and Dolley looked them over for a long moment.

"I don't see any roads, Jarry. And I don't see any smoke. Where there's a town there's smoke." She looked back to him. "We need a town." She said it as evenly as she could. She showed none of her frustration, no anger. It was her way. She strove to be unshakable.

"Let me attend to you," Jarry said, and he dropped to his knees in front of her. Dolley put one foot forward, and Jarry knelt to it. He worked the grease deep into the crevices and folds of the leather, high onto the soft uppers that reached almost to her smooth knees. Jarry had made her boots, had tooled them for her from his last flank of vicuna as part of a complete skin wardrobe: calf dirndl and vest, gloves of skiver—bookbinder's lamb, but in the heat of the trip she had consented to wearing only the boots. "Snakes," Jarry had warned her, were everywhere in the West, and she always wore the knee-high butter-colored boots. Jarry ran the back of his fingers over the curve of her kneecap. She reached under Jarry's new hat to touch his neck, a signal that he had done enough.

Jarry stood, and spread the last of the grease over his wide belt. André came running back and pulled at Jarry's wrist. Everywhere the grease nourished their leather the family gleamed. Dolley laid Gertrude in the back of the wagon, and combed the dust from André's hair. They all took turns drinking from the pitted tin ladle.

"Can we let the herd out now?" André asked again.

Jarry looked at Dolley, who nodded. Jarry led André to the back of the tanning tubs, and they began to loosen the canvas covers. "We must look like some kind of steam engine train, coming through here pulling these behind us," Jarry said, and André laughed.

When the knots were undone, Jarry left it to the boy to untie the rest, and went back to Dolley. "Jarry," she said as he was helping her into the wagon, "I think that hat looks well on you."

Jarry tried to shrug, but his smile cracked wide open.

"Père, the herd's loose!" André called, and Jarry went to help him.

Chapter 3

From the crest of the humpback crag nearly a mile to their south, a tall man with one eye closed wearing an unbuttoned duster watched the family with growing curiosity. He watched father and son pull at the ropes and loose the canvas as if the stained wooden tub on wheels was a Christmas box. He watched as Jarry passed out the bulky shapes he untangled from the khaki canvas, shapes the boy rushed to arrange in clusters of twos and threes near the wagon. André's hands flew in circles when they were empty.

The watcher couldn't make out what the shapes were, only that some were low and some high and brambly. He couldn't see if the man in the tub had a gun close to hand, or if the woman was beautiful or plain. He checked the makeshift sundial he had made on a flat scab of hard sand, then scattered its sticks and stones like a man putting out a fire. He unrolled a thick yellow blanket on the hard red rock. He chewed his lip as his hands closed over large knurled wheels and cast turnbuckles. From his saddlebag he drew a small velvet bag, and another piece of velvet from inside that, and he dismantled his gear and wiped it clean and laid it on the blanket, occasionally lifting his eyes to the distant tanners. He laid the heavy black metal tube he had aimed at the family on the blanket, rolled the blanket around it, and secured eveything to a travois which was lashed to his horse's saddle by a curious harness. He put on his black hat, mounted his dark horse, and started slowly down the long red hill toward the dots that were the tanner, his wagon and his horses.

Jarry and André were still sorting and brushing the herd when Dolley noticed the approaching rider. She watched his body, thin as the stick a magician uses to balance plates, adjusting to the pitch and roll of the horse as it walked; a man who would never be thrown, she thought. "Jarry," she said, in a calm voice, "there's a rider coming in."

Jarry moved quickly to where Dolley was leaning out of the wagon. "Indian or white rider?" He knew her eyes were better over a distance.

"He's dressed white, but he's dragging a litter with a blanket on it, the way Indians do in your books. Someone could be hurt."

André came and stood next to Jarry's legs. "We'll have to wait and see who it is." Then he said to André, "But if I tell you 'run,' you run under the wagon and out the other side and you keep running as hard as you can. You hear?"

The desert light shimmered like water running up to the clear sky, and Jarry couldn't make out the rider's face through the heat waves. Either the rider misjudged his distance from the wagon or he was impatient to have his say, because he rode into earshot in mid-sentence.

". . . could have seen you at all, without it," the rider called. "And, yes, my interest was caught. So I'm here for a closer look." He craned his long neck to look, then settled back into his caramel-colored saddle. "At a distance all this could be taken for a mirage. Funny," he said, slowing his horse, urging it into a side-step to come side-on to the wagon, "how a man can never quite trust his eyes out here. All the emptiness narrows them, maybe." He slid down out of his saddle, and motioned toward the blanketed bundle behind his horse. "I can't understand why there aren't more of these out here. They have a hundred and one uses." He pulled off his long gloves. "As the travelling salesman said." And he smiled.

There was something of the crow in the length of the rider's face and the blue-black of his straight hair. His ears looked like the lobes had been pulled to lengthen them, and his dark eyes were set deep below a high forehead. Two deep creases centered his long nose, and another pair at the corners of his mouth marked off the round bony chin. The cords in his neck stood out when he spoke, but his voice was soft.

Jarry stood silent, wondering what to do, and Dolley prompted him. "Won't you offer our guest some refreshment, Jarry?"

Jarry was still holding a tallow crock, and he held it out toward the rider. "Care for a fingerful? For your boots?" The rider looked down at his feet. "I know how important it is on the trail to keep an eye on your leather goods." The rider took his hat off then, showing brushed-back hair with no more part than the wind might give it. He reached out and scooped some tallow.

"In England they call this 'liquoring the boots,'" the rider said.

"André," Dolley said. "I wonder if the gentleman might not also care for a drink of water." And André ran to refill the ladle. The rider nodded to Dolley. She smiled, then went back inside the wagon to tend Gertrude.

"Come into the shade to have your drink," said Jarry.

The two men and the boy squatted down in the wagon's boat-shaped shadow. The rider slowly worked the tallow into his dark boots as he looked over Jarry's herd. There were brown animals and black ones, even a few green and red birds. There were mammals three feet long, and bright birds only four inches across, on arches of twisted dun wire. Some of the herd showed yellow fangs over leathery lips; all showed claws. They were posed in mock battle, or hunting, frozen at moments of animal truth. Some stood in scraps of their natural lands, others looked marooned on their plaques pinned with brass name-plates.

"That one a badger?" the rider asked.

"Wolverine," Jarry answered. "Meaner than a badger, I'm told."

"This one I know," the rider said, reaching out a shining fingertip to point out a shell. "Salt-sea tortoise. Makes a good soup."

André reached into his pocket and pulled out a pheasant claw. "Look," he said to the rider. "If you pull the strings that come out of the foot the claw closes." André pulled the tendons and let them go, and the claw closed and opened.

The rider leaned toward André. "I once knew a man who had a big hawk's claw. He mounted it to his saddle horn and tied the strings off to one side of his bridle. Whenever the horse turned his head the man got a good soothing scratch right at the horn."

"Père says I can have a horse when I get bigger. I'll remember that."

The rider turned to Jarry. "These are all east of the Mississippi animals, aren't they?"

Jarry took off his hat and twirled it around in his hands. "They are. I tried to do a bison last night. . . ."

"A whole buffalo by yourself?"

"I just wanted the head of it. A head mount, you know? But I lost it," Jarry said. "I came too late." Jarry put his hat back on. "I'll do better the next time."

The rider shrugged. "There aren't many left now of that line. The Indians stampede what herds of them they can find off high cliffs. They hunt with gravity, you might say. A most reliable weapon. And then there are the trains, with their passenger's cars that look like porcupines." They sat quiet for a moment. "But you did a nice job on that wolverine. Good eyes. Listen, can I ask you a question?"

"My wife Dolley does the eyes. Those are really white-tail deer stock."

"Not a question about the eyes. A different question."

Jarry hesitated, remembering what he had read about the Code of the West. He had read that Westerners were honest and didn't mince about with words, but he had also read that a Westerner will preserve his private business against all comers, badged or bandannaed. Jarry wasn't sure how the two balanced out. Then he remembered a rule of thumb from his days of euchre around a barrelhead in Quebec: "When in doubt, lead a scout." A question to meet a question:

"What's your handle, stranger?" Jarry asked the rider.

"Handle?" He was still slowly working the grease into his boots. He frowned.

"What's your name? If you don't mind my asking."

"I thought I called it out as I was riding in. My name is Houston."

"Not Sam Houston, is it?"

"Randall."

"I'm Jarry Kenninac. I'm a Master Tanner. This is my son, André." Jarry turned to look at the boy, who was scraping the bird claws along his pants leg. "Though now that we are in the West—what with boys running to chaps and chewing tobacco and the rest—I suppose we should start to call him 'Andy' now. What was your question, Mr. Houston?"

"Why are you—Master Tanner or no—transporting a cartload of stuffed animals across the country? No offense meant, but just what part of the East are you from?"

"It still shows, doesn't it?" He slipped his batwing hat off again and held it low, next to his hip. "We were living in Rhode Island."

"And before that French Canada, I'd say by the sound of you."

"But I moved to Providence years ago." He put his hat back on. "I'm a citizen now, no mistake."

"Rhode Island is the one that's the smallest of them all, isn't it? You can miss the coast if a gull flies in your view."

"That's the place," Jarry said. "And if you blink you can miss all the hunters left in the state. They all want to trade in their shot for bank drafts now, and only want calendars and pictures of the President on their walls. I figure we'll be better situated here in the West. I read up on it."

"You did? And you still came?" Houston smiled, to show he was joking. "Could I have another dip of liquoring? I've still got one thirsty toe here."

"Help yourself. I brought plenty of crocks. And your answer is that these animals are my samples and my advertising. The boy likes to lift them out and stand them around. Like playhouse furniture for

22

a boy. But when I find a storefront to rent I'll set out my ring-tailed cat, my tortoise, my passenger pigeons, all the rest in the front window to show what I can do."

Houston looked off to the northwest, the way the wagon was pointed, toward the green mountains André had been watching. "There aren't any storefronts out that way," he said. "Only hides stretched over poles, and those hides aren't all buffalo and mule, either. That way lies the Indian grounds. If you're planning to go there looking for hides to tan, there's a chance of the hunter being felled by the game, if you hear my meaning." He gestured toward André, to show why he spoke in a puzzle.

Inside the wagon, Dolley began to sing a lullaby. Jarry looked off toward the mountains. "I'd appreciate it," he said in a low voice, "if you could direct me to where the white man's roads run out here. How you cowboys ever know what state you're in is beyond me."

Houston finished with the last of his boot and wiped his shining fingers on his pants cuff. "I'm not sure I qualify as a cowboy," he said, "and this territory is only thinking of becoming a state. But everybody pretty much knows their own territory out here, and sticks to it, like cobblers to their lasts, you would probably say it. It's only when you wander off into another territory that you get lost. But I can direct you to the nearest town." He looked at Jarry. "I don't know if it will suit you. It's a little stranger than some. But maybe I only say that because I live there myself, and so know it better." He shrugged and stood up. "I was headed in before I saw you."

"Out riding fence, or just scouting?"

"Neither." Houston held back his words for a moment. Western Reserve, thought Jarry. "No, I've spent the last two nights stargazing from the top of that rise to the south there."

"Stargazing?" It was Dolley. She was seated backward on the wagon seat, her legs inside, Gertrude on her lap.

"Yes, Mrs. Kenninac." Houston shifted his hat a little—but the gesture was not so much a tipping as a measure of embarrassment. "I usually use a flat roof back in Hugo, but it's being tarred."

23

"Stargazing must be an interesting pastime." Dolley's smile was the first amused one Jarry had seen from her in days.

"I feel that way," Houston said. "I can only indulge myself a few nights a week. A living must be made, and the hours the stars keep interfere with my work." Jarry noticed that Houston's talk was fancier now that he was addressing a woman. Western Charm, thought Jarry. "I'm a gambler by actual trade, you see. Night work, mostly."

"Oh? And do all poker players also gaze at the stars?"

"A gambler's life isn't confined to seven card low-hole, Ma'am. But I'm the only stargazer at the tables in this territory. I trade off nights when the weather is clear. One night I deal stud, and the next night I've got my eyes on the big and little bears."

Jarry could find nothing to say. None of the gamblers in his books had run on like Houston. The man was an artesian well of words.

"And learning to watch the stars is a lot like card playing," Houston was saying softly to Dolley, who was still rocking Gertrude. "You have to sit in one place, and watch the familiar constellations march by over and over again. You have to be familiar with every combination in the sky, so you'll know when something against the odds appears."

"Against the odds?"

"Like a comet or a new planet." Houston spread his fingers wide, miming the fan of a deal, or the expanse of the night sky. Then he walked over to the travois behind his horse. "This pig-in-a-blanket is my telescope." He patted the yellow bundle. "I bought it because of the Indian trouble we used to have." At this Dolley stopped smiling, and Houston saw. "If you want to get your toy animals packed away," he said, "we can make town in a couple of hours."

Jarry and André began packing away the raccoons and fawns and the rest in the stained tubs, as Houston talked and patted his horse's neck. "When I first came here—not this territory, but one state over—the local Indians were still rostered as 'hostiles'—which meant they had their own ideas of whose territory this was, and about what the rules should be. One day a peddler came through town, and back behind his pots and clay bread pans and blue bottles he had four of these telescopes. He claimed the Navy had planned to put them on some war ships, but that all four ships had been sunk by the Greys. This peddler offered the telescopes as a means of keeping an eye on the hostiles. And it so happened that he was throwing in a set of Navy star charts to boot. Oh, and along with that he threw in a watch fob— one side engraved with the flag, the other side with the man in the moon. He never said whether that was Navy issue or not, though."

Dolley laughed at that, and wrapped Gertrude in a light blanket.

Houston went on talking, slowly, even lazily, putting no particular emphasis on any detail over another, while Jarry finished lacing in the herd. "But I was the only buyer. The rest of the townsfolk only laughed at him. It was vanity, pride going before the fall of the hatchet."

Jarry climbed up to his seat, Dolley moving over to give him room, and swinging her legs around so she faced front. André climbed up the far side and into the back. The boy's eyes were no longer on the far off green mountains. They were locked on Houston.

As they set off, wagon and the tubs side-by-side with horse and travois, Dolley prompted Houston: "Why do you say it was vanity?"

"Vanity, because they thought they didn't need telescopes. They thought their senses were enough. It turned out sad, how most of the whites out here thought they were so superior to the reds that they couldn't admit that an Indian could catch them napping. They had read that every white ever killed by an Indian had been outnumbered. So there were ranchers who stood with the edge of their gun hands shading their eyes, making a great show of vigilance, and never saw anything until the back of their head went flying by."

"But you said the Indians are on a reservation now?" Dolley asked. And Jarry knew that she had heard everything he and Houston had said while she was inside the wagon.

"A recent turn of events. The Indians rode up to a scared patrol of cavalry one day and said they wanted a paper setting them and some territory apart from the rest of this country. A treaty was scratched out as fast the quills could be caught out of a goose."

"Do they stay up there now?"

"Mostly. The reservation is run something like a cheap boarding house. The government took down names and saw the guests to their rooms, but thinks no more about it as long as they pay their tab at the bar. But they're all always back up there by nightfall. And they light huge guard fires. Against what, no white man knows. Evil spirits, maybe."

Dolley excused herself to take Gertrude inside the wagon, and Houston rode a little farther off to avoid the dust the wheels were raising. They traveled quietly for over an hour, moving steadily southwest over low hills and hard packed sand flats, then Houston urged his horse up next to the wagon again. "The town is just beyond that next run of hills," he said, and pointed. "Two and a quarter miles."

"Any vacancies in town?"

"I wouldn't have brought you all this way if there wasn't. There's an empty store near the Royal Hotel that might suit you. It's toward the edge of things, away from the drinking and the smithy, so your children would be able to sleep nights. Also, it's got a brand new roof. Ask for Jackson Watts."

"Jackson Watts."

"And I'll be leaving you here," Houston said. He lifted up on the right side of the travois harness and the horse moved off left, into the late afternoon shadows thrown by a thick snarl of high brush.

André tapped Jarry's side. "Père, was that the West?"

Jarry looked after the dim white of Houston's duster moving through a hollow in the scraggly grove, the yellow bundle dragging behind as bright as a gold coin. "I hope not, Andy. I hope not."

Chapter 4

DOLLEY'S first view of the town of Hugo put her in mind of the turnrows of a cornfield ravaged by crows. Where strong and regular lines must once have been laid out, houses with sagging roofs, stores with corn cribs and crooked lean-tos now straddled lot lines and shoved fences aside. There were yawning gates in front of houses and the sprawls of scratch lumber pig-pens behind. From the top of the last rise before the long sickle turn into the town, which was built in a kind of shallow natural saucer about a mile wide, Dolley saw two dark scars where buildings had burned to the ground. The black ash had sifted into the sandy red earth around the burn-offs like the seepings of an ink spill. The neighboring buildings had not been repainted, and high red letters reading *Thaddeus Whitewash* were just visible, with the other words on the wall lost to dark blistering and flakes. The bristly bright-topped weeds standing out against the black of the two abandoned lots were the only beautiful things she could see in the length of the town.

Jarry coaxed his horses down the main street, one of two that ran east and west, each with an odd dog-leg turn half along. They passed a two-story building that had gone down, at a slant, into a ragged hole scooped out beneath it by a mine shaft or an underground stream.

Men with young mules were tearing off its porch, using hawsers looped around the animals and rusty iron gaffs. A calico cat on the slanted roof howled, pacing from one sloping dormer to another, but none of the men in the street tried to call it down.

Jarry reined in while the mule colts pulled the hawsers taut across the street. Old nails screeched, and Dolley had to press her lips between her chilled teeth. The porch pulled free, the roof easing down to the board walk beneath as slow as a bellows closing, and the men pulled the ears of the mules, and the mules backed up. Jarry called out to one of the men holding a mule's ear. "Can you tell me where I might find a Jackson Watts?"

"Jackson Watts? What day is this?"

"Tuesday," Jarry said.

"Thursday," Dolley said.

"If it's Tuesday, he's out of town. If it's Thursday, he'll be down at the barber shop. Three days a week is all the hair this town's got."

The barbershop was only a few buildings down. Inside, a round-faced man stood on a box behind a barber chair where another man sat with his head wrapped in a steaming white towel. A second barber chair was piled with saddlebags. There were two straightback chairs, and a tin basin that plainly served as a large spittoon. The man on the box glanced at Jarry then tapped the shoulder of the man under the towel. The second man spoke as he began to unwind: "Take the chair," he said, his voice muffled but jolly. "Even a barber has to have a trim now and again," he said as he stood up out of the chair. His large nose and high forehead were red and beaded with damp. "Now that I'm back in the land of the living I'll strop one and be right with you. A new customer deserves a fresh razor, I always say."

"Thank you," Jarry said, "but I'm not here for a shave. I'm looking for Jackson Watts."

"You're looking *at* Jackson Watts," the tall barber said as he wiped his face.

"I've heard that you have an empty store you might let out."

"I've let it out more often than my pants," Watts said. "But sit, sit.

I always think better with a razor in my hand." Jarry hesitated. "Sit, I said. I judge a man by his face, and this is how I get to know it." Watts was holding a froth-topped shaving mug as big as a stein.

Jarry sat and let himself be tilted back. The bright knocking of the shaving brush in the mug was a musical version of the sound of his team, and it made him relax. Watts looped a white cloth around Jarry's throat, fastening it behind. The barber's plump fingers smelled of talc and oil, a good smell. Even before the brush touched his face, Jarry felt cleaner than he had for months. As the hot lather warmed his face Jarry closed his eyes. Watts moved the razor swiftly and smoothly, but the fingers that held Jarry's jaw, that pulled his skin taut for the passes of the straight blade, seemed to linger, to read. It made more sense than reading the bumps on a man's head, Jarry decided. When he opened his eyes he noticed a glittering line of ornaments above the big mirror he faced. A dozen or more pairs of spurs. "Are those your spurs?" he asked Watts.

"Mine? No, I'd never spur my horse. They're old collateral. The barber who used to have this shop had a lot come in who couldn't even recall what a minted coin looked like. So he shaved them for their spurs. I just leave them hang."

"A cowboy giving up his spurs for a hot shave! That must have made them feel pretty bad."

"I think all it did was make sure they rode out slower than they rode in." Watts and the other barber laughed, and Jarry smiled. The hot soap and the soft hands on his face made him a little drowsy. The spurs shone like stars to his unfocused eyes.

Outside, Dolley watched a small boy carrying the now still roof cat by its tail. André shooed the gathering flies away from his sleeping sister.

"Where did you hear about my building?" Watts asked Jarry.

"From a man named Houston. We came upon him out in the hills."

"In the hills? I wondered where he went when the tarring started. Did he say whether he was coming back this way any time soon?"

"He led us back."

"Looking out for his favorite roof," Watts said. "He's afraid I'll tear that store down and plant a little patch of yams." Watts finished Jarry's shave, and ran his fingers down Jarry's jaw line one more time, to check for stubble or character, Jarry wasn't sure which. "Clean enough," Watts said, and he sat the chair upright. Jarry opened his eyes, but shut them again against the swirl of talc. "I've got a store, all right." He began to tick off things on his fingers: "First it was a one-room school house. Then it was a church—that didn't last long; somebody shot out all the stained-glass windows. When I happened to come by the building I sold the bell to a near-sighted cannoneer back East, and tore the belfry off the top. Thought I'd attract a more level-headed class of tenant that way. It's got a new-tarred roof and new white-washed false front. And here's a novelty, the front door even has a lock and key. Let's do business."

Watts lifted his apron over his head, and took his hat and coat off a peg. He stood close to the box so the man standing on it could help him dress for the street. When they went out the sun was low in the sky and the street was filling with a deep red light.

"It's back the way you've just come," Watts said, and he started off down the board walk.

Jarry climbed up to the seat of the wagon and Dolley reached out to touch his face. "You've had a shave!" Her face was streaked with red dust.

"It was part of the deal. It wasn't my own idea."

"I want a real bath, Jarry, and a complete change. And soon." Jarry felt ashamed of his clean, smooth face. He coaxed the horses in a half circle and followed Watts.

The empty store stood at the very end of the street, next to one of the blackened lots. "The courthouse used to stand there," Watts told them. "It had a big railed-in porch, made of the same clear pine they used for the gallows—those were set off on an apron out back. The sheriff likes them visible. Well, we had a night-hanging and the whole place went up like kindling when a crying woman dropped a lantern and threw herself into the fire."

"I never heard of a night-hanging before," Jarry said, as he helped Dolley down from the wagon.

"The sheriff favors them. He points out that there's more wrong-doers out and about in the night, and they're the ones who need the lesson most. This is the place!"

Watts' store was just as Jarry had seen in his illustrated yellow-back Westerns. The entire front of the building had been whitewashed the color of a clean bone, but the sides were fuzzy grey, bare wood that showed no sign of having ever been touched with a brush. The false front towered over the billows of the wagon. On the display window glass in small silver letters was *H. Arp—Notions.*

Watts unlocked the big door and cut the cobwebs inside with the edge of his hand to clear the way. The main room was some thirty foot square, with bare wood floors and open frame walls. Flowered wallpapers, no two strips identical, filled the spaces between studs. Watts pointed out the thicknesses of floor and joists and the absence of rain stains. There were two smaller rooms in the back, one that had been storage, and another that had been the previous renter's sleeping room. André found the back door, which opened onto a wide platform, with steps down to the sloping ground, and he ran out into the growing dark. Watts lit a lantern. Dolley stood near one of the windows Watts had pried open to change the air.

"There used to be a carpet on the floor back here, Mrs., but a stageload of salesmen on a layover snuck in here and tore it all up. I guess to make them little bags they all like to carry. Now the sheriff limits stage stops to a quarter hour. So it's safe to tack down carpet again—only now there's not enough time for a traveling salesman to sell you any!" Watts laughed at his own joke.

Dolley watched Jarry walk a small circle in the middle of the main room, his head thrown back, admiring the wooden candle-chandelier that hung suspended from a tarred rope. He was smiling, and Dolley recognized the smile. He had worn it when he had seen his first red sand, his first coyote and his first Rocky Mountain. The day he had come upstairs to her lying-in bed to tell her he had traded their business for a wagon and two horses she was sure she had looked like Jack's mother when faced with the handful of magic beans, but Jarry hadn't noticed; he had been wearing this same smile.

Dolley stood rocking Gertrude in the freshening breeze and tried to show no expression while peering into the dusty corners of the big room, and under the dead-end stairs that led to a pine patch in the ceiling, steps that now served as pantry shelves. She looked at the empty barrels that smelled of pickling and of mice, looked at the bare floor with its splinters like preying mantises, and at the window glass full of pale green bubbles. Dolley thought the building was perfect for Jarry: precisely as sound as his dream of tanning the West. She took in a deep breath and let it out through the window. She fingered the old curtains with their ladders of rot and looked at the building she had seen from a distance. The complete sign read, *Thaddeus Whitewash and Ground Pigment.*

"Mr. Watts," Jarry said while Dolley stared out the window at the last of the sunset, "I believe we can talk turkey."

"Turkey? I believe you mean business." Watts leaned his head so far to the left, like a curious bird, that a cracking came from the bones. "Most people out here go about business as sideways as a woman's compliment. No offense, Mrs. I'm glad to see a man put his hand on the table."

"I have a bank draft," Jarry said.

"Come along, then," Watts said. Then, to Dolley, "I'll see if I can't get your husband out of that draft." He laughed and cracked his neck again. A curious bird, all right, Dolley thought.

When the men were gone, Dolley stood rocking Gertrude in the long shadows of the lantern Watts had hung. From outside she could hear the scuffle and click of André throwing stones. She thought about calling him in to be with her, but she knew boys always waited better in open air, so she just held silent Gertrude tighter.

Dolley knew and didn't care for the smell of the rooms. It was more than the simple smells of unwashed stone, damp cloth, and unpainted wood. The smells of abandonment, of withdrawal, were the smells of accommodation, and so warned her to take care. Dolley knew accomodation all too well. When she had just grown into her teens her father had gone off to sea hoping to strike it rich in whale oil and had never returned. She and her mother had become the traveling wards of accommodating relatives. They had all been willing, but for those kind people to make room in their homes and their lives they had had to withdraw from some parts of their houses, even from parts of their ties with one another. No one's heart, Dolley knew, could play out emotional ties endless as thread unwinding off a bobbin. Things seen and unseen had had to be unwound out of kindness to her and her mother—"the Whitetawer women." And those emptied rooms, those hugs even, had had a cold-board comfort feel these shop rooms brought back to her. The spaces had been made for her out of kindness, perhaps even out of love, but she had declined most of the space offered her, had stayed solitary in what little room she had taken up, stayed as whole as she had been coming in. She would have preferred that everyone stay as whole as she, so there would have been no demands on her. An accommodating space is a demand, she knew. And she avoided them.

To get away from them she had moved from her native Gloucester, out of the family circle, to Providence, where an unmarried aunt with no great family feeling taught piano and elocution. Dolley had found a job painting the insides of seashells with *trompe l'oeil* patriotic scenes and rocky seascapes. Then one day at the free lending library a dark-haired boy with a thick French-Canadian accent had asked her how to pronounce "Tehachapi." And other words had followed. Dolley and her aunt had quickly come to refer to Jarry as "that stage-struck boy"— a joke, because the stage that fascinated him was the kind drawn by horses in the Wild West books and magazines he read. Jarry had been struck by the West the way others were struck by gold or by the moon.

And Dolley had felt a little sorry for him, once she had heard some of his story. He had come to the States obeying his father's last words before being hanged: "Go to Massachusetts; they kicked those

33

bastards out"—words Jarry translated in a more polite form for Dolley. His father had been hung as one of the instigators of a French speakers' uprising against the English rule. For every law that was passed to impose English ways on the wild Frenchmen, an English national was killed. Jarry had been working at his father's post in the pinelands of Quebec, scraping and stacking furs, when the soldiers came. They confiscated all the furs, "to pay for the ropes we'll use," and Jarry had come south as an apprentice to a Bavarian Master Tanner.

Dolley had allowed Jarry to accompany her on short walks because he seemed as full of himself as she wished everyone would be; so full of grudges and dreams of cowboys that he didn't have much space left over to make demands on her. And because she saw him—this Canadian hayseed who no longer spoke his rough French, but whose accent still bruised most of his words—as a success story. He had fled over a border into a strange country, and had learned what he needed to know to live there with no one to help him, and with no one in need of his help. She had hoped to learn from him how to do this. Instead, here she was, in a cold bare room, filling a space Jarry had given her, the space for a loyal wife, while he attempted his border-crossing trick yet again.

She wished he hadn't decided on this place so quickly, hadn't gone off so suddenly and left her alone on a street where buildings sank into the ground and were trussed up like Gulliver, and she felt a swipe of anger at herself for letting this bother her. Rocking Gertrude gently, she looked out one of the west side windows and saw that scaffolding barred the wide panes, divided the almost black desert into small darkening boxes.

"That laddering belongs to Houston, Mrs. The man who led you here." Jackson Watts stood alone in the store's open door, a gleaming saddlebag over one shoulder. "He's been using this roof here for his big eyeglass. The last flat roof in town, this is." He shifted his bag. "As the new tenant here, it'll be yours to tell him 'go' or 'stay,' as you please. He was good for a night-owl watchman while the place was standing empty, but with a lady inside is different. Even out here."

Dolley's shoulders felt as twisted as ropes, her back tight, and her breasts tender with milk. She felt she had been too long in a heavy, specifically female harness—years too long—and wished that Watts would go so she could sit down, even if in cobwebs, and feed Gertrude. But she smiled. "You and my husband reach an agreement, did you?"

"A very agreeable man, your husband. He'll be along as soon as all the papers are sealed. I wish him and you luck, Mrs. This has never been a town for the making of big money, not since its first mine bust, way back. Sometimes it seems we've only got one good dollar between us, and we all just pass it around. Some months I'm asleep when it's my turn so I only see it in my dreams." He laughed, patted a vest pocket, and took out a match. Squat, happy Jackson Watts' pockets bulged with twigs and pipes of all sorts, briars and churchwardens and corn cobs. He lit a short corn cob, and treated her to a few smoke rings. "And this has never been a town for the spending of big money, either. So, if you'll excuse us, my horse and I will be showing our tails to this town for a while." He touched the brim of his hat.

"You're excused, Mr. Watts," Dolley said, bowing her head slightly in imitation of Watts' quirky formality. She could see that she would have to be "a good sport" to get by in Jarry's West. Watts, his eyes twinkling like St. Nicholas himself, turned and left.

Dolley went into the back and called for André. The cobwebs Watts had torn waved in the light wind that smelled of dry grass and spaded ground. In the roughly trued walls Dolley could see again the box canyons Jarry had steered them into over and over coming through the stony maze of the mountains. Still, this was better than the closed vaulted canvas of the wagon, where the grayed light and swirling motes made her feel she was surrounded by moths. André came in grinning, out of breath and with his hands dirty and his nails split. Dolley had him bring in a bucket from the wagon and she washed the children and made them pallets of packing blankets in the bare storeroom and sang them to sleep with sea songs.

As she sang she watched the darkening sky through the window. Something was wrong with the way night fell here. Then she realized

35

what it was: the sun was setting out of sight of the window. For months she had seen darkness fall while facing the spectacle of the sunset, which glowed fire red even through overcasts. For Dolley, the differences in those sunsets, the differences in the cut-outs against the sun's circle—one night a flat horizon, the next jagged as an old saw—were a sign that all the days weren't the same after all. And that last bright red light had been a kind of marker to remind them of the way to go the next day. The room that would be her and Jarry's bed-room had only a northern window. So the blue-black sky she saw now, with its patternless cold stars over the West's emptiness, was the view she would have every night from now on. She sang her sea song a little louder, to fight the sudden chill she felt.

"Aren't you glad we came the way we did?" Jarry asked her in a whisper when he finally returned. He sat down next to her on the bare floor and took her hand. She was too tired to pull it back.

"I would like to wait until we see how much business there is before I decide how glad I am."

"There's nothing to wait for," Jarry said. He let go of her hand and pushed his hat far back on his head. "This is the West, Dolley. Where men kill things as a normal thing. This is the real West. There's not even a train station here. The spur was pulled up. It's like the town is marooned. The real West at last."

"Being marooned is good for business?" She didn't want to be too hard, so she gave him a small smile, smoothed Gertrude's fore-head, and held her hand out for Jarry to help her to her feet. She led him out into the main room, where he had pumped up a lantern so it glowed hot.

"Dolley, the people out here don't need a spur. They know what they have to do, they know they have to kill things to protect their families, kill things if they want to eat and keep their strength. And men like to show other men what they've tracked down and killed. It's the measure of a man out here. And when men sit around hot stoves and spit, they like to have a mountain lion's jaws to stare into to help them hawk up their hunting stories." As often happened, Jarry's attempts at eloquence made Dolley feel a little queasy. "That's the way it's always been in the West, and that's the way it's always going to be. I came prepared: I read all about it."

He squatted down next to the lantern and put his hands on Dolley's thighs, held them as he looked up at her, his expressions made grotesque by the long shadows across his face. "We're not going to be just merchants out here, Dolley. Not like back in the East, where business is as much bootlicking as boot building." The slight sing-song of Jarry's accent always took the hard edge off any words of anger, made them a little comic, but Dolley didn't smile. "Not here," he said. "Here a man stands on his own two feet, and respects what other men do. And I'm going to put boots on them all. We're going to be a public service, that's what."

Jarry left Dolley by the lantern and began bringing in boxes from the wagon. He stacked them by the front window, and swept away the paint chips that had fallen from the ceiling onto the display ledge. He began to unwrap a few of his smaller animals from the macaroon-baking paper Dolley had gotten for him from the baker back in Providence. Over Jarry's shoulder, up the street, Dolley saw lamps and torches being lighted. Dark horses moved across yellow windows like muscled clouds. The half moon showed bright over the far rooftops.

"There will be leather repairs," Jarry said, talking to her without looking around. "Westerners make everything out of leather. And there will be the tanning business. Really big pelts, brought down out of the mountains. Business will come. I read up, remember? The West has *always* been the place to come for a change of fortune."

Jarry put down the kit fox he had been unwrapping, and crossed to where Dolley stood by table, unwrapping plates. He sat in one of the chairs and reached out and gathered her in, wrapped his skinny arms around her hips. "We will not only make a living, we will fatten you up, too. You've grown too skinny from riding in that wagon." He squeezed the fullest part of her, pressed his cheek and one closed eye into her softness, rubbed his face against her. She knew she had grown thinner in the passage, stretched and hardened by the change of weather and the work. She knew, too, that Jarry liked her pillowy. He had revelled in her through both her pregnancies. He took great comfort from her body, and the more body, it seemed, the more comfort. For him. Because whenever he held and nuzzled her in this way she always squirmed a little, inside. The gesture, so like a child's, the weakness it showed in Jarry, affected her against her will. But she abided, never let the squirming show. She knew this was part of a woman's lot, something she couldn't escape, this giving up of strength to those who weren't strong. She gave willingly to André and Gertrude, but when Jarry came to her a feeling of being tapped like a stout sugar maple always made her want to take a step away. The instinct for self-preservation. As useless in her as in the kit fox that now stood on the ledge half out of its macaroon wrapper.

Dolley smoothed the crown of Jarry's head where his hair was growing thin. She remembered how, as a girl, she had always promised herself, the way girls with early romantic notions did then, that she would only marry a sensitive man. And Jarry was that, but sensitive in the way a compass needle is: always trembling a bit, only able to hold a true course in a calm sea, and crazed by magnetism—in his case, the magnetism of the West. She smiled to herself, noticing how words of sea and sailing, from a life she knew well but that Jarry could never have lived, fit so naturally into her thoughts about him. As when, soon after they were married, she had suddenly seen that Jarry's brave border crossing had only been a retreat before a rising tide, a retreat to a farther shore. His move south had been a voyage in search of an Antarctic—a frozen world, where he could wrap himself in furs and watch an unchanging landscape. And this move West, she knew, was another voyage with the same compass.

"Jarry, the only dead animal I've seen in this town was a cat a boy was carrying by its tail. I hope, Jarry, that you haven't come to the wrong town."

"That was a boy." Jarry said. "The men are in the mountains. Or in the desert. Where the buffalo roam. The men I came to work for don't spend all their time in town with the flour sacks and the church mice and the farmers. You should have studied." He started to wag a finger, but her expression froze his hand at his side.

So Jarry stood and crossed the room and stepped out the front door, still speaking to Dolley over his shoulder. "Do you want to know what *I* see, Dolley? I see a need for me, for us. Did you notice there are no antlers, no horns to be seen? Not over any doors. Racks of antlers should hang over every door. I read that horns mark the doors in the West the way lamb's blood marked the doors of the faithful back in the Bible."

"Jarry, come back inside."

"These people need someone to help them be the faithful, Dolley." He turned to her and patted his chest. Then he made a rolling gesture with his hands, mocking himself the French way.

"Come back in with me, Jarry," she said, and pointed at the chair he had vacated. "If people hear you they'll think you're odd."

"Not here, they won't," Jarry said, but he came in and closed the door. "Watts was telling me about some of the characters here, real colorful Western characters. He says the sheriff here, Temiz is his name, is from Turkistan, if you can believe it. And also that he keeps a woman who looks like a bird. . . ."

"How can a woman look like a bird?"

Jarry was at the stove now, opening the rawhide tie on a half sack of coffee. "I don't know that. I only know what Watts said, that she looks like a bird, and that she's supposed to be the local witch, pickpocket and saver of fingernails for spells. He said to tell you that a woman as pretty as you had better watch out where she drops her trimmings. I told him we knew how to protect you from witches."

Jarry chuckled, enjoying his story. But Dolley felt the run of a chill down her back. She knew a little something about the kind of woman who might pass over into magic. Any woman might be attracted— there were so few ways for a woman to avoid the steps laid out for her, like minuet steps chalked on a bare floor—but few finally crossed over. Jarry and her own flirtation with magic had both been parts of her first summer in Providence, the summer, too, of shell paintings.

She had studied magic, did her own bookish research into the Beyond, and had done it secretly: her aunt would have put her on the first train back to Gloucester if she had known why Dolley had taken out the wild tales of Washington Irving and his fantastic Sleepy Hollow, the tales of E.A. Poe and of Walpole, and the others she had slid into her bag while her aunt was busy trying to teach Jarry to pronounce *piñon.*

It would have meant worse for her than just the train if her aunt had known that once a week she accompanied the one woman friend she had made, a woman who affected the deepest violets in her dress, to a conjuring meeting. In her own circle the woman called herself a "witch"—a word that had at first made Dolley giggle even as she had tired to touch the magic the others conjured into the gathering room. Jarry had been useful to Dolley while she tugged at the doors of this cabinet of curiosities—he had been her cover. She had let her aunt think she enjoyed being courted by this dreamy, backward boy, thinking all the while that when she left him, when she flew away, he wouldn't feel abandoned, so full of strange ideas was he.

But those first polite séances, the table knockings and number games and crystals like soap bubbles had only been the carpenter's Gothic, the gingerbread. Inside the house of magic, waiting for her to enter, had been the witches' cauldrons: hunger for power over others, the joining with animal ways in ceremonies, the flashing insights promised in the transports of blind rutting. At the very threshold, at the last minute, Dolley in her shift and stays, her hair teased to stand out like a cat's, had been pulled back from the seductive door of the occult—literally. Like a hero in one of his yellow-back adventure yarns Jarry had glimpsed her through a badly drawn curtain, and had crashed through glass to carry her off. It had been thrilling, in an embarrassing way, to be carried off that way. But she hadn't known when to make Jarry let her down. It had taken too long for her to fill again, and Jarry had made use of the opening to marry her. A cautionary tale about half-measures, she told herself.

But here she was doing it again. She had let Jarry carry her away again, but not beside. She had been "beside" him, in the way a heart might be, for not so much as one mile in fifty. She had known many a woman to stand her ground and turn her back when her man had gone off at some odd dreamer's angle. Dolley had come, not because she believed in Jarry's dream, or because she was frightened of making her own way, but simply because there had been nothing else she had truly wanted to do with herself. A sour, puckering excuse.

"Some honest-to-God characters," Jarry was saying. "And the roof Houston likes to use for his big eyeglass is the one I've just put over our heads."

"I did hear that."

"I guess that will have to . . ." He yawned before he could finish his sentence. "I had better bed down the horses before I fall asleep standing up."

The moonlight was bright and marbled, a spill of vanilla at the horizon. The few scattered clouds were as thin as ribbon snakes. Leaving the wagon in front of the store, Jarry led the horses toward the ash-floored alley to take them to the back where the trough was. The horses were tired and Jarry was drowsy. He leaned against the big animals and spread his fingers on their cool hides to soothe his driving blisters. The moon's shape-shadows made it difficult to see into the black of the alley, but Jarry saw that there was something there, close to the wall of his store, only a yard away, standing as tall as the window ledges. Jarry tried to slow the horses, but the tired animals plodded on, carrying the lead wagon away with them. As the tanning wagon passed him, Jarry heard a sound as harsh as the wagon's smell. It was a raspy whisper, a sibilant word Jarry couldn't catch, and it came from the deeper shadow—the sound of a windy cavernous voice, a voice Washington Irving might have given his Headless Horseman.

There was a flash, a grey-white loop in the vanilla moonlight, a rope that arced above Jarry's head and hit the tanning wagon like a snake striking. The horses stopped now, their ears back. Leather creaked in the dark alley and the rope tightened, striking Jarry across the neck and throwing him to the ground. Hooves struck his back, tore his

41

collar, as a stuffed whitetail deer was dragged from the wagon and out of sight in the dark alley. From where he lay, Jarry could see the far end of the shadow of his store and saw the horseman appear, dragging the stiff deer behind. He rode straight out into the desert. Jarry got to his feet to watch, but soon the horseman was only another black patch against all the others. Then there was shooting: the sound of six shots, accompanied by six flashes mixed the red and yellow of rock candy. Someone was shooting Jarry's dead deer.

Jarry waited until the desert was dark again, then he tied the horses' reins to the back of the driver's seat—tight, so they would think they were hitched—and sat a water bucket at their feet. His head felt cold. His hat had fallen off and landed under the wagon. He would have to crawl on his hands and knees to retrieve it. He decided to leave it where it was. Then he went inside and locked the shop door.

Chapter 5

"Excuse me." The words mingled with the shop bell hung on a spring above the door. Dolley, who was soaping buckskins on the table top, looked up and smiled. "But could I interest the Mrs. in a calendar bee?"

"Mr. Houston! Please come in."

Jarry saw, with an unconscious nod of approval, that Houston didn't remove his hat—not for Dolley, nor for the simple act of passing through a man's door.

"Good morning," Houston said, and he wrinkled his nose. "Those spirits are a bit strong, aren't they?"

The sign painter, kneeling in the window display area nodded his head but didn't look around. With a steady hand he drew the long curls of the "s" in "Master Tanner," backward on the greenish surface of the window glass.

Houston stood next to Jarry and they watched the sign painter. "I realize that you are still unpacking, but as I'm sure you know, social contacts are the best door to good business." Jarry looked to see if he was being mocked, scoffed at like a greenhorn, but Houston's face had a serious set. "I've come to invite Mrs. Kenninac to attend a bee, and open a few doors. If you will permit me."

Jarry turned to Dolley. "You hear? A bee."

Dolley snapped a small buckskin, with a crack like wash to be hung on a line. "What sort of bee did you say this was?"

"A calendar bee, Mrs. Bring your writing quills, and I'll supply the cream paper as a store-warming gift."

"I don't know that bee," Jarry said. Dolley was already searching boxes for her quills and ink jar.

"That's because calendar bees are only found way out here. Away from the railroads, almost off the track of the jackass mail, even. Once a year all the ladies in town—and a few of the shopkeepers— come down to my cabin with their blank pads and we make Chinese smoked-tea and put old shirts on backward and have a calendar bee."

Jarry watched the sign painter from the corner of his eye. He was enjoying the deep brown of the wet paint, like one of his dreams spilling out onto a smooth pillow, enjoying the mingled smells of saddle soap and mineral spirits, enjoying Houston's talk, enjoying standing in the right place at long last.

"Out here we have to order a lot of things by mail," Houston was saying, as the painter, holding his brush with both hands like a man with a too-large sidearm, crossed a 't.' "But it seems that back East the calendar printers figure us all out here to have lost track of the time. When we order calendars or almanacs they try to unload old stock with New Year strips pasted crooked on their tops. Every year I get one we can trust, from an astronomical society in England. They know their stars and their days over there at Greenwich. Their calendar has the moon phases, and the correct number of days in February. And I for one wouldn't want leap year to come upon me unawares."

Jarry heard Dolley laugh at that. She came up between the two of them then, and handed Jarry her quills and ink jar. "If you two will excuse me, I'll change into something more fit for opening doors," she said.

As Dolley made her way through the tipped boxes and upended trunks to the bedroom she heard Jarry ask Houston to help him lift the tanning tubs down from their cartwheel platform. As she dressed, Dolley heard the two men horsing the wooden tubs under the back porch just outside her window. Then she smelled the sour sharpness of boiled barks drifting in. She knew it would again seep into her clean linens even past the cedar lining of her chest. She slid her leather-bibbed dirndl skirt down over her white lace blouse with ruffled cuffs, a favorite. Jarry had told her when he presented her with the leather clothing he had sewn for her that she would be responsible for making women see that leather wasn't only for men, that it could be proper and feminine looking, even alluring, if tanned and tailored with a fine hand. "Keep an eye on the underdeveloped market," he'd told her when he had presented her with a doeskin foundation garment. She was slightly more amused than insulted.

In the box where she kept this garment, Dolley kept a ribboned packet of smooth, colored-paper. She slid a few sheets inside her blouse. The paper felt cool against her skin, made her stomach flutter as she listened to the men outside her window.

"Watts tells me you've been using this roof for your spyglass."

"I have. But I understand the new order of things. Women in the house makes for a change. Even out here."

"No, I want you to use it. As much as you like. It would make us sleep easier."

"Oh?"

"Watts tells me you make a good night watchman."

"There's nothing much out here to watch for. Our Sheriff's very thorough. Though come to think of it, some of us do watch out for him."

"I saw something."

"What?"

"I didn't see it, no. But something. Or nothing. It scared the horses, and the offer stands."

Dolley walked out into the main room, past the kneeling painter who was too absorbed to notice her, and out onto the front board walk. She walked to the corner of the store and looked around. Jarry stood with his hands in his pockets, but she could see beads of sweat standing on his face. Houston leaned, at ease, against his scaffolding.

"I am ready now, Mr. Houston."

The two men moved toward her. Between them, out in the dry country, Dolley saw a bright red wagon slowly making its way toward the town. She found her quills and ink on the hitching rail where Jarry had put them.

"I'll mind the children," Jarry told her. "You be sure to tell everyone where we are."

"Where are we?"

"The old Arp place," Houston said. He offered his arm, and Dolley accepted. Jarry waved and went back inside to watch the sign painter.

"I'm sorry," Dolley said once they were out of earshot, "that my husband bothered you with those tubs." They were passing in front of the burned-out lot, and Dolley saw pages of the newspaper-sized catalogue Jarry had had printed before they left Providence. The sheets were scattered over the ashes, making almost a harlequin design against the black. But some of the pages were shredded as if torn by wild animals, and Dolley wondered what would have attacked loose papers.

"Because toting those keg tubs is harder work than lifting five cards at once?" Houston leaned to look into her face, smiled to make her smile. "It's not that I'm afraid of 'honest' labor, Mrs. Kenninac. I just have my preferences."

They walked in silence until they came to the tipped and sunken building. "How long have you lived here, Mr. Houston?"

"I've been in and out of this slit trench of a town just over four years now, Mrs. Four years ago this was a stop on a little jerkwater I used to ride from one lining track site to another, one card table to the next. I was fluent in Mandarin and poker and maritime knots, but rusty in table manners and English. Still am, I suppose."

Dolley saw that Houston was trying to impress her, but she didn't know how to react. "What," she asked, to keep him talking, "is a 'jerkwater'?"

"It's what railroaders call a train on a branch line. I worked for the railroad then, as a translator for the Chinese crews that shoveled the beds and pounded the crossties and laid the tracks. Some of the beds and banks out there have more Chinese bones than gravel in them. But when the town got a new sheriff a few years back he decided the railroad was a bad bet, and hired his own men to pull up the tracks and haul them down to the blacksmith shop. He's got a lifetime supply of horseshoe metal now. So the railroad bosses scratched this town off the roundhouse map and gave the sheriff's jurisdiction up for dead."

"It surprises me that a man like you would stay in a town cut off from the world."

"A man who moves around much is like a blister beetle. He has to store up a stock of poison in him, just to protect himself on unfamiliar ground. Keeping up that stock of poisons was poisoning me, too. So, I've been making my compass smaller. I sailed around the world, then rode across the country on rails, and now I ride a horse on a circuit of small towns in sight of the same Indian mountains. But I look up and out, too. I'm not cut off from the sky here. The railroad didn't go up there, anyway. Neither did the old tubs I sailed on."

"My father was a sailor."

"It's a big ocean," Houston said with a smile. "What's his name?"

"He was lost at sea," Dolley said.

Houston nodded. "It's a big ocean." Just ahead of them a woman was switching a chocolate-colored mule, and the mule was kicking in the staves of a rain barrel. The mule gave one last kick and the barrel split. "After I came ashore was when I was almost lost. I stayed with the railroad until I saw that I was almost as comfortable breathing the crew's joss sticks as I was fresh air. I'd quit the ships to get a job in the fresh air. There's nothing like a ship at sea to put the stink into a man's lungs for fourteen months at a time. Then there I was, getting addicted to that Chinese smoke. I admit I was tempted. Going over the line into a floating world is a lifeboat a lot of men take, have you noticed? So they don't have to face what they've made of their own."

47

They had come to the end of that stretch of board walk and had to wait for wagon traffic to clear. "This town is more my home base than a real, anchored home for me. I spend a lot of my days riding out the spoke roads, searching for the perfect poker game and uncharted stars." He shrugged. "It's not as colorful as it might sound."

"Perhaps not, but your speech certainly is." Dolley nodded to passing women. She noticed that they all wore bonnets nearly identical to the Rhode Island best she was wearing. She decided to go bareheaded and untied her strings.

"Talk is like anything else physical," Houston said. She was conscious of how intently he watched her as she folded her bonnet and tucked it into a dirndl pocket. "At least for a man. If a man goes without talk for too long he's likely to go overboard when he gets back to it. When I was a sailor, I used to go months without speaking a word of English, except to my boots in the morning. Months of sitting around waiting for a ship gone light to wander into Tangier or Shanghai. Or someplace that just smelled like Shanghai. And neither poker nor astronomy involves a lot of talk."

The alley traffic cleared and Houston stepped down into the large kidney-shaped puddle of mud made by water the mule had kicked free. "Is it true that men back East lay their coats across a mud hole?"

"I believe you're thinking of Englishmen. I'll go around, thank you."

"Wait," Houston said, raising his hands. "Do you contra dance, Mrs. Kenninac?"

"Yes, I do. Why? Does one dance at a calendar bee?"

"No, not at a calendar bee." He began to hum, and his right foot stirred in the mud. He hummed a quick-step tune, but the scale was vaguely wrong, exotic. "Here," he said, and reached up to take her right hand in his left. His warm right palm moved to the small of her back and, still humming his oddly-keyed tune, he swept her off the walk and through the air, her unheld hand folded against his chest, her legs sailing over the thin flashing skin of water, her hair flying free of its comb, making her head feel light on her neck. And then she was on her feet again, on dry clay. "I didn't get to contra dance much in Shanghai, either," Houston said, and he bent to retrieve her lost hair comb from the puddle. "We'll rinse this out," Houston said and slipped it into his pocket. Dolley felt flushed. On the walks around them women stood watching, some scowling, some smiling.

Dolley had trouble remembering what they had been talking about on the other side of the water hole. Then she did. "Chinese must have been very hard to learn," she said.

"If you think their language was hard," Houston said, "you should feel their paper. They have paper so strong they chain their prisoners with it."

Dolley touched her stomach where her soft paper rested. "Do you think me a foolish woman, Mr. Houston?"

He looked honestly surprised by the question, stopped and blinked his eyes as if trying to guess where it might have come from. "Of course not," he said. "No. But I'm serious about the Chinese paper. Hold out your pointer fingers."

Dolley stepped aside, against a storefront, and she looked into Houston's face. His eyes were steady, his face as open as a clean white plate. She could easily take a man's offered arm, or give the back of her hand to acknowledge an introduction, but individual fingers were too plainly instruments of touch. A hand is a social thing, a finger a private one. Houston waited, his eyes a soft, cat's green. Dolley held out her hands, index fingers pointed straight at him. "Ready," she said.

Houston took from an inside pocket a strip of woven green and yellow paper. He took Dolley's writing quills and put them in the paper's place. He blew a gentle puff of air over the end of the paper and it became a tube. He slid one end of the tube over one of Dolley's fingers. She felt the tube, still warm from Houston's pocket, close over her fingertip like a living thing. Then Houston guided her other finger into the other end of the tube.

"Chinese handcuffs," Houston said. He took her elbows and moved her arms apart. The paper squeezed her fingers until she felt the beat of her pulse in their sensitive tips. Women passing by stole quick looks at her hands. "Now, Mrs. Chinese outlaw, let's see you escape from me."

Dolley pulled and twisted, laughing with Houston, biting the end of her tongue as she concentrated, but the paper held her prisoner.

"Then," Houston said as he reached out a single, crooked finger, "the lawman takes a hold like this . . ." He hooked the center of the tube with his bent finger and, smiling and walking backward, he slowly drew Dolley along the wooden sidewalk. She kept moving her head from one side to the other, laughing and dropping her head to hide her smiling, red face, then lifting it again to see her captor. In the past two days this man had led her out of the desert, given her flight, loosened her hair, and placed her into bondage to him—the full history of what a man can do to a woman—and now he was taking her to his home, and she was laughing.

"Mr. Houston, let me go."

"You have fallen prey to frontier justice, Mrs. Kenninac. And it is ruthless."

"This isn't frontier justice the way it's told in Jarry's penny dreadfuls."

"What can you expect for a penny?" Houston asked.

JARRY watched the way the sign painter scrabbled around in the window space, watched the way one eye closed to let the other better gauge the plumb of a letter line. Jarry enjoyed watching work—a man painting, or a woman knitting, or even a ditch digger squaring earth with an expert hand. Jarry knew he should just watch quietly, let the man work in peace, but his excitement crept up from his arms and his chest, seemed to gather in the tips of his fingers, and the warm spot where his voice impatiently waited. "My handle's Jarry," he finally had to say. "My wife is a painter, too. She paints miniatures. She colors all the eyes for the animals I mount. I think women are special about eyes, don't you?"

"Can't say," the sign painter said.

"They can look all the way into men's eyes and babies' eyes and each other's eyes and I know they can see things, things they don't always tell us men. The eyes are supposed to be the windows of the soul."

"Windows get dirty awful fast out here," the painter said, and Jarry wondered if the man was listening to him at all. He decided to take a different tack.

"She was painting when I met her. Down in Massachusetts. At Plymouth Rock. Not eyes, though. I got her into that. She was painting panoramas and patriotic scenes on the fore-edges of books. You've seen those, probably. When you look at the edge of the pages you don't see anything, but then you cock the book a little and there's a scene on the edge?"

"I don't believe I have, no." He was finishing up now, *Master Tanner Jarry Kenninac*, reversed, in wet brown on the imperfect glass pane.

"Women who wear diamond buckles on their shoes, they buy those kinds of books when they're on vacation. When I saw Dolley's *Sundown Over the Mayflower* on a white calf *Sartor Resartus* I knew I had to have her. And she painted Plymouth Rock on the insides of sea shells, but I didn't like them so much."

The painter twisted a smelly rag around the hairs of his brush and turned to Jarry, a puzzled look on his face. "Did you say your wife paints realistic eyes?"

"Yes. Dolley is very . . ."

The painter grinned now. "And she used to paint sea-shells down by the sea shore?"

"Plymouth Rock. That's where your forefathers first landed. Mine came from . . ."

But the painter had started to laugh, softly, and then he recited,

> The law's tall Turk lurked
> Beneath the dry draw's bridge work
> Until the railroad's work was jerked

"I know someone I'm going to send to meet you two," the painter

51

said. "You should like him—he makes up his own tongue twisters. That was one of his. And I think he might be a customer for your wife, too."

"A customer? Is he a hunter, or trapper, or what?"

"Oh, he's trying to be a little of both. It's not usually all that black-and-white about who's what out here. Or about who wants what from who." He held out his open hand toward Jarry. "Me, I'm an exception."

Houston towed Dolley along the board walks to the last cross street, then down that walk to the last house, a small unpainted cabin with heavy coats of tar over all its joints. The tar rounded every corner and made the cabin look like something that had been sewn rather than carpentered. At the cabin's gate, Houston took Dolley's wrists in his hands and slowly moved her hands closer together. The paper loosened on her fingers, and he traded her back her quills for his handcuffs.

"This is it," he said. She heard a violin being played inside. "I hired the best fiddler in town to play. He only knows old tunes, but he plays them well enough."

"I like old tunes," Dolley said as they walked toward the porch. "I like *Turkey in the Straw* more than anything."

"That was requested once, and old Dewey there said he'd learn it as soon as he could mail away for the sheet music. Dewey doesn't get much contra dance work. The cigar box fiddlers get that." They went up the washed stone steps, and Houston opened his front door for her. He took off his hat and stood aside for her to enter.

Everyone in the parlor had an improvised easel in his or her lap. They were all nodding to the music played by a fiddler who sported a blond derby over his graying but still blond hair. Dolley recognized the music: a Bach ricercar, a tune that moved along in a sweet mechanical rhythm, like meshed sudsy hands on a washing board. While Houston sketched a few introductions, Dolley took stock of his furnishings. The chairs were all of a deeply polished red wood. An oriental tapestry covered an entire wall, and on the window glass there were small paintings of spiraling dragons and fish in transparent green paint. Tiny brass bells and a huge glinting sword hung from wooden knobs and painted nails, and a stack of palm-sized books stood in the center of the mantle. Food hung from the open roof timbers. Not Chinese delicacies, she was relieved to see, nothing monkey-faced or man-shaped. Simple food was hung in the air like a constellation the stomach was familiar with: deer meat and hams, ducks withered as old purses and darkened with wood smoke, baskets of berries just at eye-level fit for pinching into. Over the fire hung a coffee pot, and next to that a pot of thick white soup. A very pale woman held a spoon and leaned over the pot, her sharp nose almost touching the handle. Houston's telescope occupied one corner of the room, and his much-valued astronomical calendar hung where sunlight fell full onto it. A tobacco humidor filled with quill pens stood on a low table in the middle of the room.

Two women patted the open cushion between them and smiled at Dolley. She joined them. "What a lovely leather skirt," one of them said, and the other nodded over her drawing of a high tide on a June 28th. "I'm Marilyn," the first one said. She wore a bright flowered dress with a Mandarin collar, and had the cheekbones of a gypsy. "And this is my daughter Carla," she said, nodding toward the second, who was a tall woman with a shy smile. Over the divan where they sat a canary sang in a very small cage.

"I didn't expect to hear canary song out here," Dolley said to Marilyn. The sound reminded her of Providence parlors, of fainting couches in tapestry slip-covers and of cool breezes healthy with salt. The bird cocked its head and watched her. The thin feathers above its beak and the crusts in its cloudy eyes told Dolley it was an old bird, but its song was beautiful.

"That's the last of its kind," Marilyn said, tilting her head back, not to look up at the cage, but as if to catch more of the light coming from the window across from her. She smiled, and a small purring stirred in her throat. Then she said, "It belongs to poor Evie Bonner. Her canary and her dithering brother are her life. She's gone back home to fetch some asafetida she bagged and then forgot."

"Our sheriff gave it to her," Carla, the daughter, added, and she shook her head. "The canary, I mean."

Marilyn laughed. "His ways are mysterious. Foreign, you know." She set her pen down and laid a hand on Dolley's forearm, obviously preparing to tell what she thought was a fine tale. "This town died once, died a natural death when the mine went hollow. Then came Mr. Sheriff Saz Temiz, riding in half lost. The story is that he built a campfire in the middle of this very street, and went to sleep right in the road. When he woke the next morning, flocks of canaries came out of the trees and roosted on his arms and shoulders. One of them," she laughed, then her voice dropped to a whisper, "lit and sharpened its beak on the nail of Saz Temiz's toe—thought it was a cuttlebone! Now, those yellow birds were all descended from the canaries the miners had taken down into the mine to warn them about the black damp. When the miners went bust, they set the birds free. And because the oldest of them didn't fear men, none of them did. With a welcome like that a man would either be spooked off or stay put for his life. Saz Temiz stayed."

"And this is the last one."

Carla nodded. "When people started to fill up the town they brought the fowl pest. And the buzzards that trail even the cleanest of wagon trains got all the rest. Even a sheriff can't keep buzzards out."

"That's sad," said Dolley. "My children would have liked to have seen a whole flock. They like pretty birds."

"So do buzzards," Marilyn said. "Bright things attract hunters and scavengers, is the truth of it. They don't last. . . ." She leaned toward Dolley, and nodded her head in the direction where Houston was pouring cider into bright red cups. "You better watch out for buzzards yourself, Dolley."

"No buzzard could carry me off," Dolley said, trying to sound sure of that fact. Then, more to change the subject than to advertise, she began began telling them about Jarry's work, and about the store, all the while readying her best quill pen.

Setting pen to paper, Dolley noted that the coming year would indeed be a leap year.

WHILE Dolley sat shading in phases of the moon to come, Jarry laid Gertrude down for her nap and went to his tubs to make up a fresh supply of stock solution. As he gathered up the scrap paper and old leaves for the fire, Jarry stared out across the hot red sand pan of the high desert around him. Everything was still, and distant. Features were farther apart than he'd expected they would be out here, as if the landscape he had read about had been painted on an India rubber balloon which had then been inflated with heated air. Even the smells, all there on the winds just as the yellow-back books had said, were far apart, thinner than he had expected, like tatters of old flags. Jarry had expected the scents of the West to be bolder, but his boiling potions easily covered the smells of hot rock and blown sand and sage with the cutting aroma of industry. But he had to work, and, after all, his work would preserve what was best about the West, wouldn't it?

Dolley came back to the store just before suppertime. She was laughing to herself as she came in. She had her calendar on cream paper rolled under one arm, and one finger and the opposite thumb were locked in the bright Chinese handcuffs.

"Look, Jarry," she said. "I've got my hands buttoned up wrong."

Chapter 6

Jarry took a deep breath and slid the long shaft into the narrow slot. He put his weight behind it, driving the shaft home, adjusting the angle, forcing it a little, nearly knocking the wind out of Dolley as she tried to hold her ground. She had been delaying this, though she knew Jarry would sleep easier once it was done, but now everything else had been sorted out and it was time. She held the low, curled footboard while Jarry pounded the rail pins into the slots to secure the frame. Lying so long in the wagon, in the extremes of heat and cold and damp the family had ridden through, had warped both sides, swelled and twisted them, and Jarry had to hammer hard to force the brittle pieces together.

Once the dark mahogany and iron bed frame stood ready for the mattress to be tipped from where it stood against the wall, to be squared up and made up, Dolley had to rest a moment. Jarry came around behind her and squeezed her shoulders. He looked down into the open space of the bed frame as if in it he beheld his most prized possession. "I guess you can take it from here," he said. He left her alone in the room, and a minute later she could hear him slapping leather, tucking and folding his samples of skins that she had hung out over lines and beaten like rugs that morning. It had been the same when they had moved into their first home. He had put the frame together, then left the rest to her while he went about minding his business.

Dolley looked through the empty frame and saw a scattering of dusty miller leaves on the floor beneath. They must have fallen off the last of the Providence bouquets she had arranged for herself in the closed bedroom, one every Sunday after Jarry went downstairs to his Westerns. The slight false roses of the plants had all gone, pressed into her own books or thrown into the dust bin, and these leaves must have been wound into the thick bed clothing along with the bedrails. They had packed quickly, nearly been catapulted from their home by the force of Jarry's eagerness—and by his oversight in not asking for a decent grace period. She had not been given the time to do the usual, to air out and scrub and wash and wipe like a nurse cleaning instruments after a botched operation, before finding herself thrown first into a cinder-blackened train car and then into the deep creaking belly of the wagon. These leaves, once part of a small but regular time of arranging her own beauties, her own antidotes, were dead now, as curled as dry pine shavings, and in need of being swept out before she could finish making the bed. But she was too tired to sweep any more just then. Jarry's vigor in the name of a clean start, his second wind after a stumble, his memory as short as any skinned-kneed child, had always been something Dolley had joined in with as her duty. She had always been a good listener, nodding in the planning stages, but now she was tired. The months of effort in the name of making this change a hopeful running-toward had taken as much strength as she was going to let be tapped. Or almost: now she planted her feet firmly, and pulled the mattress to its balance point, then let it drop across the frame any way it would. The mattress broomed the air and she heard the scuttle of the dry leaves of the dusty miller. She laid down on the crooked mattress, one of its corners bent up like a fainting couch, and found it suited her just fine as it was. Someone else's turn to move. She lay that way, across the bed, enjoying herself not moving, a long while. She listened to Jarry slapping and tucking leather in the back room, and to Gertrude trying to talk to her father. Half asleep, she heard the tinkle of a bell.

"Dolle-ee!" Her name, loud as a blast from a ram's horn, as full of yearning as an animal's mating cry, sounded from the main room. She felt a chill run down her backbone and splash over her thighs. She levered herself up on one elbow, facing the bedroom doorway. Through the thin dividing wall she heard Jarry's careful steps, his boots almost whispering.

"Dolle-ee?" The voice was loud and grating, like an old machine works straining.

In the main room Jarry found a towering, almost-gone-to-fat cowboy. He wore a black and white bandanna over his hair and his left eye. He wore a beaten copper bracelet on each wrist, wide as a gladiator's. He was puffing like the giant at the base of the beanstalk. He showed a round brown cavity in one of his front teeth as he called Dolley's name again. Then he turned and saw Jarry.

"Hey, you! Is there a Dolley here?"

Jarry nodded. "She's my wife. She's busy just now. How can I help you?"

The big man's jaw worked back and forth, chewing the question like a tough piece of meat. Jarry moved behind the counter and laid his fingertips on the wooden case that held his knives and gouges.

"The sign painter sent me," the big man said. Then he cocked his head and moved his lips silently, a distracted look on his face. He shook his head, dismissing some thought, then smiled at Jarry. "I'm here for Dolley."

"Do you have a skin?" Jarry asked. This was a good sign, Jarry knew, having their first customer before they had time to unpack.

"Do I have . . . ? The sign painter said you were a strange man." The big man was still smiling, but he had begun drumming his fingers on a support beam.

Jarry kept his voice slow and patient. "People who come to a tanner come because they have a skin they want preserved, or an animal they want stuffed." He heard Gertrude begin to cry.

"It's stuffed I want," the man said. "And the skin's right here." He pointed at his half-masked face, and Jarry saw that the man was trying to be funny now. "I'm for Dolley," he said, summing up. "The sign painter says she used to paint seashells down by the seashore—only he didn't say it as fast as I can!" He laughed, a sound like an iron pump pumping dust.

The big man's eyes shifted. Jarry turned and saw Dolley crossing from the bedroom to comfort Gertrude. The big man moved to follow her. Jarry, his leg muscles fluttering as he moved, blocked the way. "We didn't bring any seashells with us," was all he could think to say.

"I don't want a shell. I want your woman to help me." He rocked from one foot to the other, like an impatient child, and watched the doorway where Dolley had gone. "It's because of women that I'm here," he called in the direction Dolley had gone. "It takes one to know one," he said, sounding simple again. Dolley held Gertrude and stood rocking in the lee of a wide wardrobe, the spot she would have chosen at the approach of a cyclone.

"If it wasn't for women why would men do anything decent at all?" the big man said to Jarry. "There would be no reason, would there? But the women are coming. They're coming for sure." He leaned toward Jarry, and spoke more softly. "See, I've got this problem." He touched the bandanna where it came down over his forehead. "My name's Hart," he said. "Samuel Hart. And I've got this problem."

"Jarry Kenninac."

Hart nodded, then lifted the bandanna to show a drooping eyelid with a diagonal red scar running across it from brow to cheekbone. "It was because of a woman that I was gambling and lost this. And now because of the women. . . ." His voice rose in a bellow again: "I've come to see Dolley!"

"Because of which women?" Jarry tried.

"All the women. All of them that are coming." He tucked his huge hands in his vest pockets like a banker meditating over a deal. "I can tell they're coming, soon, too. I knew it when I heard about your wagon coming in. A woman bringing in a baby is like the bell that the leader of a flock of ewes wears—it's a signal for others as gentle as she to follow. Every other woman out here was married when she came, and had her children here. Yours is the first to come carrying a baby in. Next will come the women who want babies but can't get them made back where they come from." His voice dropped to a confidential tone. "It's like the territory is doing a slow male coaxing, you know? Little by little convincing free women that the part of them that exists between their legs can come out here without being dirtied, you see? So, I know they're coming now, bringing their wide wagons this way. And I want one!" Hart leaned back then, looked up at the ceiling and, so quickly that Jarry could hardly sort out the words, he recited:

> *I want a woman with a warm wide wagon*
> *I want a woman with a warm wide wagon*
> *I want a woman with a warm wide wagon*

He lowered his head and nodded. "A baby in a wagon was always the clue for me to move on. But this time I'm going to meet the flood head-on." He touched the cloth that covered his scarred lid. "But, there's this. And the sign painter said Dolley does eyes."

In separate rooms, Dolley and Jarry both let out tense breaths. "We can do that," Jarry said, drawing out the *we*. "There will be days when you'll swear you can almost see out of it."

"Don't need to. Just need it to be seen. I can stir up a good line about the gold dust I'm bound to hit any day just as good as the next man, but I can't talk a new eye into this hole. A man looks like me needs all the being-seen help he can get." He smiled.

Jarry said, "I thought you cowboys all got mail-order brides."

"Who can write?" Hart said. "And would *you* trust a pony express rider to bring *your* wife across country?" Hart laughed loudly, and Jarry could hear the quiet sparkle of Dolley's laugh as well. "Bouncing up and down on leather all day gives them strange ideas."

Jarry had heard about men who swung back and forth from idiocy to brains and back again, and wondered if he was meeting one now. "We can start on that eye any time, Mr. Hart. Is now a good time?" Jarry was circling, his finger through a hole in his pocket, not wanting to push his first customer too hard.

Hart spread his huge hands on the counter and hoisted himself up. He stretched out and covered the countertop from end to end, his beaten-down boots nearly touching the wall. Jarry had to bend and scoot under Hart's legs to reach his supply shelf. The smell of the man's sweat was a sour fog.

"I don't like surprises," Hart said when Jarry moved toward him. His voice was threatening once again. "So why don't you tell me what you're doing as you go along?"

"No surprises," agreed Jarry. "I understand: rattlesnakes, bush-whackers. . . ." He spread his tools around Hart's head. "What I have here is a little glass bowl with a hole in the middle. I'm going to slide this glass under your eyelid."

Jarry slid one edge of the tiny bowl under Hart's upper lid, then pulled down the lower one and popped in the bottom edge of the mold. The veiny, grey flesh that remained where Hart's eye had been removed showed hazily through the glass. Hart's lid wouldn't close over the glass and he scowled.

"Now, Mr. Hart, what I have here is a metal tube that I'm going to fit into a hole in the glass." Jarry pushed in the tube until its taper wedged it tight, a stalk straight out from where Hart's eye had once viewed the world. "Now relax while I melt some paraffin."

Hart lay still, but began whistling a crisp march tune. Jarry lit a small oil lamp and set a cube of wax in a pan over the flame. He looked toward the storeroom and saw Dolley standing in the doorway. Gertrude was quiet again, and Dolley stood watching Hart with her arms tight across her breast. She had never liked this part of the eye-making process. They had made human eyes four or five times. They had even once made one for a woman. Her eye had been pierced by a seabird while she had been unwisely taking the air too close to a rook-ery on one of her first walks after giving birth. It was while Dolley had been carrying André, and the woman proudly told her, "And all the while it was being pecked out I never took a single finger from my child's bottom." The day she came in to pick up her eye, as she sat patiently while Dolley painted the iris to match her own, then unraveled a red thread from an old sweater to make the veins, the woman had told Dolley, "Something will happen to you, too. Mothers all lose something."

Jarry nodded to her across the hot pan, and tipped his head in the direction of the whistling giant behind him. She smiled weakly, and held a finger to her lips so he would not speak to her. She had not forgotten those first fierce shouts. Jarry turned back to Hart with the pan of melted wax.

"Now I'm going to pour this wax down the metal tube, and it will seek out all the space of your socket. The metal and glass will pull most of the heat out, but you'll feel some. I need you to lay as still as possible for a few minutes after I pour." Jarry held Hart's forehead, then tipped the wax into the small tube. Hart lay still, and Jarry said, "Mind saying how you lost the eye, Mr. Hart?"

"A low hole card."

"In a fight over a poker hand?"

"A fight *with* a poker hand. It was Houston."

"Randall Houston?" Dolley spoke before she thought about it. At the sound of her voice the giant on the table smiled and, excited, tried to turn his head to see her. "Oh no, Mr. Hart," she said, quickly stepping to the counter. She took his round face in her hands and righted his head on his spine. "You must not move just now."

"Yes, Ma'am," Hart said, as obedient as a school boy. His smile, between Dolley's hands, was so wide that Jarry was afraid the man's jaws would become dislocated.

"You said Mr. Houston had something to do with the loss of your eye?"

"You know Mr. Moon Man, I saw that."

"Moon man?"

"The way he's always staring off into the sky. Everybody knows too much moonlight addles a man, and I guess he proves it with that spyglass of his. He tell you how it has a hundred and one uses? I mean, who can count to a hundred and one?" Dolley took her hands away from Hart's face. "But the moon got to me, too, you know. The game I was in with him was the night of the harvest moon, you see. And I had promised a lady something bigger than I had the cash to deliver."

"Oh, what was that, Mr. Hart?" Dolley was relaxing, sure now that she could handle the big man.

"Nothing less than a new life, Ma'am. It was a big promise, but it was what she needed. So I had all my stake on the table, and Houston was dealing. I swear still that I saw his hole card spinning. And if you don't know poker, Ma'am, a hole card's job is just to lie there real still. So I offered to show Houston the fine engraving on the barrel of my Texican pistol, and he took my eye. Blood ran down my face, excuse me for saying so, all over my money. Paper money at that, and that doesn't launder up like silver does."

"Dolley, do you need to sit down?" Jarry asked. She had gone as pale as the puddle of wax in the bottom of his melting pan.

Dolley remained where she was. "I don't believe I understand."

"See, Ma'am, the edge of a fresh deck playing card can be as sharp as one of Watts' razors. And Houston can throw a card as accurate as an Indian throws a buffalo spear. Is this mess ready to come out of my head yet?"

"Nearly," Dolley said, and she started to move toward a window, but Hart turned to look at her and reach out to hold her by the wrist. "Mrs.? I want you to know that the woman I was gambling for was a good woman." Dolley nodded. "She left me not because I was scarred, the way some would, but because I couldn't give her the new life she needed. . . ." Dolley put her hand on Hart's big hand, and he released her wrist. She moved toward the window, and Hart called after her. "I agreed, Mrs. I agreed she should go find it."

Jarry stepped in between Hart and Dolley. He twisted the mold stem and its cherry pit of hardened wax out of Hart's socket, and set the wax in a cool pan. "What we'll do now," Jarry said, "is make a casting from this wax to use as a model to carve you a new eye out of a plug of smooth Brazil wood. Rosewood, some call it."

"That might be something good to tell the women," Hart said.

"Then Dolley will paint it."

"Good. A woman knows what a woman wants, knows when a man's recipe's got the right flavor to it." He rearranged his bandanna. "Wood, huh? *How many wood eyes would a woodeyedchuck chuck if a woodeyedchuck was wise to wood eyes?* No, too easy. And you've heard the wood eye joke, I'd guess."

"What joke?"

"No? Good. There was this dance," Hart began, still lying on the counter, his hands folded on his chest now, his ankles crossed. "And this dance was just for cripples. The dance hall was filled with stump-legged women, cross-eyed men, and retards, and what-have-yous. A lot of harelips, too. There was this one boy who had just got him a brand new wood eye. And this boy wanted to dance with this hare-lipped girl. I guess she had pretty hair, maybe. But the boy was too shy, and he was afraid she would notice his wood eye and make fun of him."

Dolley listened to Hart telling his joke, without taking her eyes from the window. She noticed that something was coming in out of the desert, moving slowly toward town. It moved slowly, but raised a lot of dust as it came. She thought she could make out men on horse-back, and some kind of animal she couldn't identify, all whirling around and cutting off one another, slowly circling toward the edge of town.

"But, finally, the boy got his nerve up, and he walked up to this harelipped girl and he said, 'Would you like to dance with me?'"

Dolley was sure now that there were two men on horseback, and they were worrying some running animal. Then the animal fell, then was up again, running. On two legs.

"Jarry!" Dolley called without turning from the window. "Jarry, quick!" She heard the clatter of Jarry's boots, and Hart grunting as he levered himself down off the counter.

"What is it, Dolley?"

She pointed and he followed her finger. The men on horseback

64

were laughing and whipping with short branches at the running two-legged animal.

"It's only an Indian," Hart said, somewhere back over her shoulder. Dolley felt like an avalanche was about to descend on her. She slipped past Jarry and Hart and hurried to the door. She was out on the board walk and moving toward its end before Jarry could catch up with her. There, at the edge of the walk, she felt like a woman on a pier, watching a storm approaching from the open sea.

The white men, on matched buckskin mares, both with their shirt sleeves rolled, cut their horses sharper and sharper across the path of the running Indian. Dolley hadn't recognized the runner as a man because of the enormous shaggy cape that hung from his shoulders almost to his knees, and the horns attached to the part of the robe that was gathered into a cowl. The robe was such a deep brown that it was almost black, but with copper lights that flashed when the Indian turned sharply, or when the branches the men switched him with slashed at the nap of the robe, which was as thick as a black sheep's fleece.

Jarry and Hart stood next to her now. Hart crossed his arms across his chest and looked impatient. Dolley felt that if the runner could reach the safety of shore, reach the edge of the board walk, that he would be safe. But the men were crowding him more closely now, cutting their horses so close that their strong haunches struck the runner, finally knocking him to the ground. He got up, but before he could run, the second rider kicked him in the chest, and he fell to his knees. They were too far out for Dolley to be able to see the kneeling man's face, but she could see the sun move on the bright red and yellow band that held his cape in place as he looked from one rider to the other.

"Here," Dolley called, cupping her hands. She felt the blood rush into her face, felt a strong wind gathering in her lungs. "Over here," she shouted, and she felt Jarry take her arm to keep her from jumping off the end of the walk and running out into the desert. The kneeling man looked in her direction, the horns on his cowl sharp as listening ears, then the riders surrounded him again. He tried again to stand,

and this time one of the riders struck him in the face with the butt of his rifle. The riders rode back a little distance then, and leaned their heads together.

"They won't ride him over," Hart said.

"Are you sure," Dolley asked, turning to him.

Hart nodded. "They won't tear the robe, not after this long a hunt."

Dolley turned back in time to see the second rider draw out his rifle. The man on the ground quickly picked himself up, and before the men could cut him off again he ran toward town. But he ran more awkwardly now: he had gathered the robe around him so that it covered his arms and his chest, and he was running with his head down. He looked like a woman trying to keep off an unexpected rain. The men on horses rode slowly after him. They each had a rifle in one hand, their short reins in the other. The runner was only a hundred yards from where the board walk began, but was running with his head down. "Here! Here!" Dolley shouted.

One of the men on horseback turned in his saddle to look in the direction of her shouts. He raised his gun in a friendly wave, then began riding toward them. Jarry wrapped his arms tightly around Dolley and tried to pull her back, but she struggled against him. The rider guided his horse through a small gully, and slid out of the saddle on the gully's near side. He positioned his horse across the path he had just ridden, and rested the barrel of his rifle in the smooth trough of the saddle. He was so close now that Dolley could hear the gun being cocked.

The runner in the dark robe, followed closely by the second rider, still ran with his face protected, watching his own feet. He almost pitched forward when he came to the shallow gully, then he strained to hurry up the near side, as the rider had known he would. When he came over the lip of the gully his arms flew open with the effort, and his head came up. The waiting rifleman calmly squeezed off two shots quicker than the running man could close his robe again.

The running man went to his knees, his face a bright copper flash before it went down again. With clumsy hands, he gathered the robe around him as best he could, twisted its folds one side into the other, and tucked his head in tight against his chest. He looked like a small dark cactus. Then he pitched over into the red dust.

"Jarry, do something!"

"There's nothing to do," Hart said. "It's all done now. That was clever, wasn't it—the hunter knowing where the Indian's head would come up?"

The riders moved to the body, and unwound the robe. This they carefully folded and tied, and laid across the rump of one of their mares. They slipped a loop of rope around the dead man's ankles. He was all copper and buckskin and crow black hair now. The rope was secured to one man's saddle, and they rode off, dragging the body behind them.

Dolley was crying now, her hands held out toward the desert, watching the men ride away.

"Are you all right, Mrs.?" Hart's voice was gentle. "It's only buffalo robe hunters. They'd never hurt you or yours."

"But they killed that man, and now they're dragging him away."

"Don't worry. They'll cut the body loose on reservation land. They only hunt for the skins, they don't eat the meat."

Jarry held Dolley against him, and spoke softly across her back to Hart. "But buffalo hunters are supposed to hunt buffalo."

"The Indians are the only ones who can find buffalo around here anymore."

"I found one, just a few days ago," Jarry said. Hart looked skeptical. "Truly. He was dead, but had only been for a maybe an hour."

"How did it die? The Indians kill it?"

"It had been hit by a train. The locomotive was derailed, down on its side."

"Oh, that explains it," Hart said, nodding. "Everybody knows bison hate trains. They'll chase one down if they see it. That's why the railroads organize so many sport hunting parties. But buffalo robe hunters without train tickets would starve if they didn't hunt robes the way you just saw."

"And people just let these, these, so-called hunters murder Indians like that? That's sickening."

"This is Sheriff Temiz's territory, and he makes all the laws. Including the hunting laws. He says that white men and Indians have always killed one another, and he's not going to be the one to change something that's been going on for so long. He likes the old ways, you see. He's not too happy with the buffalo hunters taking up new ways, but he knows that a man has to stay with the livelihood he knows."

"Jarry, I'd like to lie down," Dolley said. Jarry helped her to their bed, the dusty miller crackling under his boots, and called Andy in to sit with Gertrude. He sat with Dolley and ran a cool cloth over her forehead and cheeks.

"I'm sorry that you had to see that," Jarry said.

"Don't be sorry," Dolley told him. "You'd better not be sorry. I'm not. It was a good reminder, for both of us."

"A reminder? Of what?"

"Of what this place is really like," she said, gesturing toward the street. "Of how it operates. Houston and his card tricks; buffalo *robe* hunters. After so long in that wagon it would have been wonderful to be be surprised, to find that this town would be just the way your books said it would be. I needed a reminder that people are alike everywhere. And if you've got any sense, Jarry, you'll let today scratch out those yellow-back book words that brought us here. Hart isn't the only one who needs a new eye, or two."

"You should try to sleep now, Dolley. I'll make some lunch in a while and wake you." He laid the cloth on her forehead, and walked quietly out of the room. Andy had fallen asleep with his hand on one of the rockers of Gertrude's cradle, and she slept, too. Jarry took his pipe and went out onto the front walk where his smoking chair sat. Hart was waiting for him.

"You didn't let me finish what I was saying," Hart told him.

"Oh? Then go on, please. I'd be interested in hearing the rest."

"All right, here it is: The girl is so happy to be asked that her face lights up and she says, 'Oh, *would I! Would I!*' The boy jumps back a step and shouts at her, 'Harelip! Harelip!'"

Chapter 7

JARRY sat at the table, his face close over the tin he used to keep his untended cigar out of the drafts that would burn it up before he got back to it. The light of the lamp was watery, the fuel diluted by seeping damp in the root cellar of *Hawkshaw's Necessities*. The book in front of him was a familiar one, but this time he didn't shiver when Pathfinder was caught in a sudden snow squall halfway up Bloody Boot Mountain; he didn't sweat when the hero's faithful Indian Big Axe was whipped by the one-eyed villain; his fingers didn't twitch as the sage scratched against the flanks of the wild roan horse Snake Killer. He was distracted by the foolish giddiness of the plot. Reading this, his favorite Western novel, had always transported him out of his troubles. He took a quick look at the cover to make sure he had the right title. But something about the book had changed.

Jarry laid down the yellowback novel, and took a puff on the cigar. The cloud rose into his face until he felt sooty as a coal miner. He got up and walked to the sideboard, and took out one of his work books. Back at the table, lifting his elbows absently as Dolley laid out plate, fork and knife, he stared into the etchings of cross sections of mammals and birds, trying to find a feeling of a "natural logic" prevailing in all things that the skeletons and charts of chains of being usually gave him, their ladders of form from insect to man; the feeling that everything living fit together according to rules, that there was harmony in the fit of all the pieces. But the feeling wouldn't come. What came in its place was a cold clamping in his shoulders: the ladder of life suddenly seemed a warning flag, with its ocean-cool precision, its surgically sharp divisions between cold-blooded and warm, between predator and prey, its efficient use of incisors as punctuation.

Dolley came up behind Jarry and looked down into his book. She wrinkled her nose at the illustration: *The Ghost of a Flea.* The flea was man-shaped but scaled, with long curling fingers like joined shells, and a pointed tongue that flowed out from its mouth, whisking and eager. No living flea ever looked like this, Dolley knew, but the sketch showed its true spirit, all right: a cup in its hand to catch blood. *Fleas were once thought*, the caption told its enlightened taxidermy students, *to be the ghosts of greedy men turned away from Heaven.*

"Jarry? Are you going to keep your nose in books all day?" Jarry was surprised to find Dolley at his elbow, and even more surprised that the sun was almost down. Dolley touched his shoulder. "Supper will be on in ten minutes."

Jarry laid the book on the table and reached out to gather Dolley into his arms. She smelled of wind and sun dried linens, of vanilla and flour, and he held her tightly around her thighs. Solid thighs make a man feel there is something that can be depended upon, Jarry thought. Skinny thighs remind him that everything is going to wither away. He listened to the sounds of her stomach, and she put her palm, smelling of peppers, over his ear to hold him against her. So she heard the wagon first.

She heard creaking wood, then the puffing sound of horses' hooves in dust. Then she saw the wagon. It might have been driven off a tray of fancy gingerbread men. The big wooden box of its body was a celebration of wood and chisel and saw blade. Scalloped jungle palms were carved into the corner-posts and painted an oily-looking emerald green. Along the sides were paintings of flat faces with red scars. Below these, looking like the shag on some strange beast's belly, hung strings of feathers and shocks of Indian corn. From the top of the wagon, from the center of the top, rose a stubby flagpole. It looked like the wire of a paper-souvenir bird. There was no flag on the pole.

Dolley gently turned Jarry's head until he faced the window. As the wagon passed in front of the store the driver looked up. On his face as he looked into the display window was the slight smile of a man who has seen many follies. The setting sun put flame and blood in the colors of the murals, some of which was reflected in the face of the driver, a face that was creased with wrinkles and crow's feet as deep as the lines inside a man's palm. One eyebrow rode noticeably higher than the other above a surprisingly delicate nose. Jarry quickly got to his feet, and moved to the front door to watch the wagon pass.

The mural on the back of the wagon showed a tall muscular cowboy in a painted desert. He was surrounded by threatening Indians and snapping wolves. The figure wielded a bullwhip while he drank down some amber liquid from a bottle. The label of the bottle had been scraped away, leaving bare weathered wood. It was clear that the man driving the wagon had been the model for the mural. But it must have been some years before, or the muscles had existed only in the artist's eye. The man wore a black hat, both in the painting and in life, with the severe brim and domed crown religious sects favored. The face beneath the hat brim looked as cool as stone.

But the man's boots! The wagon driver wore the Western boots of Jarry's dreams: deeply tooled, black and high arched, with enormous undershot heels and corn-gold stitching. Jarry smiled. If there were more men out here who favored such fancy boots, this was indeed the perfect place for a good tanner to be.

The driver reined in in front of an empty storefront across and four doors down from the burned-off lot. He climbed stiffly down from the seat and reached back up for a canteen. He carried this with him as he went to the back of the wagon and sat there on a wooden step just below the door.

D<small>URING</small> <small>DINNER</small> Dolley found herself feeling grateful that the strange man had come to town. Seeing the stranger in the red wagon had snapped Jarry out of his brooding. He said little at dinner, but he smiled. When dinner was done and he had lifted water onto the stove to heat for dishes, Jarry announced he was going for a walk.

The last of the red sunlight was raking across the wooden side-walks making wide shadows at his feet. When he looked up the street toward the red wagon he saw that it had almost doubled in size in the time it had taken him to eat his dinner. One side of the box had lifted up, and poles at its two free corners held the side high; it looked like a porch belonging to a short man's shack. Some kind of tent material hung down from the roof edge, light from the street lanterns high-lighting the creases in the fabric. Under the makeshift roof, two fig-ures stood, one dark and one light. In the hard sunset light, the tall thin shape of the wagon driver could clearly be seen moving around the back of the wagon. A familiar cricket-legged motion told Jarry that the man was pulling off his boots. Then he walked around the corner of the wagon, out of sight. The two figures, who looked like a man and a woman now that Jarry was closer, still stood under the tarp.

Jarry approached the wagon slowly. He cautiously approached the first figure, the woman, and found she was headless. The second one also was without a head. They were just cut-out shapes of a man and a woman, thin as planking. They had taken him in because they wore real clothes, fancy and formal Eastern clothes to Jarry's eye. He moved away from the headless couple and up onto the board walk. The stranger was peering into the dark glass of the empty store, one finger inside his mouth vigorously rubbing his teeth. He cocked his head to watch Jarry's approach. White foam showed at the corners of his mouth. He took a short drink from his canteen and swirled the water in his mouth. Then he reached down, lifted one of his boots, and spat the thick white foaming water into it. Then he did the same with the other boot, smacking his lips as he leaned against the window ledge to pull the boots back onto his feet.

"Baking soda," the man said before Jarry could ask. "Cleans the teeth, and keeps your feet fresh, too." When he saw that Jarry wasn't going to move on, the man tipped his head forward then took a step in Jarry's direction. "It's too late for my kind of business. You'll want to come back tomorrow."

"I'm interested in your boots, is all." The man's face took on a pull-the-other-one cast, so Jarry added, "I'm the new tanner here. I'm always interested in learning a new last . . ."

"New last. . . ." The stranger crossed his arms over his chest, and he scowled.

"A man's trade can lead him into doing things that might seem strange," Jarry said. "But they've got to be done." He felt awkward standing there with his hands useless at his sides, so he hooked his thumbs in his back pockets.

The stranger seemed to be giving Jarry's words serious consideration. Then he nodded. "That's the barefaced truth of it all, isn't it? I'm one who knows that well enough." He took a step toward his wagon, a wet sound coming from his boots as he did. "And I think good boots are as important as a good horse, myself. And one's as hard to break in as the other."

As the man spoke, Jarry leaned forward, into the wind of the man's soft voice, smiling too at the sight of some kind of needles tucked in the band of the man's hat. Cactus, maybe, Jarry thought.

"Leather, tanned or alive," the stranger went on, as he retrieved a bottle from in a blanket under the driver's bench, "can make a man feel good and strong as an animal sometimes. Like he's gotten inside this powerful skin and the original heart's taken over beating his blood for him." Jarry nodded, and squinted with concentration, trying to catch every word. "These particular boots," the stranger continued, upending the bottle and emptying it before he finished, "are buffalo hide." Jarry stared at the boots, their darkness, the sags in the side where the leather had worn to a buttery softness. "And sometimes," here the man leaned toward Jarry, and Jarry lifted his eyes again. The man's face bore a mischievous grin now. "Sometimes they make me feel like I've got the blood of the big bull that used to rush through him. You understand that?"

"Yes I do." Jarry felt his arms twitching.

"You got any beer?" the stranger asked

"Beer?" Jarry almost patted his pockets to see if he had a bottle. "No, I don't."

"Well, that's all right."

Jarry did reach into a pocket then. "But I've got some tallow for those boots."

The stranger laughed a high whinny that made the knot in his throat flush red. He ran his hand across the offered grease, like a faith healer making a pass, and came up with four fingers full. "I'm Jarry Kenninac," Jarry said. "What's your handle?"

"Handle? Oh, my Christian name blew away a long time ago. People call me Swing T." He bent and rubbed the tallow into the buffalo skin boots. Jarry saw a large knife in a sheath centered on his belt under the back of his coat.

"Swing T?"

"Swing T."

Jarry put a broad smile on his face before he said, "Swing T is a kind of name I never ran across before."

"Came to me from an apprentice job I had. When I was young I lived where everyone wanted to be in a good, clean trade, and I chose one with some purifying fire to it." Swing T wriggled his fingers in the air in self-mockery. "But I was too slight. I even grew a big beard, thinking it would give me added weight." He laughed. "But bushy as I was, I was still too light for the hammer. I had to whale a horseshoe nail again and again if the horse wasn't to come out running on stilts. The cracker barrel boys would sit around the forge, eating pickled eggs and calling out 'Swing that T!' Because the hammer was shaped like a 'T,' you see? And it got shortened, and I live under it now. It's

74

comfortable."

"You're not a blacksmith now?"

"I went on *rumschpringes* more than a dozen years ago and haven't been back. They probably gave my apron away by now."

Jarry didn't know the odd word, it came through only as a string of growling sounds, but he didn't want to seem too ignorant. "What business are you in now?" he asked.

"The soul-catching business," Swing T said.

Jarry was worried now that he had come across an eccentric preacher, a circuit rider with the Gospels simmering so long in his brain pan that they had seeped through, like a stain through buckskin, and colored everything the man saw or did. Jarry didn't want to talk religion, he wanted to talk buffalo hide boots, or about living in the West, something that would help him stay put.

"I'm a photographer, you see," Swing T said with a grin that let Jarry know his discomfort had been a little trick on Swing T's part. "I'm sure you've heard it said that some believe taking a picture of a man steals a piece of his soul at the same time."

"You take daguerreotypes?"

Swing T shook his head. "Wet plates. Daguerreotypes are pretty old-timey these days."

"You take pictures for magazines about the West?"

"Sometimes I do, though that money pool is drying up anymore. You have to have something new every time. Most of my plates these days are of my friends around the front there. Did you meet my friends?"

"I saw two headless dummies."

"Me, I prefer to call them false fronts." He shrugged. "But either name is likely to make you confuse them with a lot of living people." Swing T's expression changed, but it was too shadowy for Jarry to see where it ended. "Let me show you my operation, as one tradesman to another," Swing T said, and he led Jarry around to the other side of the wagon. "These false fronts are hollowed out behind," he said. "For folks to stand in, see?" And he stood first behind the man, then the woman, stooping so that his neck lined up with the cut-out. "Folks stand behind these fancy dress dummies and get their pictures taken. Then they mail them back home to make their people think they're successful Westerners. This way one size of clothes fits all. Fat folks are a little more trouble, but loose a few pins and we're there."

"That's clever."

"Just business. Making a living out here asks that a man can do a little conjuring. Everybody's got to have their own tricks just to get by." Swing T stepped farther into the deep shadows under the canopy, and lit a lantern. It was almost fully dark now. Jarry looked into Swing T's studio on wheels. The walls were hung with pictures of people in fancy clothes and buckskins, still men and women in cheap coffins, and the odd blurred horse or two. There was a thin dark blanket over a narrow plank bed, lanterns and candles in corners, and a few things Jarry didn't recognize—engraver's gouges, copper plates, Mexican pasteboards for the Day of the Dead. "Those last are just personal," Swing T explained, pointing to each in turn. There were boxes wrapped in blankets under the bed, and at its foot stood a gangly and goggle-eyed thing, its head a black concertina of folds, with a long black veil than hung down its back. It was a camera, Jarry knew that, but it still looked spooky in the flickering shadows. The bare floor had the look of oak worn to soft furriness. The interior air smelled of vomit and beeswax and strong salts, a smell not too far removed from his own tanning baths.

"As with most things in life, the most fun part's on the under-neath," Swing T said, and he knelt down and held the lantern so Jarry could see under the wagon. Eight small kegs were slung in nets and tied beneath the wagon floor, giving the whole shambles the look of an unstable raft. "Full up to their bungs with flash powder," Swing T said. "This wagon's got more full teats than your best milch cow."

"I make up my own tanning chemicals," Jarry said, "and my tubs are on wheels, but I have to have a building. I have a family."

Swing T frowned and held the lantern up close to Jarry's face. "You're a French Quebecky, aren't you?"

Jarry started to shake his head in denial, but knew his speech was a bright pin stuck in a map of the continent, locating him precisely. "A long time ago," Jarry said.

"Some marks never wash away, do they?"

"Some do not, no."

Swing T still held the lantern close to Jarry's face. Jarry couldn't see Swing T's face past the lantern, but refused to blink or turn away.

"You have a good face for the West, Jarry. As long as you don't talk, nobody would know you weren't born and raised out here." Swing T lowered the lantern. "Jarry, let me buy you a drink, and we'll talk some business. Here, you can look at these on the way." Swing T pried off his boots and handed them to Jarry.

The wind was coming out of the west, and it worked its way through town in corkscrews. It picked up loose ash from the alley next to the store, where Dolley stood in the front window, and set it spinning up the street, smudging signs and hissing on glass until it overcame Jarry and Swing T so they made black footprints on the board walk.

Swing T led the way through the pitted Dutch door of the saloon. A man with a bandage on his head stood behind the bar, spitting on some warm bottles to clean them. The room was empty except for a woman with hair like a swirled mop, and a man chasing a mouse around a table top with some playing cards. The smell of old drink slapped at them like a wet rag, made Jarry's eyes burn. Swing T marched straight to the bar, laid his wide hat on its stained top and looked back over his shoulder at Jarry. Jarry joined him, and they ordered beers.

"Jarry, would you be willing to play the wild Westerner in a few wet-plates? Dress up and grit your teeth, and generally carry-on in a frontier spirit for the camera? You've got the face I need for a new idea that's come to me."

Jarry had a flash of worry. This was how men talked to women they wanted to flatter, whose stays they wanted to loosen. "I'd have to hear more."

"I don't want to say too much here; too many ears." No one else had entered the bar. Jarry made a quick count: there were only ten ears to hear Swing T, if he counted the mouse. "But I've got an idea for a few kinds of pictures never seen before in the Eastern papers, or anywhere else." He held his hands up as if to quiet Jarry, who had said nothing. "I'll pay you, too. Seventy-five cents each time I set off the powder. Good wages for standing still."

"I have to move one entire hand to get that," the bartender said.

"Well, move two," Jarry said, putting a dollar and a half on the bar. "We've got a deal to drink on."

WHEN JARRY LEFT the store to investigate the stranger, Dolley fed and dressed André and Gertrude. Then she washed herself head to toe, digging away with her nails any red spot that looked like it might be part of the land. She put on a short slip and some tall white stockings. She moved nearer the warmth of the stove, and stood twisting her hair dry in a thick towel. Then, the towel still in her hands, she walked slowly from one window to another, looking out. Dolley was a sea captain's daughter; she knew how many points there were to a compass, how many degrees around the horizon. She looked and felt her way through every one of the 360 that surrounded her. She stopped at the window that opened onto the burned wall next door. The wall was slug-gray, a bubbly wash that seemed to sag toward the ground.

But the scarred wall was now the most comforting view she had from any of her windows. The other doors and windows opened into endless-looking rolling red space. The real life of the legendary West, the tooth and claw she had seen bared the day before, might appear again from any of those directions. But a building, even a burned building, was something which might come to hold the kind of people she could understand. She had met no one here she could understand. Except for the close mother and daughter, who had charmed her with that closeness as much as their words, the women at the calendar bee were almost caricatures of her aunts, too good and too in love with their needles and thread. Huge Hart, who could be so love-struck at the very idea of women, saw nothing amiss in the killing of a man for a robe. She had thought Houston to be someone she could reach out to—though she knew she shouldn't do so—but his attack on Hart was a terrible thing to hear. And Jarry . . . he was always wanting to be wherever he wasn't, soaked like a wick in a man's notion that life would be better over just one more hill. When her honesty was at its hardest she admitted to herself that she sometimes wished he would go over the next one and leave her behind. She would be sorry for her children, but for herself? A shrug would likely cover it.

And loneliness wasn't cause enough for her to indulge in any gerrymandering silliness. It had been with her most of her life, and by now was no more distracting than her own shadow. Why was it bothering her today? That Houston? Maybe she had accidentally wicked up a bit of Jarry's oil; maybe, without knowing it, she too had felt that in moving on she would find someone to be her match. Dolley smiled at herself. Such dramatics!

And she already knew some of the places that thinking you could find someone or someplace ready-made to suit you, someone or some-place waiting "out there somewhere" for you to find could lead you. In her short flirtation with occult circles back in Providence she had met many who had been looking for this—in fact, it had been top-most among so many other things. They had stories galore about loving the wrong types, both for the excitement—which they admit-ted—and because they didn't have to do the work of making any of their own decisions—which they didn't admit. There had been some pock-cheeked family-circle lechers whose families had slept them-selves into flinching idiocy, knots of the most miserable kinds, every one still distracting themselves by imagining the problem was they hadn't found their perfect match. They came to peep into crystal balls and fans of painted cards; always looking, looking and never finding. Better a mirror, Dolley knew.

And if she had never felt she belonged anywhere or with anyone, that was surely her shortcoming, a kind of bruise left by the buffeting of her early, homeless years. Enough, she told herself. Find your hands something to do and your mind won't wander off. She turned away from the window, and went to gather up water and soap.

Half an hour later there was a knock at the door. The *Open* sign hung from an old pot hook on the front door, but someone stood outside on the walk, knocking. Dolley was rocking Gertrude in the canvas sling that had been her trail cradle. She checked the knot on the kerchief that kept Gertrude secure, and went to open the door. There she found a small woman with her head bowed so far her chin nearly rested on her collarbone.

"Yes?" Dolley said.

"Mrs.," the woman said in a whisper. "Do you remember me?"

"Remember you?" Dolley had to lean far over to see into the woman's face. It was craggy and rubbed looking, and a strawberry nevus with the dry look of clay covered one cheek. "Yes, I remember you." She had been at Houston's calendar bee, in a back corner, her face red with excitement, but she hadn't spoken a word that Dolley could recall. "What can I help you with?"

"Do you have all your notions in, Mrs.? All your dry goods and millins?"

"My . . .?" Had this woman come to offer charity, a welcome in the currency of house goods? The dress she wore looked like a girl's dress onto which six extra inches of odd cloth had been roughly stitched to accommodate the woman's height. She surely had nothing to give anyone. "I have most of what I need, yes. And a few extras, for any who are without."

"Oh, no, Mrs. I'm not here for a handout!" The woman looked as if she might run away in fright, so Dolley laid a hand on her arm.

"I see. I have some tea made. Won't you come in and join me?"

The woman smiled and nodded, drew herself up with a dignity that made Dolley think of a child playing grown-up. Dolley led her to the table, and poured her a cup of tea.

"I don't believe we were properly introduced," the woman said.

"I heard your name, but you don't know mine. It's Bonner. Eve Bonner."

"Pleased to meet you, Eve," Dolley said and she put her hand under Gertrude and patted gently, hoping she would remain asleep through their conversation.

"It's an easy name to remember," Eve said. She leaned over the table toward Dolley, then added, "'Eve,' but not like the first woman, my Mother used to remind me. But like the end of the day, when all the deviltry is afoot. Mother always used words very precisely." Eve tried to assume her dignified posture once more, but her eyes kept darting toward Gertrude, her grin almost uncontrollable.

Dolley smiled. "When Gertrude wakes up, you can be properly introduced to her, as well."

"To be straight forward, Mrs., it's your children that have brought me here. I wanted to tell you that I'm the town's nanny for hire. I'll give you better penny-weight value per hour than anyone else. Guaranteed."

"Well." The idea of leaving her children with this odd stranger started Dolley's head shaking before she knew it was happening.

"I know what you're thinking, Mrs., but I have papers. Wait." She had a badly worn beaded bag through a loop at her waist, and snapped it open and took out several pieces of folded paper. Each was a written testimonial. "Evie can't read a stitch," one note said, "so none of us have to write any lies. She's an angel with children, and I would trust her with their very lives." Some made unkind remarks about Eve's intelligence or her looks, but all were unanimous about her caring for their children.

Dolley talked with Eve another half hour, under the pretense of tea. At the end she decided the woman was sane enough, and when Gertrude woke, she let Eve rock her. "I've only got my raggedy brother Increase to care for in this world," Eve said. "And the less caring for, the better he likes it. You know what men are. And, God is merciful, but he didn't make me with looks enough that I'll be having anyone want to give me children of my own." She shrugged. "Some have

81

looks enough that a hundred men would want to give them. . . ." She squinted. "That's Houston's box ladder, isn't it?"

Dolley turned her head toward the window behind her. "That's his scaffolding, yes."

"I thought as much. He scavenged it when the paint store there closed. The town's grown dingier and dingier since. All that paint going to waste in them beautiful cream-glazed jars. The owner used to let me lift up the lids and look in on the colors." She blushed, and whispered again. "I think he enjoyed watching me bend over when I looked down in. You know what men are. And I liked it, too. But don't tell my brother!"

"And the paint's still there?"

"Yes, Ma'am. When they hung his wife, the paint seller decided to move along."

"They hang women here?"

Eve looked at Dolley as if she were a simpleton. "Of course, Mrs. And that's only right." Eve's face took on a stern expression. "According to my mother, the Bible says that women are more guilty than men nine days out of ten."

"Well," was all Dolley could think to say. She looked beyond Eve, out the window at the blistered and faded wall across the black alley. "Who owns that paint now?"

"Owns it? Nobody owns it, Mrs."

"Someone must own it."

Eve shrugged. "It's like a horse set free to see what kind of grass it can find. The doors are always unlocked. Folks take what they want, the few who want it. This town never had much use for painting itself up. Except the woman who was hanged, of course." Eve's voice dropped. "Don't you want to hear her story? It's a good one!"

"Not now, Eve, thank you. I would rather look at the paint. Would you show me?"

"Now?"

"Now," Dolley said. "And you can carry Gertrude."

As they made their way down the steps and across to the blistered building, Dolley called for Andy. He came running with an empty snakeskin in his hand.

"What are you going to do with that?"

"I'm going to make a tie from it," Andy said. "For when we have company." He rolled it around his finger like thread around a spool.

Eve led the way up the charred steps onto the back porch. There was no knob in the door, but Eve took a railroad spike off a barrelhead and slipped into the gap where the knob had been, and the door opened without a creak.

"Look at them jars, Mrs.," Eve said as Andy moved quickly into the room. And they were fine jars, Dolley had to agree, even if they had too much of the look of funeral urns for her own taste. The were rows of the earth jars, some as short as a foot, and others more than a yard high. They were dusty, but even in the low light and through the dust, their glazes shone. Each lid had a knob in the middle, and the knobs were painted different colors. These identified the paint inside. Smaller jars and pots stood empty on table, their tops next to them.

"Why are we in here?" Andy asked.

"I need some paint. And you're going to help me pour and carry it."

"Wow. Do I get to paint, too?"

"I think so. I think I'll be in need of an apprentice on this job."

"Do you like to help your mother paint?" Eve asked.

"I do! But she usually tells me I can't do it because I'm too little."

"Well, Andy, this time I'm too little, too. But I think I know how to boost both of us up."

LATE THAT EVENING, Jarry sanded Hart's eye while Dolley bathed the children. He had returned from his talk with Swing T walking like a sailor getting his sea legs. She had gently helped him to his rocker and told him of her meeting Eve, and Jarry had told her as much as he could remember of his conversation with Swing T.

"And you're going to go with him?" she had asked.

"Day after tomorrow. He's going to pay me six-bits for every wet-plate he does of me. It's a bit of revenue coming in, Dolley."

"That's not much money for doing such a strange thing. And I still don't understand why he wants your face."

"Well, most would say they don't understand why you want it around, either."

Jarry rarely made jokes, particularly at his own expense, so Dolley knew he was excited about what he was going to do. "Well, I just hope he gives us a copy of the pictures. I know Andy would like to have a picture of you being a wild Westerner." This came out more mocking than she had intended, and she gave Jarry her best smile to carry it through the awkward moment. She left Jarry in his chair, put the children to bed, then retired herself, slipping off with the sound of the sandpaper gently rocking her as well.

Chapter 8

THE next morning, Jarry finished the eye blank. When he handed it to Dolley she held it carefully, as if it were breakable, or alive. She turned it over and over, rubbed her thumb inside its smoothly cupped back, where the wood would ride against Hart's skin.

"Smooth enough?" Jarry asked.

"Yes, nicely so," Dolley said. She wondered if she should go find Houston and show him this before taking it to Hart.

"Could you take it to him today?" Jarry asked. "We could use the benefit."

"Is our money gone?"

"Not yet. But we could use the walking advertisement."

Dolley knew how hard it was for Jarry to go out and drum up business, how uncomfortable it made him. "I could take my things to his shop right now. Did you think to ask him where it is?"

"I did. He told me all I had to do was ask anybody to direct us to the 'beehive.'"

"Are you sure you heard that right?"

"The 'beehive.' I'm sure."

"Whatever that means. I'm sure someone will be able to direct me to him. He's not a character anyone's likely to overlook."

"Do you want all of us to go? A smithy's no place for a lady."

"I've been in a blacksmith shop before, Jarry."

"Not alone."

"I think Hart is the last man on earth I need to be afraid of. Except, of course, for you, Jarry. But it's good of you to look out for me." She gave him a kiss on the cheek. "I'll hurry back. Don't let the children run you too ragged."

The sun was bright and the yellow dress she was wearing glowed. She found herself wishing she had a parasol to twirl, as silly as she would have felt actually doing it. It was that kind of a day. She decided to walk a while, to try to find the smithy on her own before asking anyone to direct her. A blacksmith shop should be easy to find, either by the sound of the hammer or the smell of the quench. And this would give her a chance to give the town a more thorough look.

Everything she passed seemed used up. The herringbone ripples in the lot of ashes, the dark balloons of the paint blisters on the seared building next to it: both belonged to dying streets. Through the empty window frame of the building that had sunk into the ground she saw an enormous grandfather clock that had toppled and split its casings, and all the spilled brass gears and bright glass shards made an angular fountain shape across the tilted floor. She saw that the building had three cells along its far wall. Each of the barred doors hung open and blankets were humped on the floor. Even the jail seemed used up.

A small girl stepped out of the tipped jail, her legs crazily askew as she negotiated the change from sloped floor to level walk. "I was reading my father's initials," she said to Dolley, smiling. "W. C. B. It's all I know about him. Do you want to go in and see with me?"

"No," Dolley said. It was not that the little girl's request was so odd that she said no, not that the floor was so skewed. It was that the exhausted sadness that came to her when the Indian was killed returned now. As if folding its wings after having temporarily taken flight, it settled gently but heavily on her shoulders and heart. "Not right now, thank you. But, could you give me directions to the gaming hall?"

She had expected a fancy building with music pouring out of it, but the door the little girl directed her to could easily have led to a potato cellar. Inside, there were boards and wheels of many colors, but no music. There was a piano, painted an appropriate brothel-red, but the old woman who sat on the bench was busy counting change into a small purse. Kidney-shaped table tops rattled with tossed chips, and men in cocked hats shuffled cards, the sound like the dry husk of a locust call, or her own deep dry breathing. Just inside the door, seated on a high black stool, sat a boy not much older than Andy. Still he had an old man's voice when he said, "Ladies two-bits for the house," and held out his puffy white palm. Dolley quickly opened her bag to find the coin, but when she lifted her eyes the boy's hand was gone. In its place was a grown man's hand, also held out to her. She looked up further and found Houston.

"Allow me," he said, and put his hand on her elbow. She stood a moment without moving, to show him she made her own decisions, then she allowed him to lead her into the room proper.

He led her through the room to a small section marked off with a velvet rope where a sign hung that read *Family Gallery*. Inside the ropes he showed her to a small round table with a fringe of Irish lace. The top was glossy white paint. She sat down, and Houston ordered them two lemon drinks.

"I wouldn't expect you to drink lemon water, Mr. Houston."

"In case I should lean over the table to speak," he said, and did so. In a near-whisper he continued, "I wouldn't want my breath to keep you from staying close enough to hear what I have to say." His face was only inches from her, and she turned and looked out across the room. No one at the gambling tables was dressed like Houston. The other gamblers mostly wore mismatched once-Sunday clothes and farming wear; a pair of trousers, say, and a red flannel shirt with tobacco stains; or the reverse, a white shirt and string tie with denim and split farm boots. Dolley didn't know if clothes made the man, but she knew they showed where a man was comfortable and capable. Houston must do quite well in this room of inept dress-ups.

"I came here to find you," Dolley said. "I want to ask you something, and to show you something."

"I thought you might be looking for me. But let me show you something first, while we talk," Houston said. He took a white handkerchief from his breast pocket and laid it in the center of the table. He folded one corner across to its opposite, making a triangle. He took a small knife out of a sheath somewhere inside his coat. Its handle was a stained-tooth color, and was scratched with another triangular design: sails. Scrimshaw, Dolley knew. Houston slid the tip of the knife inside the fold of the handkerchief and slit the length of it. He did the same thing with one of those halves, and slit the second according to some odd design Dolley couldn't make out. She watched his hands, the sure way they handled the knife and passed it through the thin cloth, imagining them shuffling cards, imagined the right one sending a card sailing into Sam Hart's surprised eye. The lemon drinks came, and she sipped at hers.

Houston spread the white pieces—five triangles, a square, and a diamond—on the white table top. "You're wondering," he said. "How I could put out a man's eye with one of these." A playing card appeared in his fingers, and he snapped the edge of it. His habitual one-corner smile was gone; his mouth was a straight line. The wedge-shaped lines in his forehead were dark now.

"I do wonder," she said.

"Hart came by to gloat that he told you the story."

"Why would he do that?"

"When Sam Hart sees a pretty woman, he starts right away jockeying to be at the head of the line for her attention."

"I didn't come here for flattery, Mr. Houston. And what has that to do with him coming to gloat, as you call it?"

Instead of answering, Houston gave his full attention to moving the white cloth scraps around again. "Big, smiling Sam Hart is walking around with one eye because even a gambler has a right to protect himself. Hart had a sawed-off muzzle loader. In his hands it looked about the size of a hat pin, but it could have killed me twice—once going in and once coming back out." His hands continued their shell game with the cloth.

"And you don't carry a gun?"

"You would rather I had killed him than blinded him? If I had had to draw a gun he would have killed me. Or I could have been shot by one of the ones before him."

Dolley felt a chill, and took her hand off the glass and placed it in her lap. "You've done this before."

Houston nodded slowly, keeping his eyes on her. "Three times. You've gone a little green, Mrs. Kenninac." She touched her throat, and he went on. "A gun is kept in a gun belt, but cards are right there on the table. A practical decision. And I've got 52 shots, where a gun has at most six. I've never taken both of a man's eyes, I want you to know." He shrugged. "After one, the fighting was over, usually. And there's no pain when you cut an eye, did you know that? No nerves there."

He didn't seem to be trying to excuse himself, Dolley thought, so much as to make sure she understood the true scale of his woundings. She shook her head *no*.

"But there is always a lot of blood. One man did come after me, with one eye and blood streaming down his shirtfront. And do you know what I did? I ran like hell." He shook his head, wondering at the memory. "The others just left the table."

"And after you cut Hart? I suppose you went on with your game?"

The softness that had crept into his voice as had tried to show her he had thought of consequences was gone when he answered her now. "I stropped the card off on my boot top to clean it. Like running a knife in the ground." Every word was as hard as iron. "A man's entitled to make a living." He held her eyes for a moment, then pointed down at the table. From the seven pieces of cloth he had made a white animal, the two big triangles, a small one, and the diamond making the body, the square and the rest making a sharp-chinned face with alert ears.

"A cat!" Dolley said, smiling in spite of herself.

"Symbol of curiosity," Houston said. "And there's some curiosity about you at this table." This was said in the voice he had used walking her to the bee, soft and teasing. Behind her, Dolley heard the click of the number wheel coming to rest.

"I never know what you're going to pull out of your sleeve, Mr. Houston."

"This time it's a tangram," he said. "Something I learned on the China Sea."

"A sailor acquires unusual skills, doesn't he?" She wondered for a moment what her father might have been like. She couldn't imagine him being anything like Houston. But every ship must be a different world, every voyage with its own exotic knowledge, its own games to be learned.

"You can make almost any animal shape with them," Houston said. "If you'd like these, you can have them." He smiled. "The handkerchief has never been used."

Dolley imagined what it would feel like to carry the soft cut shapes with her, to puzzle out shapes for her children and try not to think about where the pieces had come from. "I think not," she said. "If my children want animal shapes, we have windows filled with them."

Houston shrugged and swept the pieces to the floor. "There was something you were going to show me?" he asked, his voice cold.

The eye blank was warm in her palm. "No," she said, rising from her chair. "It seems that I no longer have it."

OUTSIDE again, at the head of the street, where the smell of sugared coffee rippled in the wind like a thick sheet, she saw a short length of railroad rail hanging outside a corner window by an alley. This seemed a likely sign for a smithy, but there was no written legend, and a second-story smithy was most unlikely. She stopped two women and asked if the rail marked Hart's shop.

"No, Mrs. That's the sheriff's office," answered the younger of the two. "He had his jail sink under him a few weeks ago and he had moved up there until a new jail can be built. I guess sinking into a pit will make a man seek high ground." She smiled.

"Amen to that," the older woman said.

"The smithy is in the beehive. Just follow the dogleg here, and you'll see it on your left soon enough. Come, Mother," she said, and the pair started away.

Dolley frowned, but followed the woman's directions. At far end of the dogleg the road curved slightly to avoid what had once been an enormous tree. All the trees in this valley were low, shrubby things, most of them with shaggy leaves that gave off bad smells. This tree would have been taller than anything Dolley had seen for at least a hundred miles. Now only the great gray bull's eye of its stump remained. On its flat top a dog lay sleeping.

Dolley looked up from the stump and she saw the beehive. Of course, she thought. It was an enormous round kiln, curved red brick courses three standing men high, with a domed roof out of which black smoke curled like a pig's tail. It was almost as tall as it was big around, and it did look like a beehive. She looked around at the giant stump and knew, had it still been standing, the scale of the tree and the beehive would have been a perfect match. Dolley knew, in fact, that "beehive" was what this kind of kiln was called. She had seen one before, near the railyard in Boston. And she knew that kilns this big were used for firing bricks. What better place for a smithy?

The giant side-sliding iron door was open. A huge, upturned horseshoe above it served as Hart's sign. Dolley walked through the fan-shaped apron of filings and soot that had been tracked out into the sand and stood in the doorway. Now she smelled the smithy, the iron and manure and fire, and she felt the insect-husk scratch of chaff in the air as she inhaled. The smithy interior was black as pitch after the sun of the bright October day, and all she could make out was the opening of a big iron pot that stood in a cone of light colored sand. The pot was full of glowing coals. Then she made out Hart himself.

He was standing over the heat, holding the lid of the pot by its built-in bellows. He wore a leather apron ornately studded with silver rivets like a fancy stirrup. A wide lanyard around his neck was tied to a pair of goggles that flashed as they caught the embers' glow. Hart sniffed at the glow, then put the cover back on and gave the bellows a pump. He had not noticed Dolley.

"Mr. Hart?" she called.

He turned slowly, a man used to being surrounded by hot metals. "Dolley!" he said, and straightened his apron. He lifted his bandanna off a hook and settled it at a slant on his head, covering his empty socket. Only then did he smile at her. "I'm deep roasting some pork. You came at just the right time."

"That's kind of you, Mr. Hart, but I'm afraid I have supper to make myself."

"Your family." He nodded. "Once, I ate alone for a full year by the calendar. You're here are business, then?"

"Yes."

Dolley stepped into the smithy. All around hung twisted iron, curved iron, greased or rusted iron, barrels of nails and slag with thin skins of rust, black tools and smoothly planed lengths of new wood. Dolley put her basket on the seat of a pedal-driven grinder like a spinning wheel of gray stone.

"I've just finished something," Hart said, gesturing for her to come around the fire. "Tell me what you think of it." What he showed her had once been a farm buckboard. He had trimmed its sides and flipped the frame over, bottom-side up, so that its primitive stiff springs and iron-collared axles were now topmost, and the planks of the buckboard's bed rode only a foot above the quench blackened floor of the smithy. The harness had been remade to a new angle, made into a yoke that stood rigid about a horse's height above the floor, braced with wood like a miniature railroad trestle. "It's for salvage," Hart told her, as he patted the big iron and wood hoop of a rear wheel. "A smithy has to be a kind of knacker's yard for implements past their primes if it's going to keep the smith in iron stock.

Without stock you can't make soup; can't raise cattle, or people for that matter; surely can't be a smith—stock is everything. So, I might hear of a wagon or paddlewheel thresher that's gone down in the belly, or a rider might stop and for a shoe he'll give me the location of a Conestoga wagon down a wash, and I go out after that iron. You know I do. Until now I've had to stand out in open country and cut the implement to pieces so I could carry it back in a wagon. Now I can just put my shoulder to it, topple it and pry it up onto this lowboard here, and cut it up when I get back. I invented it!"

"That's wonderful, Mr. Hart! I am very impressed."

The big man beamed at her. Then he gave the big wheel one more affectionate pat.

"I've come about your eye."

Hart stopped smiling. He looked up at the smoke hole, then back down. Then he stepped very close to her. He rubbed his chin and the rasp was like a far-off locust. "Have you heard the news, Dolley? Have you heard what the sheriff's done now?"

"The sheriff? No, I'm sorry, I have not."

Hart nodded his head again and again before he could speak. "He turned back the train. He sent the women off into the hills, told them to go around. He told them they weren't welcome here. Not welcome here!"

"I'm sorry, Mr. Hart."

"I told you they were coming, Dolley. And they tried to. They tried to come here, but Temiz turned them away."

"I'm so sorry, Mr. Hart. We can cancel the eye."

"No, I'll be needing it. See, I'm going to take this iron knacking wagon and go after them."

"Do you know where they are?"

"No. I'll just start out. I know I'm meant to find them, so I will." This reminded Dolley of Jarry and his search for a "real Western town." She tried to imagine what unmarried women suffering the hardships of a wagon train journey would feel if this giant and his topsy-turvy wagon should suddenly appear out of the dust and offer to take one of them home. She wished she could think of some way to help him not scare them away.

"Do you perhaps own a suit you could wear?" she asked.

"No, Dolley, no." Even in the dim smithy Dolley could see Hart's smile, the way he looked at her as if she were a child. "The woman I'm going out for won't want a man to hide himself inside some starched suit where all the cloth and creases match up. She'll want a man whose parts don't match up too well. Things in people can match up too simple, you know? And that makes them fit only for another simple soul."

Hart took the lid off his firepot, and used a long rod to spear a black lump out of the coals. He gave it a gauging look, then dropped it back in. "The woman I'm going out after will be looking for a man like a cut out of a cliff—all the layers hard and separate and in sight, showing what his ground is made of, and showing a body where to mine for what's wanted." He shrugged, and smiled at her. The glare of the firepot gave his face the red, high-boned look of a painting of Asmodaeus. But, if he looked like the red devil, his words were, in their way, sweet and gentle. "And if I show I'm that kind of man, I'll get that kind of woman. They're getting harder and harder to find, Dolley. More and more folks are learning to smooth themselves out, show no cuts, no seams, you know?" Hart turned to Dolley as if to ask her a question, then turned away. She wondered if he had intended to ask her what kind of woman she was, or even to tell her.

Now he drew another black lump from the fire. This one he sat in a cool iron griddle that stood on a tripod next to the firepot. Holding it down with the iron spear, Hart used a towel to wipe it clean. Dolley saw that it was a bite-sized piece of the pork he was roasting. She watched closely as Hart trimmed off the burnt hide. There seemed to be no guile in the big man, none that she could see in his plan. For Hart it truly was this simple: display what kind of man you are, be just a bit of a peacock about your layers, and out of the flood of possible mates the right one will find you. Simple, like the rough grace of the way Hart prepared his meal and offered to share it with her.

Dolley knew she didn't share Hart's feelings. She had always felt herself drawn to men who kept their secrets under cover, men with secrets that might burst out of them like milkweed pods scattering seeds. She was drawn to men with split lives, broken images, of mismatched extremes, men who might follow any fork in the road, you could never predict which. She never let anyone know this, of course. She had never told anyone how she was drawn to men who, like P. T. Barnum, mixed children's delights with suckerism, and men like Henry Beecher Ward, who had spat hellfire then sniffed violets at his adultery trial, and even John Wilkes Booth—and these were only the "B's." If Hart was right about a man and woman needing another like them, then what kind of woman did this list make her?

"When a woman has herself all smoothed out and covered up," Hart went on, "that's the kind of man she wants—or maybe has to have, to keep themselves smooth—whether she really wants him or not. A lot of them might want a man who's all sweat and spitting, but it would wear on their smoothness, and so they pass. Me, I want an old-fashioned woman, one that shows off the kind of ores *she's* made of. I don't want one who is always busy trying to paint everything over smooth."

"But isn't that what your new eye is for?"

Hart laughed. "I've got a little something to ask you about that. But later. Right now I want you to try a bite of this." He held out the bit of pork on the end of the iron skewer. Good manners, Dolley reminded herself, and she took the pork off the point. It was black on the outside, and a pale shrimp color inside. She popped it into her mouth. The sweetness of the flesh inside the crunchy black jacket was a delicious combination. Hart was waiting, an expectant look on his face, and she nodded.

When she had finished the pork, she took the eye blank out of her paint box. "I need you to sit for me, Mr. Hart."

"Sit?"

"I need you to sit down with me for a few minutes while I paint this blank to match your good eye." She looked around the smithy.

95

Sunlight shone down through the smoke hole, and small lanterns hung at ninety degree intervals around the circular wall. It was bright enough for the hammering of horseshoes, but too dim for detail work. "Would it embarrass you to sit outside while I did this?"

"No. Everybody already knows what this cocked bandanna is about." He took a sooty three-legged stool out from under a bench then gave her a "Ladies first" bow.

The beehive opened onto a kind of village common, marked off on one end by the big stump where the dog slept, and on the other by a well ringed by a steep cone of mortared field stone. Hart set his black stool down near the well. Then he frowned. "You need a stool for yourself."

"I can manage standing, Mr. Hart. The top of this well is wide enough to hold my paints. And this will only take a few minutes."

"No, you need a stool. And all mine are . . . *Hey!*" Hart shouted, spying a man in a suit crossing the street. "Lady here needs a stool to sit on." The man stopped, bobbed his head, and went back into the doorway out of which he had just come.

"Really, Mr. Hart, I'm fine standing."

"I can't sit while a lady is standing. That's a rule. And here he comes."

The thin man in the dark suit carried a whitewashed stool to where Dolley and Hart were standing. He sat it down in the red dirt of the road near their feet, touched the brim of his plain dark hat, and went back up the street without saying a word. Dolley heard hard soles on the board walk behind her. Hart's shouts and the stage comedy production of bringing the stool had drawn an audience.

"See?" Dolley heard one woman say to a small boy. "That's what you need, good manners."

"If you would sit down, please," Dolley said to Hart. They were seated less that six feet apart, and the whorls of Hart's warm brown eye were as clear in the sunlight as the chambers of the nautilus shells she used to so carefully cut in half and paint in imitation of pinwheels. Dolley opened her basket and took out her pallet, an old school slate. She took up two of her paints and squeezed out a small button of brown, and double that of white. She took out two brushes and her painting glove. The glove fit loosely on her hand and was stained with the colors of other painting jobs, but she never washed it. It had once been trimmed in French lace, and had belonged to an enormously fat woman who used to pay Dolley to paint mildly scandalous scenes on the fore edges of her leatherbound romances. The woman had noticed Dolley admiring the gloves one day and promptly gave them to her. When Dolley protested the woman had said, "The red no longer rises to a man's cheek with quite the rawness I like when I slap his face with these. I'm afraid they've gone soft, and I shall have to buy a fresh pair." The memory still made her smile.

Dolley placed the blank near one corner of the slate, then looked again at Hart. The brown was very close to Hart's own color, but would have to be lightened just a bit. "Try not to squint so much, Mr. Hart, and this will take only a few minutes."

"I'll try, Ma'am, but anything other than fire-colored light makes me squint pretty steady." His eye was in fact watering as Dolley brushed on the first layer of white background.

"Do you have to wait for that to dry, like on a house?"

Dolley turned to find the woman who had recommended good manners to the boy was now staring over her shoulder.

"Hello," Dolley said. "No, I only have to let some of the spirits escape, and it will be stable enough that each color will hold its line."

"You'll paint the brown next and then the black on it."

"That's right." She heard other footsteps behind her now. Hart was smiling, enjoying the attention given his eye by the gathering crowd of women. Dolley laid the brown on the white now, bearing down just hard enough to make sure the colors mixed. "This needs to evaporate a minute," she said.

"Let me," a woman said, and before Dolley could stop her she had lifted the eye into the air, holding it between forefinger and thumb, and was gently passing it back and forth.

"Please . . ."

"This is our midwife, Mrs. You can trust her hands with anything."

Dolley hurriedly prepared her black and, squinting at Hart to find any flecks, a tiny dot of emerald green. When Dolley looked up, the midwife gently laid the eye back in its place on the slate. "Like a babe's palm," the woman said, more to herself than to Dolley.

Dolley finished her painting as the women watched quietly. "Would one of you please reach into my basket and take out the jar with the red threads and the tweezers in it." The midwife lifted out the jar and took off the top. Dolley pulled a pin out of her hair and put it between her lips, then she pinched a short thread with the tweezers and lifted it out. She held the thread on the slate with the tweezers and used the pin to pick it apart, into hair-thin fibers. She touched one end of each of these fibers to the white of the eye and the paint drew the thread into its evaporating surface, making perfect likenesses of veins. This made the women applaud.

"You may squint now, Mr. Hart," Dolley said. And he did. The women began moving away, and Hart stood up from his stool to look at what Dolley had done.

"I don't look in a mirror much," he said, "but I'm sure that's a good likeness of me."

"This will be all for now, Mr. Hart. In the morning we'll glaze it, and you should have it by tomorrow night."

"That's fine," Hart said, but he was distracted, looking up and down the street. "But could you come back inside for a minute?" He set her stool up on the board walk, and carried his own back into the smithy with them. When they were inside the beehive, Hart asked, "Could you make me a second eye, Dolley?" He spoke almost in a whisper.

"Did you see something wrong in this one, Mr. Hart?"

"No, it is very fine. It will be a good fit for everyday, for business. But I want something special, something for private times."

"I don't understand."

"I would like an eye that will show a woman what I feel inside,"

98

Hart said, and he began to scissor the bellows on the fire pot. The capped heat roared louder. "I like my pork *crackling*," Hart said.

"Mr. Hart, brown eyes can show just fine what a man feels."

"Oh, I know that," Hart said, as he scissored even harder. The room was growing hotter, and Hart had to almost shout over the roar of the fire and the wheeze of the bellows. "But I want something that will make being alone with me different from being alone with anyone else. When I find a woman, she will be everything to me. I want her to see that," he pointed at his covered eye, "I want this to open and tell her how I feel about her in the dark." He gave the bellows one last heave, then lifted the lid off the firepot. His face glowed in the glare from the coals. Dolley quickly stepped back, away from the heat. Across the fire Hart said, "I want a fire-red eye."

"Mr. Hart, all you have to do is to keep thinking whatever it is you have in mind right now, and you will have your fire-red eye. I won't have to do a thing."

Chapter 9

Jarry spent the next morning on his back, his hands behind his head, watching pyramids of gray shadow come and go on the whitewashed ceiling in the bedroom to avoid the embroidering women in the main room. At the calendar bee, some of the women had promised they would come calling one day, and this was the day. They sat in an egg-shaped ring, tiny silver needles rising and falling in yards of cloth. Jarry had tried to read but the clicking of embroidery rings being snapped on and off distracted him.

"Dolley," one of the women said in a lecturing voice, "we find it hard to believe that you never learned to embroider!"

"My mother could knit, and I did all our darning. I suppose our family could only learn one needle skill each. And I could never catch up with any of you now. Everything you're doing here is so beautiful."

"These patterns reach way back," the same woman said, obviously ready to lecture on the subject. "Before there were worked silver and gold, before some clever Jew learned to cut and polish diamonds, there was English needle and thread."

"And Irish, Dear."

"Yes, Joyce, and Irish. Embroidered gowns used to mark the ones who were blessed to stand out as examples to their people, to be royalty, the way crowns do now."

"And fine gloves, Dear."

"Gloves, Joyce? Please!"

Jarry was pleased that Dolley had visitors. It would cheer her up, at least for a few hours. And they would teach her things, things she could turn into work. She could now add embroidery to the children, the cooking, and the mending, all the women's work that filled her hours. Jarry knew that a woman's life was not an easy one, that work filled their days, but the one time he had thought to say anything to her about it, he had also pointed out that there were fewer women in madhouses than men. A body had to have work to do. Jarry had nothing. He had sharpened his knives, cleaned and curried and smoothed his small, still samples, and carved a plug for an eye. He had reread his manuals, dipping into the sections he had always skipped before, like the chapters on natural dyes: brown from walnut roots, red from madder, green from sweet hickory ooze. But reading was not real work.

Being a photo model wasn't work, either, to Jarry's mind. But it would pay.

He went out the back way, through the children's bedroom. He walked slowly up the alley of ashes. At the head of the alley Jarry turned, and looked at the front of the store. He could barely make out the brown lettering on the glass in the shade below the porch roof. He needed something in front of the store to draw attention to it, something to make people want to walk down and take a closer look, something impressive. But then he knew there was nothing impressive in his displays. The buffalo head, that would have been something! But he had lost it. He walked through town with his head down, walking without seeing his feet, until he stepped off the end of a sidewalk into a large mud puddle. A mule brayed at him, and Jarry made a disgusted face at his boots.

Jarry leaned against the end of a hitching post to wipe the worst of the mud off his boots. Awkward on one leg, he teetered sideways.

He steadied himself against one of the horses tied to the hitching rail. Then he saw that something thick was draped over the horse's saddle. It was the buffalo robe hunters' trophy. It hung down over the horse's hindquarters like a skirt. Someone was on the far side of the horse, adjusting the robe.

"How much for the skin?" Jarry called across the horse's back.

"You're too late, Tanner," came the quick answer. A woman's voice.

A short, wide-hipped woman stepped around the horse. She wore scarves and feathers and shimmering cloth that had once been crisp and elegant, and now was as broken-in as a familiar pair of boots. She stepped out far enough to face him, but she kept one hand on the buffalo robe. Her eyes were bright green in the sunlight, with deep night pupils. She was almost a full foot shorter than Jarry, but she looked him up and down as if she towered above him. This had to be Coulisse, Jarry knew, the woman Watts had talked about, alternately wringing his hands and licking his lips. She was both the sheriff's woman and someone tilted enough to fancy herself a witch.

"You're the stuffer," she said.

"I'm a tanner, yes."

"And your wife paints things. Like plug eyes for deer and badgers and sometimes big galoots with romantic ideas."

"Well, she used to paint sea shells."

"This isn't much of a country for those," Coulisse said, with a smile that withered Jarry a bit more. Her voice was low and husky, like a woman aroused. Her skin was dusky, pocked, handsome. "She'll find plenty of one-eyed men, though. Especially in this territory. Tell me," she said, "is that how men court back where you come from, by adding plug eyes and other false pieces to the body? There must be a lot of disappointed brides."

Her voice, so low, cool and comforting even when insulting, confidential even in the open street—Jarry remembered where he had heard its like before, when he had felt just this tone winding around him like slow smoke: a tent show mesmerist Dolley had once taken him to see, in the early days before they were engaged. The animal magnetist had swung a crystal on a velvet lanyard, and it had winked with much the same rhythm that Coulisse's glittered nails now hid, revealed themselves, then hid again in the thick dark pelt of the buffalo robe. Jarry took a deep breath and looked off down the empty street to clear his head. Somewhere a banjo was playing, a sound like buckshot in a pie pan.

"Where is the hunter who took this robe?" Jarry asked.

"He's busy. And the robe is mine."

"Yours?"

She nodded, smiling.

"I'll give you twice what you gave him for it."

"Now, that's an interesting offer," Coulisse said. "If you could do that twice, I'd probably let you have the thing, out of hand."

Something was wrong in the way she was amused by this. "How much did you give him?"

She pointed to the flight of red-painted stairs that the mule stood under, half way up the alley where Jarry had stepped in the mudhole. "Those boys ought to be just about finishing up right now, getting in their last groans and grunts before they go off snoring." Jarry felt his face going red. "I don't mind standing here talking across one horse's ass," Coulisse said, "but don't make me feel like I'm just talking into another one. Tell me, why do you want this robe so bad that you'd offer a lady twice what those boys are getting?"

"I didn't . . . I'm a tanner, is all, and I want to display this robe in front of my shop."

"You didn't make it. So this is just another false part, like that eye, then?"

"I didn't, no. But I could. If I got my hands on a buffalo I could certainly tan a robe this fine. And that's the truth."

Coulisse's nails were pulsing in the robe again, like a cat readying its bed. Two girls, neither over twelve as best Jarry could judge, came laughing down the red steps. As they walked out of the alley and up onto the walk they waved to Coulisse, who nodded at them, and said,

"Thanks." She pulled the robe off the horse and held out one end of it to Jarry. She tipped her head to show him how she wanted it folded. They worked to put a fold in the thick robe. Surprising Jarry with her strength, Coulisse lifted the robe free of his arms. "I'll be going," Coulisee said.

Jarry moved back to clear the way, and stepped into the same mudhole he stepped in earlier. Coulisee laughed. "Right back where you started," she said, and went on her way.

At Swing T's wagon, Jarry waited while a thin woman with no expression on her face had her picture taken behind the cut-out dressed as a man. Swing T tipped his hat to her, pushed his false-front people face to face, roped them together, and threw them into the wagon. Swing T looked over Jarry's outfit. "May Ned Buntline bless us," he said. "A longrifle. I haven't seen one of those in ten years." He ran a finger along the barrel as if measuring it. . . . "It will be good for the pictures, make you look like a real pioneer. But we may have to knock a few dents into that hat. It's a little too clean."

Swing T and Jarry climbed up onto the seat and Swing T nickered at the horses. "These clouds should blow off later," Swing T said, "and give us more light. The valley we're headed for is good territory for taking old-timey pictures," Swing T said. "Sort of like the back parlor of the West. Everything looks just the way the magazines say it should. Don't know, though, how much longer it can last. Good pictures are going to get harder to take around here." He leaned toward Jarry. "From under my breath to under your hat, I don't think the sheriff's cobbled-up paradise is going to last long, and when it sinks, new people, new sights are going to run in and fill the hole."

"The same devil drove me out of the East," Jarry said.

"What devil would that be?"

"You know, *Fashion*. Every week a new way, a new cut or dye or button count shine, all on a whim. I thought things would be more set out here. And while things aren't exactly like the books told me, I think this place is safe from that devil, at least for a while."

"You believe so?" Swing T shook his head. "Back in the wagon here I've got a hard spine book. . . . That's what I need now, come to think of it." He took out a small pouch of tobacco and a tin box of papers. "Wish I could kick the habit," he said. "With every bag of tobacco the wagon gets heavier and heavier." He shook some of the rough-cut shag out into his palm and kneaded it with the thumb of the other hand. "You smoke up a pouch of this and the company sends you a book for the coupon at the bottom of the pouch. Books with hard spines. About Jefferson, maybe, or about Sam Adams, or even about some Russians with big families who all hate each other. I read them when my stomach keeps me awake. They make the horses work harder, though. But, how can a man pass up something free, even if it's only a book?" He rolled the cigarette and lit it. "I wish I could kick it, but this hardspine coupon habit is a hard one to break." He inhaled deeply and blew the smoke out of the side of his mouth, like a man spitting. "Now, where was I?"

"Saying something about a book."

"Well, this book is the story of a doctor who builds a man from pieces of dead men. Of course, this is a book written by a woman— they know how many poor pieces make up a man, don't they? Now, this stitched together man gets up and walks around, but he's never right. Too many of the doctor's flaws are sewn right in him, with bad results. I think Temiz's territory is like that poor puzzled soul: just parts of Temiz sewn together, using poor lost people as thread. He doesn't let anybody come through here who doesn't have some part of him in it. So, the territory has no life of its own. Bad results, like I say." He nodded. "Like I said, from under my breath to under my hat."

"You come and go as you please. What part of Temiz does he see in you?"

Swing T turned to look at Jarry, and sucked air in through his teeth. "I've wondered about that myself. When I first met him—out in the desert where I was roasting a turkey I'd swapped for a hardspine about a certain Garden in Persia," Swing T winked— "he came swooping down on me like a hawk. On his saddle where most have a slip for their rifles Temiz has a wide leather pouch for an enormous sword sickle! Here I am, sitting by a pit roasting a turkey, and up rides this bristle-faced man waving a huge sword. At first I thought maybe I'd gotten some of the wrong kind of weed mixed up in my cook fire. But he circled around me like a hunting bird, and declared that I was in his valley, and he had some questions for me. Not being the fool I look, I said, 'Yes, sir.' First thing he asked me was why I came here from where I was. I told him straight out, and he didn't ask me any more questions. He just took a turkey leg and rode off. So it was something to do with my travel reasons."

"Because you came out to take pictures."

"Not a bit of it. What I told him was how I spent my first sixteen years in the northeast, on the spreads of my faith, hoeing the bastard toadflax back out of the cornrows. And how I'm out on *rumschpringes*, that's what they call it in my faith when a man goes walking about to see the world before turning his back and taking his final baptism. Most make it back in three or four years, and I've been gone thirteen. But I know I'm going back some day. I'm part running away from my home, but part preparing myself to go back and live the life I was born to. I'm just a little overdue."

"And that's all you told him?"

"Seems it was enough to—Jarry, look at that!" Swing T was laughing so hard he could hardly point.

Jarry had thought Swing T and his wagon, with its hell-red murals and flash-powder teats, likely to be the oddest sight to be had in this desert. But coming up a small rise, they saw an even more exotic traveler riding along the ridge top. The wagon must have begun life as an ordinary Conestoga, but now the canvas cover only extended for half the wagon's length. Even the hoops had been removed from the back half. The driver clearly was a woman, seated by herself on the bench, watching them approach. With the sun shining behind the wagon her hair glowed like polished chestnuts, hanging down to her shoulder. She wore a wine red shirt and a corn-colored straw hat.

In the open space of the back of the wagon was piled straw and something Jarry didn't recognize. Plodding behind, tied to the tailboard on a loose leash so that it could approach and eat whenever it pleased, was a gold animal taller than a horse. Jarry had seen this kind of animal before, under a small cloud of flies in a sideshow. "My Lord, it's a camel!" Swing T said.

The woman reined in her horses and waited for Swing T's wagon to finish its slow climb. "Good afternoon," Swing T said, and he stood up to sketch a tiny bow, Jarry did the same, but a heartbeat slower, so that the wagon see-sawed and he almost fell out. "My name is Swing T. Photographer by profession. And this is Jarry Kenninac, Master Tanner." Swing T's voice had the smoothness of pomade.

"Che-Marie," the woman said, in a voice so quiet she had to repeat it before Swing T and Jarry could sort it out. But there was nothing shy or timid in how she held her shoulders, or the fox-eyed, measuring way she looked them over, deciding if she needed to run or snap.

"That's a camel," Swing T said again.

The woman's eyebrows rose a mocking touch, then she looked back over her shoulder. "Yes, it is," she said, as if Swing T were a child pointing out a kitty in a parlor.

"Where are you taking him?"

"I'm taking her," Che-Marie said, softly, "that way," and she pointed west.

"From that way?" Swing T asked in a teasing voice. Che-Marie only smiled. "Do your travel plans allow you time to entertain a business proposition?"

"I do have to meet someone. What did you have in mind?"

"Stealing a bit of your camel's soul."

Che-Marie didn't fall for Swing T's jape the way Jarry had. "You want to take her picture."

"Yes. And I'll pay you two-bits a shot."

"I'm only getting six, myself," Jarry said, wanting to be part of the conversation.

This brought a smile to her face. She tipped her flat hat back, and the sun lit her face. It was wide across the cheekbones, to give room to her long pointed eyes, and her nose was tiny between them. Her smile was wide and squarish. Whenever she moved her head, one of her shoulders would rise or lower in a rhythm with it. Her posture was cat-like on the high seat, as if she were curled around some warm center and took care not to lose touch with it.

"I think I can spare a little time. You are honest businessmen, I trust?" She readjusted her bright hair with the barrel of a small pistol Jarry hadn't seen until that moment.

Swing T took a small bag out of his pocket, shook it so they all heard the clank of money, then he tossed it into the camel's hay.

Half an hour later Jarry was seated on the back of the camel, wearing his batwing hat and holding a stick as if to tap the sides of the animal's neck. Sitting on the camel was uncomfortable. Its strange fibrous hump made Jarry think of some of the carcasses he had had to mount where the bones had been shattered. The animal was so tall that every time it shifted its weight Jarry was nearly thrown off. Swing T had set up his camera, and every four pictures he handed Che-Marie a silver dollar. The flashes, slower burning that Jarry had expected, didn't bother the camel at all. She looked at Swing T as if wondering why he went to so much trouble for these tiny flashes, but she didn't even twitch.

"Stay up there, I'll be right back with you," Swing T called, and he ducked inside his wagon.

Che-Marie walked up and laid her hand on the side of the camel's neck. "I told your friend that this is the last of the camels from an experiment down toward the border. They thought they could ranch them, raise them and use them for following the cattle. One desert is pretty much like another, they figured. The camels thought otherwise. They died." Hearing this in Che-Marie's softly musical voice was like hearing a sad fairy tale.

There was a flash. "Wonderful!" Swing T was behind his camera again. "If you can put more expressions like that on Jarry's face, I'm offering four-bits a flash!"

Che-Marie looked at Swing T and smiled a tolerant smile.

"He's going to sell the pictures with the story, except that he's going to leave out the part where they all died," she said.

"If I asked you again where you are taking her," Jarry said, "would you just point that way?"

She smiled, and turned her face away for a moment. "I'm meeting a man down in Bisbee. We've got a trade going."

"What are you going to get for her?"

"A lion."

"A lion?" Jarry's first thought was that he was glad they had met up with Che-Marie before the trade; what would Swing T have him doing with a lion in the interest of the Eastern papers?

There was another flash. "Keep listening, Jarry, but look this way!"

Jarry looked at the camera, and asked Che-Marie, "Why do you want a lion?"

"I don't want a lion. I didn't want a camel, either. But a lion is worth more than a camel once you get to the coast. I'm just trading my way across the country, working my way up in value each time." Jarry wanted to say something about himself, but he couldn't decide what that would be.

Flash.

"What kind of animal are you going to trade for when you get to the coast with the lion?"

"An infant," she said.

Flash.

"We're all set," Swing T said, his voice surprisingly quiet, his eyes glued to Che-Marie. "You can get down now, Jarry."

Jarry slid down awkwardly, the camel doing her best to ignore him completely. Che-Marie led the camel back to her tether at the rear of the chopped Conestoga, climbed up a set of small wooden steps, pulled them up with a rope, and set herself, cat-alike, atop the folded quilt that padded the bench.

"Perhaps we can do business again sometime," Swing T said.

"As long as things stay containably crazy and askew, I won't be back this way."

The urge to climb up onto the bench with this fine-looking woman, to ride next to her and ask her everything about her life, fluttered through Jarry like a bright bird through a bramble, and then it was gone. When she released the brake on the wagon and urged the horses forward, Jarry began to walk alongside. But as the camel passed it noticed him, and tried to bite his arm. He had to jump back. He stood and watched the wagon make its way back up the ridge.

"You look like a man in love," Swing T said, coming up to him. "You've got a green look to you."

"Tell me," Jarry said, "why didn't you take any pictures of Che-Marie?"

Swing T waved a dismissive hand. "Ah, they'd never sell. That woman's too strong, too sure of where she's going and what she's trading for. She would have developed out looking like somebody's sweet niece. I'd just be throwing my plates away. No one wants to buy a picture of someone they don't know looking happy. I can only sell pictures of people in peril, in distress, poor jokers who have taken wrong turns, lost souls. Too many people turn up happy, and I'll starve to death, Tanner."

Jarry glanced over his shoulder, but all he could see was the yellow wink of the haystack at the back of Che-Marie's wagon.

Swing T looked with him. "You missing your woman, Jarry? You'll be back to her in a few hours." Jarry shrugged, and turned his back on the woman on her way to own a lion. He walked with Swing T back to the wagon, Swing T talking the entire time he broke down and packed away his equipment. "You're lucky to have a wife, Jarry. The only voice I hear in the night is the one coming up out of my belly, the only warmth from the cooked-down sand in the bed warming pan. Sometimes the wind catches the junipers just right, and the wild evening primroses, and it comes up like a whiff of shoulder or fancy bath salts. That will make the horizon seem a lot further off, I can tell you."

With a forefinger that looked to have been broken and badly set,

Swing T pointed out into the desert "West of here, where all the brown sand is blown out of the red, there are cactuses as big as a body, bigger. And when you've been out here on *rumschpringer* as long as I have even a saguaro can shimmy." He spooned a little baking soda out of a big box under the wagon seat, shook it into a cup of water, swirled it around and swallowed it down. "Jarry, I'll wager you never took a knife and cut a little round hole in the side of a cactus, cut away the needles to spare your belly, never felt the pulp, juicy and cool, like a powdered woman's skin when the window's been left open of a night. I'm sure you haven't, having your family with you. A man on his own does what he has to do, and tries not to let shame hold him back. Like most of us out this way, I make the most practical use of what little there is to life in this territory. Thinking up new uses for old things is the key to living out here."

Jarry wondered if Swing T's tone of voice was more one of bragging or of sorrow. He couldn't tell. Both were there. Swing T climbed up into the wagon seat, and Jarry climbed up beside him. "A lot of people try to make this country into something romantic, I know," Swing T said, as he gently started the horses moving. "But it's mostly just empty, that's all. If empty and blank and nothing are the dimensions you're calling for, we got them. But that's about all. There are more men like me, Jarry, not all of us picture takers, but we all travel out here just to write or draw about this territory, because it's the last one not shining itself up for statehood, and we picture it all romantic and exciting for people who have never seen it, and we make a dollar from our pretending. We find the romance in all this scrub and scorpions."

"It's there."

"It is, if you want bad enough to see it that way. You can fill up three dimensions of nothing any way you like." He smiled. "I know I do."

"It was the drawings and the daguerreotypes and the stories in the dime novels that made me come out here."

"Then you probably saw me before. I've never had many stories

I was willing to charge only a dime for, but I got to stick out my chin and pose a few times. Erase the beards on half your Buffalo Bills and you'll find this face here."

It could be true, Jarry knew. He looked at the faintly visible line of crumbling rock at the base of the cliff Swing T was driving toward. "But the drawings and the stories got the country right. I've seen clean white rock falls like that in a hundred drawings."

"You have? We'll take another look, and find out if we see the same thing."

Swing T drove his team close to the cliff, and pulled up on a small rise. He motioned for Jarry to climb down. "I'll get my camera out, you take a quick scout for a level place to stand."

Jarry walked down the rise and approached the first large white stone. It was a skull, as wide as a man's chest, with an enormous gash along one side. Looking around, Jarry saw the knobby sticks of a litter of leg bones standing up out of the sand. And more skulls, the symmetrical boat shapes of pelvic bones, vertebrae like stacks of coins that had fallen over. Some bones were badly broken, some smooth and whole, all were clean and bleached white. They stretched off for a dozen yards each way, and filled the half dozen yards between Jarry and the cliff.

"Is this what you remember seeing in your dime novels?"

"No."

"This is an Indian buffalo jump, an old one. The Indians are very scientific hunters. They understand the science of gravity very well. They cut a few head out of the herds and then drive them off that ridge up there. When they land they break their fat necks. Then the Indians ride downslope and cut off the meat and horns."

"Don't the Indians have guns?"

"Stand with your foot on that skull, right there." Swing T ducked under the cowling of his camera, lifted something out of a black box and slid it into the side of the camera. "Hold it." There was another slow, bright flash, and Swing T came out from under the cowl. Jarry saw that his boot had left a black scuff on the dome of the buffalo's skull, and he stooped to clean it to match the bleached whiteness of its company. "They have guns, all right. Increase Bonner, protected by the umbrella that shelters fools from harm, even rides up there and sells the Indians reloads. But they do it this way because they have always done it this way." He did more juggling of holders and glass. "Now, point your rifle off to your left. Mean look, now, mean look." Another flash.

"A tradition, you mean."

"To hear the Indians tell it, its more they're treading water waiting for the flood to subside."

"What flood?"

"Us." Swing T looked up at the ridge. "I'm losing the light, we've got to hurry. Do you think you can lift one of those skulls?"

"I know I can," Jarry said, remembering how he had been lodged inside one not so long ago.

"Good. We'll finish up with that."

Jarry lifted one of the bleached skulls, and held it against his chest, so the staring eye sockets faced Swing T's lens. Swing T poured more powder. "We are the flood," he said. "At least that's how the Indians see it; we have flooded their territory and forced them to high ground. But just like any other flood, we will subside some day." A slow burning, and wriggling spots before Jarry's eyes. "They figure all this territory that used to belong to them is going to be the same underneath once we whites have all evaporated. And they figure if *they* stay the same"—Swing T threw a cracked glass into the scrub—"then the land will welcome them back someday."

"That's a wonderful belief," Jarry said, smiling just as the flash went off.

"Indians are stupid that way," Swing T said. "Nice smile, Jarry. I'll title this shot *A Big Western Appetite.*"

Sunset was glowing along the top of the ridge. There wasn't a cloud in the sky, but the red light was giving way to the color of water boiling in a pot. Jarry thought he heard a roll of thunder. "That's all we have time for," Swing T said, and he began packing up his equipment.

"Now we go up on top."

"If you want another picture why are you putting the equipment away?"

"Oh, it's not a picture. I've already taken pictures up there. And I have to save some plates for another job. What I want is for you to do a little reading for me."

"Reading. Can't you read?"

"Of course, everything from a blast power ingredient list to the Latin on a Jesuit map. But I don't read that French of yours."

"Someone speaks French out here?" Jarry was amazed.

"Did." Swing T nodded. "Just hold on, and I'll show you."

Swing T finished lashing his equipment in and under his wagon, closed the door and slid a tiny horseshoe through the hasp. "This way," he said, and he started up a gently angled path on the rocky rise, carrying an unlit lantern and a coil of thin cord. They only climbed some five minutes before they came out on the open top of the bluff. Jarry looked around. The country was subdued but beautiful with the sun brightening the colors. The sky was still a clear blue, but a stubble of grey cloud or dust was gathering where the sky met the washed tan of the northern horizon. The top of the bluff was a mosaic of bare rock, each piece bigger than a man lying stretched out, each a different shade of red. Near the center was a stake wedged into the seam between two slabs. A thick rope with a pigtail knot around the stake ran a few feet, then disappeared down an eyebrow-shaped opening between two clashing shades of stone.

"Down there," Swing T said.

Jarry walked to the opening and looked down. The opening was about two feet wide, and smooth-edged. The rope disappeared down into a darkness that was more maroon than black. "You've been down there?" Jarry asked.

"Me, my camera, my plates, the whole cat-in-the-bag of me. Room to stand up without cramping. And a few surprises."

"Surprises?"

114

Swing T smiled. "I won't spoil them. You'll see." He set the lantern down on the rock, took out a match and lit it. "You just get yourself down there, and I'll lower the lantern right by you."

"And when I get to the bottom?"

"There's French written on the wall. I can't read it. I even came by a book of French lessons, but the only word I could pick out was 'gold'."

"It's a message about gold?"

Swing T lifted his hands. "You tell me, Quebecky. And before you ask, yes, we'll split any more gold we might find."

"*More* gold?"

"He had a few doubloons on him." He reached in his coat pocket and pulled out a brilliant yellow coin, as big as Jarry's palm. "This one will be your fee for the reading."

Jarry reached for it, but Swing T folded his fingers over it. "Reading first."

Jarry found that Swing T had tied knots in the rope, to help hands and feet stay put, and he descended easily, his back against one side of the rock chimney, the swaying lantern following just above him. The chimney stayed close until the last few feet before the sloping bottom. Jarry dropped the last few feet, and stayed in a crouch while he got his bearings.

When he finally raised his head, he saw what had once been a man sat opposite him, facing him.

"Find the surprise yet?" Swing T called down, his voice echoing off the rock. Just behind his voice, like a second echo, came the sound of distant thunder.

Jarry wasn't shocked much by the remains. Mostly, he was impressed. The man's boots, sitting next to him against the wall like a pair of nesting birds, were a fancy pair indeed, with stars and lacy circles and angels and crosses. His hat, the rags of it that remained, would have been big enough to shade a surrey full of women, his chaps were wide and studded. His empty holster had once been fine-tooled, but there wasn't much left of it. Jarry envied the corpse his outfit.

Over the dead man's shoulder there was red writing on the wall. Jarry couldn't help but grin. He had at last dropped into a scene from one of his penny dreadfuls. A dead cowboy, in a secret cave, a mysterious inscription on the wall, and the hero—Jarry laughed a bit at himself—the hero being the only one who can read the inscription. He knew he should feel badly for the dead man, but he mostly felt excited for himself, happy. He stood straight and walked across the cave. The inscription ran from the top of the wall to the bottom. It had been done in red chalk, and it was indeed French, as Swing T had said. But it was an old French, Jarry's grandmother's French, "Formal as the Sun King himself," his father used to say. It had some words that had died before Jarry was born, but he could still read it.

The others came for the gold. Their books all say it is here. The old ones hid it, the Captain has read. May they find it. I came for my own reasons. But I fear I have come too late. The Indians have—Jarry didn't recognize the next word, it looked like "receded."—*I still hope to find a tribe that will let me join, to help them hunt the mighty bison, to join them in their dances, to help them fight the whites as my grandfather fought the English. I know if I can but find them, they will let me join them. How have I come to be here? I told the others the truth of why I came. They think I am a fool, and when they found no gold here, they blamed me, that my foolishness weakened their deservedness before God's eyes, they blamed me as a Jonah. I was left here. I believe this was meant to be, that when the tribe comes to save me, they will see*

The bottom line of the writing had been washed away, either by a seep or by fluids that had escaped when the dead man's skin had burst years ago.

"Can you read it?" Swing T's voice echoed down the chimney. "Is there gold?"

"No gold," Jarry shouted.

"You'd better come up. A storm's coming, I think." And the thunder was indeed louder. Jarry reached the rope, but moments later the thunder was directly overhead and the walls began vibrating with it. Jarry put a hand over a knot and looked straight up. The pale afternoon light was flickering, like a candle about to be blown out. Animal bellowing echoed down the chimney and red dirt was falling in Jarry's face. It wasn't thunder after all, but the sound of dozens, maybe hundreds of hooves pounding past overhead. Hooves of what? Jarry couldn't sort any shapes out of the flickering shadows. Horses? But horses didn't bellow, did they?

And then it looked like a twisting snake was falling into his face, diving into the rock divide to escape the hooves. Jarry turned his head and was struck on the side of the neck by the falling rope. The hooves had severed it. The animal rush went on for only three or four more minutes and then the shadows were gone, replaced by a drifting red haze of dust.

"Swing T!" Jarry called for what he judged to be nearly half an hour, and there was no answer. The red dust had settled over the lantern and the room glowed like the internal organ of some huge beast. A huge beast Jarry had to escape. There was enough rope, but no one at the top to catch and secure it. The rock walls were close enough that Jarry could have tried jamming himself against one wall, with his feet on the other, and shinnied up. But he knew he wouldn't have the strength for it. It had to be the rope. "Swing T!" he called again, and again there was no answer. Jarry saw a star in the deep sky and knew it was nearly sunset.

He had to have some way to wedge the rope at the top. There was nothing but the old French explorer. Jarry knelt down next to the body and tucked both hands under the femur, and heaved. The rotten pants split, the remains of the tendons twisted then popped like overtaxed fish line, and the femur came loose in his hands. He tried to tie it into the end of the rope, but the bone was so thin and the rope so thick that the bone slipped out every time he tried to throw it up the chimney. So Jarry returned to the body and tore loose the other femur. Discs of the backbone fell on his hands like poker chips, and the entire skeleton collapsed. Jarry centered the huge hat over the bones as best he could. With a bit of the lantern cord, sawn against a rock, he tied the femurs together, so they formed a shallow X, then once again threw the rope and bones straight up the chimney. It wasn't until his sixth try that the bones landed across the chimney and the rope could support his weight. He tied the lantern cord to his belt, then started climbing to the top. If he fell he would land on the lantern, and possibly burst into flame. This encouraged him to keep his hands tight above the gripping knots. The hole was less than thirty feet deep, and Jarry was soon climbing out on top of the bluff, lying on his back panting for a few long minutes before drawing the lantern out behind him. He would need it soon; the sun was nearly gone.

Jarry looked downslope and saw that Swing T's wagon was gone. Jarry held the lantern to the sand where the bluff broke and started slanting down. The hoof marks there were layered and layered, slashes one atop the other until no shape could be made out. There were no animals in sight, either; no lights. The desert looked empty. Jarry faced the setting sun, knowing Hugo lay in that direction. He didn't know whether the town was due west, northwest, southwest.... All he could do was set out, and hope for the best.

"Just another day in the West," Jarry said to himself, and he started down the path.

Chapter 10

"I was no more than ten the last time I was tempted onto a roof." Dolley spoke into the darkness beyond the chimney. She knew Houston was there, waiting for the clouds to clear off and the stars to come out. She was fresh from her bath, and her throat still felt moist under its dusting of powder. "It's steep here," she added, meaning, "Where are you?"

"It's flat on this end," came Houston's voice. He was invisible against the dark block of the chimney, but she could see his outstretched hand. She was almost lifted off her feet when he tugged her up onto the flat. "Walk slowly if you have acrophobia." He held her hand and led her to where the telescope stood just past the chimney. She could make out Houston's face now. He wore a look of curiosity, but he asked nothing. Instead he said, "This end is flat because this is where the bell tower stood when this was a church. Watts took all the pieces down and put them back together in his backyard. The best view of any outhouse in town. Perhaps you've seen it." He was smiling now.

"I haven't had that pleasure," Dolley said.

"Built himself a little round seat so he can face any direction." Before Dolley could decide if he was joking, Houston turned and pointed into the sky. "A fine night for gazing," he said. He turned back to her. "In all directions."

"I wouldn't know one star from another," Dolley said.

"That's only because you haven't cared enough about them," Houston said. "You probably don't know one tree from another."

"I once did. I don't now." The breeze felt good, running over her skin, drying her powder.

"But I'll wager you can tell one baby from another," he said.

"Certainly."

"And one man from another?"

"Mr. Houston, you are teasing me."

"I'm only pointing out that your life has been full enough without the need of stars."

"My life has *not* been full of men."

He gave no sign of having heard her. "But if you had been born out here, it might have been different. There's work enough for a woman in this country, but it's stingy about beauty. Tracing the stars after the children have been put to bed is as close as most women out here get to touching something beautiful." He bent to the telescope, swiveled it until he found what he wanted. "Here, take a look."

He took a step away and motioned for her to look. She felt the warmth of his eye in the eyepiece. When she settled her eye against the warm rubber she saw a bright diagonal of hard white dots running across the circle of sky Houston had chosen for her. Some tribes in Australia," Houston said, "think those three stars in Orion's belt are men, chasing the women of the Pleiades. The stars are only cold and distant if you look at them that way."

The white sparkles were beautiful, but she knew that bent forward this way her hips were slanted out toward where Houston stood. She straightened up and moved away. "They're like pearls, you mean. They pick up the warmth of the wearer—or the watcher in this case—and that gives them their luster." The wind was rising again, scuttling across the dry hard pan of the dark country. It broke against the buildings of the town and shot up, lifting Dolley's hair from her neck, tangling it. She tried to smooth it as Houston went on talking.

"That's good," Houston said, and he pointed. "The middle star of the three is called Alnilam. That's the name of a string of pearls. And you said you didn't know anything about stars."

"You're teasing again. But you do know a lot about them, don't you."

"Oh, I don't know. I used to think that if I kept looking in every part of the sky that I could find an uncharted star, or an eighth planet, some pure light nobody had put their name on, and I could put my name on it. I thought that would be a fine thing, to write my name forever in the sky. But, really, I was like that cocky guard I told you about, the one who was ever-vigilant, but looking the wrong way. I was spending so much time trying to discover something no one else had found that I didn't see all that was right in front of me. Things everybody else already knew about." He looked at Dolley, hesitated, then looked away again. "I don't try to discover anything new in the sky anymore. I just keep looking at the things I've already seen, because they're so beautiful. But I try to look around in the daylight a little more, see if I can pick up any traces of a path." The last few words came out with uneven spaces between, as if they had to be found at the last moment.

"The sky is the most beautiful part of the country here," Dolley said. "I used to love the sunsets on the trail. Waiting for them is how I got through the days."

"The air here is too clear for really beautiful sunsets," Houston said. "Things afloat in the air really bring out sunset lights. I remember. . . . Do you mind another of my old sailor stories, Mrs. Kenninac?" She shook her head.

"A few years ago I was on a spice steamer just out of the Sandwich Islands," Houston began. He was standing very close to her, the two of them leaning against the warm chimney, which was as tall as top of Dolley's shoulders. When Houston spoke his breathing stirred the hair on her brow. "And the sunset lit up in red ribbons, like a dancer's scarves. And then at sunrise the light came up blue. Not just the sky, the light from the sun streamed down bonnet blue, blue as a field of papoose root. All because an island near Java was dying, thrown up into the air by a volcano. I wonder why it is that pressure escaping all of a sudden like that will make things more beautiful everywhere in the world."

They stood quiet. Out of the chimney came the sound of logs popping in the fireplace below. "Sometimes I can see your wrists when you're cooking over the fire."

"You look down our chimney?"

"I have my own pots to attend to," Houston said. He stepped up on a protruding brick ledge and leaned over the top of the chimney. His face was devilish and long in the orange light. From inside the chimney he lifted out a small round pot that hung on a thick iron hook. "Care for some soup?" He asked. He hung the pot from the telescope tripod, and lifted the lid. "Doughball soup. The cold up here will sink into your bones otherwise. Jennice Skoda at the cafe makes it up. Folks call her 'Skoda from Dakota,' but she's really from Wyoming."

"She was at the calendar bee."

"That she was." Houston blew on the handle of the big dipper that stood in the pot, then handed it to Dolley. She scooped up some of the thick soup and sipped it.

"This is very good." She tried to take another sip, but the words came out before she could lift the dipper the last inch: "How much does Skoda from Dakota charge you to make this delicious soup?"

"Exactly what you're thinking she charges me." He hadn't hesitated.

"I'm sorry. That's none of my business. It must be the unaccustomed height." She dropped the dipper back into the pot.

"A man on his own attracts friends in a country like this, Mrs. Like most of us out this way, she and I make use of what little there is to life in this country. We make do with what there is until the proper thing comes along. All in the name of pioneer spirit." There was a metallic sound, as Houston began turning some part of his telescope.

"I've overstepped my bounds, Mr. Houston. Forgive me."

"I once jumped ship just to take the measurements of the Venus de Milo. Do you want to know what they were?" He was taking something out of a bag and screwing it onto the telescope.

"Are you trying to embarrass me, Mr. Houston?"

"Thirty-seven, twenty-six, thirty-eight, and you have nothing to be embarrassed about." He swiveled the telescope to a new angle. "Now we've both overstepped. But bounds are for parlors, Mrs. There are no bounds on a dark roof unless we put them there. And to my way of thinking you might just be coming inside the bounds I'd want you to be in." He was turning to look out across the desert, and then back to her, his face half-lighted then eclipsed, like a moon furiously running through its phases. "And you're entitled to know what kind of man is prowling over you while you sleep—in case a hole ever opens up, you should know who'll come falling through." He turned back to the soup pot. "I should have warned you, Mrs. Skoda always makes her doughball soup with a generous pour of beer in it. I'll put the lid back on for now," he said when he turned back. "Now could you take just two steps back?"

"Why?"

"I'll show you."

Dolley stepped back. Houston made some final adjustments and turned the telescope toward her. The Pleiades appeared on her bodice, the stars following her curves, winking brightly on the smooth satin. When she turned, the stars shifted, winked and slid over her dress. Delighted, Dolley laughed.

"A little something I'm working on. But there was nothing smooth and light enough to try it on, until now. Now, Miss Alnilam, what brings you out onto your roof at this time of night?"

Dolley kept her eyes on the shifting stars while she answered. "Your scaffolding."

"Really? I thought you probably flew up like a night bird."

She looked at him then, and shook her head. "You have a way of mixing compliment and rudeness that can be very off-putting, Mr. Houston."

"I've been told that before." He spoke softly, but it wasn't an apology.

"What I meant was I wonder if I might borrow it for a few days." Even in the dim light, Dolley could see that Houston was surprised. "I wonder, too, Mr. Houston, if you could turn off these stars. And if we might finish your friend's soup down below."

Inside the store, Dolley first stood a minute, listening to the breathing of her children. Then she took two hot pads out of a drawer and crossed to the west window and opened it. The small soup pot appeared from above, dangling on a thin line. Dolley brought it in then untied the bow. She put the pot in the middle of the table. Houston let himself in, walked to the table and pulled out her chair for her. He walked around the table and pulled out the chair opposite, which struck against the side of a wooden tub that set beside the stove.

"Oh, excuse the tub," Dolley said. Houston smiled, leaned over and prodded a few of the bubbles with his finger, watched them pop and dissolve.

Dolley felt her face flush. To ask a man into your home with your bath water standing by the table! She turned her full attention to dipping out the bowls of soup. "I'd forgotten that was there. Usually Jarry drags it out and empties it behind the house, but he's gone out with that man who drives that little red wagon."

"Swing T? The photographer?"

"Yes."

"The preserver is having himself preserved?"

"I don't know what he is doing, but he said it would bring . . . that it was a job."

Houston stirred his soup without tasting of it. "Now that we're out of the wind, tell me again what you said that sounded like you wanted to borrow my scaffolding."

"I do."

"I can't help but ask: what do you plan to do with it?"

"Move it over here," Dolley said, and she pointed over her shoulder, out the dark window. Houston looked over her shoulder and frowned. "I want to paint a mural," Dolley said. "I want to paint a mural on that blistered wall, so I have something to look at when I face that way."

"What do you plan to paint?"

"Something with water in it, I think."

"Water? How about a twenty-foot high wash tub? Or my boots when I've been riding in the rain?"

"I'll decide once I'm on the scaffolding, thank you. I've never painted a mural before, and I'll have to plan as I go along."

Houston smiled. "This territory is full of folks with busted plans, or who have been busted by their plans, so starting off without one is probably a good move. Mrs., I'd be pleased to move my scaffold for you. Tomorrow soon enough?"

"That would be fine, Mr. Houston. Thank you." Houston tipped back in his chair and again struck the bathing tub. "I'll empty your tub for you," he said.

"Certainly not! No. Jarry can hardly drag it, but it is his job to do. No."

"Drag it, Mrs.? No. Let me show you the lazy gambler's way of emptying a tub." He nodded his head toward her, a kind of bow with just his hat, and left the store. He was back in a matter of minutes. He carried a coil of copper tubing.

"Moonshiner's friend," Houston said. He walked to the window near the stove and pushed the curtain back. He cupped his hands around his eyes and peered through the bubbly glass, out into the ash stained lot, then turned back toward the tub. He carefully straightened the tubing into a long arc, like a low, copper-colored rainbow. He put one end of the tubing into the bubbles and held the other while he slid the window open. "Pardon me," he said, and stepped out over the window sill.

Dolley waited, but Houston didn't climb back in. She walked to the window. Outside Houston, bareheaded, was bent low, his lips against the open end of the tubing. His neck was pale where the collar of his coat kept it covered, and Dolley could see the cords there stand out in the moonlight. Houston pulled the tube sharply away from his lips and the soapy scented water began to splash softly onto the ground, vapor rising from it as it passed through the cooler night air.

Houston held the end of the tube with one hand, and reached the other into the stream for a moment. Then he raised his wet fingers. He patted the water onto his chapped face. He never looked up, and Dolley didn't know if he was aware of her or not. Houston put his fingertips in the water again, and this time held them to his lips.

Dolley stepped back from the window, and turned her back on it. She went over everything he had said on the rooftop, then nodded to herself. "The soup," she thought. "Of course. He's intoxicated. That's all."

THE thunder of the stampede that had nearly marooned Jarry had called up real thunder in answer; the red dust seeded the clouds in their passing. A steady warm drizzle hovered overhead. The hard weather lashed the town, rain hammering on the rooftops and cutting deep sluices down the tracks of the main street and pooling in the alleys. The flashes of lightning were like Swing T's magnesium flashes, freezing outlines on Jarry's pupil, like the images of murderers penny dreadful detectives found in the eyes of victims. The flashes showed how the black clouds flowed in off the Indians' mountains. Jarry saw the rushing line moving east, with hard claps above the clouds, saw how it rolled past Hugo to spread out flat and wool-grey and scatter in thin plates above the high desert to the east, even allowing some star light, like fringe at the bottom of a shroud.

This was the first rain in the territory since their coming, and Jarry knew the land needed it. But there was something too violent about it, something feral that Eastern rains didn't have. The rain seemed to sink cold teeth into the ground, to worry it like a wolf tearing at flesh. And the flowing cuts and jumpy rivulets in the street made Jarry think of an animal with its flank slashed open. He had thrown away the empty lantern miles back, and he now moved slowly down the muddy street toward the low light Dolley had set in their display windows.

Then a dark figure was outlined against the window light. One minute the street had been empty, all sensible life beaten indoors, and the next someone was blocking his way. *Swing T*, Jarry thought, and his anger at being left behind returned, despite his exhaustion. But two more steps brought him close enough to see that it wasn't the photographer. It was someone small, a small man wading, shoulders hunched like a bird with its feathers ruffed. He walked head down, and every few steps he would stoop down to scoop mud out of a rut. There was enough light for Jarry to see that the small man carried a miner's pan, and he sluiced the muddy water around and let it sprinkle down out of the bottom of the pan. Then the little man poked through the mud left behind. Prospecting. But for what? These streets, even Jarry knew, were not paved with gold. Then the small man drew something with a dull glint out of his pan and slipped it into a pocket of his coat. He threw the mud out in a rooster tail behind him, and walked closer to Jarry's porch. Keeping one eye on the odd prospector, Jarry stepped under his porch roof, finally out of the rain.

"Mr. Tanner?" the small man said, and Jarry turned to face him.

The rain had soaked through the brim of the small man's wide soft hat, and it hung down almost covering his eyes. He stepped up under the cover of Jarry's porch roof. When he took off his hat he slid it off backward, so the trapped water splashed out into the mud, away from where Jarry stood. He turned his hat slowly in his hands, like a preacher, as he spoke.

"My name is Increase Bonner," he said in a high voice.

Jarry nodded. Increase turned his hat halfway around before he spoke again. "I reload," he said, with rhythm, almost piping it. "I come to ask if you need any reloads or shot."

"You make new bullets and shot out of spent ones."

127

"I do," Increase said, sounding happy now. "Miss Lynn, down the schoolhouse, says I'm like the lamp peddler in the Aladdin story." He pointed out into the street in front of Jarry's store. "It's always good looking down this way when it comes down hard. Something always turns up in this stretch here." His hand returned to his hat brim. "You knew this used to be a church."

"Watts told me, yes."

"Did you know that lead in stain glass windows is exactly the same as what makes the best shot?"

"No, I didn't."

"It spooks some people, you know? And so they don't like to buy my reloads. They'd rather send away instead. The Sheriff, now, he wouldn't have any other kind than mine. He tells the hunters, 'You don't know where that outside lead has been!'" Increase laughed, a small wheeze. "No matter how much I pick up here, more always wicks up with the next rain. The way a splinter worries itself out of your hand, you know, or like the ground just pushes up more lead from down mine level. But the ground can't do that, can it?"

Jarry shook his head.

"Would you be needing any reloads or shot tonight? I deliver at more hours than the stork."

"I don't believe so, no."

"Well," and the hat made a complete revolution before he finished his thought, "if you do decide you want something, just call on Increase Bonner. I'll give you a better penny-weight price than any mail-away can." He thought for a moment. "Business cards?" he asked. "I also print cards."

"There's an idea," Jarry said, trying to be polite. He just wanted to get inside.

"I could make you up a sample. Take the spelling off your window."

"Fine . . . but what's the cost?"

"I'll give you a better penny-weight price than any printer around."

Jarry tried to smile. "I'll look at a sample."

"Good. I'll be getting back to my harvesting now," Increase said. He put his wet hat squarely back on his head and walked back out into the mud.

Before he even took off his wet boots, Jarry went to the doorway of the bedroom. Dolley was breathing evenly. He was in no hurry to tell his story. He would just stay up until she awoke.

The way the rain beat against the oiled paper on the roof and loudly conducted its bubbly overhead search for leaks made Jarry turn and count the kitchen kettles, just in case.

He made a pot of "late coffee," half as many grounds as used in the morning. He took off his clothes and wrapped himself in a long doe-skin, then stoked up the fire. He had walked so long in the hard rain that his ears crackled, as full of water as if he'd been submerged in a pool for hours. The skinny falls of rain coming off the porch roof began to show a dance hall pink as Hugo moved a little further on toward the sun.

Jarry stood up, pulling the doe-skin tight around him, and took down a book titled *Watson's Quantulucunque Concerning the Animal World* from the sideboard, and took it to the table. He turned again to the "Superstitions Debunked" chapter, to the engraving of *The Ghost of a Flea*. Jarry squinted at the flea's eye, cold as a fish but ravenous at the same time, looking out of the corner of its socket right at him. Jarry had seen that look before, recognized just such a cold, round eye elsewhere. But it hadn't be alive, hadn't even been an engraving. It had been glass, the staring eye of Swing T's camera.

Chapter 11

THE whitewash soaked into the wood like fresh churned butter into a biscuit, and so two coats were needed. It had taken almost two days to scrape down the wall. Two days through which Dolley and her helpers—Andy all of the time, Jarry those times when Evie Bonner could sit with Gertrude, and even Houston, who showed up and stayed half an afternoon, wearing an old bee-keeper's hood to keep the flaking paint off his face—worked in a steady shower of black curls and powdery ash. The whitewashing took only a morning's time as the day was bright and a warm wind moved gently across the desert. The breeze was gentle, and swept down out of the Indians' green mountains and so was fresh. A hawk tipped and circled above the building, watching its own shadow move across the white wall. The sun coaxed out the full color in everything around them, made the few late dark purple flowers sparkle in the brittle brown of the beaten-down tumbleweeds.

Dolley knew this was the kind of day that made some love this faded and scoured-out country, but she was only grateful that the wind dried the wash so quickly. Houston had had the idea to dig a foot-deep trench at the base of the wall and most of the black ash fell into it and was covered over with sand, and more was dampened down with drippings from the wash. But there was still burned wood laying on the lot from the gallows fire. Dolley pulled on a pair of old duck gloves, kicked away some of the sand that had gathered around a piece of burned wood a good foot long and pulled it free.

She stood a long moment looking up at the wall, its off-white stretch cut into sections by the black bars of the scaffolding. Houston and Jarry had claimed an old set of steps from the sunken jail and propped them against the scaffolding; using these Dolley could climb to the second level without the loss of dignity she'd suffered when it had at least been dark and no one had been able to see her climb to the roof. Now she paced the gritty sand from one end of the blue-white to the other, held her hand up to divide its height into fingered sections, which she marked with black nicks at each of the corners. Jarry, Andy, and a number of curious attracted by the novel smell of someone whitewashing, all breathed as quietly as they could. Dolley, with no look back at her audience, climbed the jail stairs, her neck craned as she walked as if keeping a target in sight. On the second level she moved to her left, reached as she could, and made a single black chop mark. At the back of the small crowd, Evie applauded.

Dolley moved with increasing speed, sketching in what soon came to resemble a long pole against a clear sky, with feathery, shimmering charcoal lines echoing its trunk that caught the moment when the trunk would have tottered before sliding down into its hole. With the burned wood she sketched in the crow's nest (fat-bottomed as a wash tub), and the spar, and the slats nailed to the pole for climbing, all the ropes, iron and wood she remembered so well from the ships in bottles her Mother had carried from charity room to charity room. Dolley remembered the names of some of these parts as she sketched them in: "Head of the gallant mast, the gallant mast cross-trees, crow's nest—Sleet's patent type, monkey-rope to keep you from being carried off."

Dolley moved down to the lower level of the scaffolding and drew the mast down. It ended not on the deck of a ship, but on a stretch of rocky New England earth, the rocks created with a few swipes of her black wood as solid as any in the landscape surrounding her. Jarry hadn't known Dolley could be an artist on such a grand scale, and he watched with a huge smile on his face as she climbed back up, created another land mast, shrunken by perspective, rooted in an even rockier ground. These filled the top two-thirds of the left side. She came down to ground level now, and drew a sooty, curved-side triangle that touched the ground on one side, and ran off the side of the building on the other. Dolley leaned into her work, and when she stepped back everyone saw that the triangle was the front of a boat, seen from a high angle so that it was clear it was filled with furs. Dolley turned from the wall for the first time then, and smiled at Jarry. He knew this was her nod to advertising his business.

She walked slowly to her right, slashing at the wall as she moved, and under those slashes rocks appeared that told the watchers this was a channel, or the edge of a harbor the boat was floating in. Dolly again mounted the stairs and walked to the very end of the first level. There she began another slim pole, but one which quickly widened out, became an upturned milk funnel with mysterious black and white eyes in it, round as a skunk's. She stepped down to the ground and, with one long graceful curve, turned the funnel and eyes above her into the prow of a large ship, with its opening for anchors and lines, a ship moving toward her, up the channel out of the sea. Then it was back to the first level to create a horizon, part rock, part sea, part distant cloud. Dolley then returned to ground and began walking toward the crowd. Several voices began congratulating her, but after a small nod and smile for their benefit, she turned to face the wall, giving the sketch a hard eye at this critical distance. She nodded again, and returned to climb to the very top. She moved quickly from one part of the sketch to another, again slashing quickly at the wall, moving left to right, then down a level, and then down again. When she had worked her way down to the sand, she had written a number inside each outlined area of the sketch.

"Andy!" she called, and held out her arm toward the back of the abandoned paint store, like a conjurer setting up a trick. Andy ran around the corner, then immediately came back around leading a goat with a miniature wagon yoked behind it. The boy from whom Andy had borrowed the goat and cart followed behind, steadying the load.

Dolley turned to face the people gathered in the alley. She smiled and said, "I had planned to have my husband and son help me with this part, but perhaps more of you would like to assist me, as well? There are plenty more brushes inside."

"Yes, Ma'am," one young man shouted, and the others laughed, but many of them nodded. "Inside this wagon," Dolley announced, "are eleven glazed urns, inside each is a mixed paint. On the outside of each you'll see a number." She pointed over her shoulder. "The numbers on the urns match the picture. All you have to do is grab a brush and fill them in." She tossed her stick down in the sand. "I'm a bit tired, so all I'm going to do is some cooking for anyone who does my work for me. I hope you all favor hot cakes." She smiled and walked toward the store.

As Dolley passed through the crowd, Jarry began handing out brushes to the eager volunteers, adding in a serious voice, "Those doe-skin gloves, which I tailor special to each living hand, will clean right up with a few dabs of my special blend saddle soap. . . ."

DOLLEY fed the volunteer painters their flapjacks through the window next to the stove. Jarry tended Gertrude—Evie had insisted on being one of the painters on the topmost level of the scaffolding. Dolley lifted a stack of dirty plates off the window ledge, and stood in the window for a moment, looking at her mural. The volunteers had done a pretty good job of filling it in. There were a few areas, she saw, where she would have to do a bit of touch-up, a place or two where the color might even have to be changed, but overall it was good work.

The mural was her memories of the Nantucket of her child-hood, with a few improvements. There were rows of land masts with spars and crows nests all along the shore, manned by men who brandished speaking trumpets. Dolley imagined them keeping watch for whales, and then shouting down to harpooners when they sighted a spout. Lines ran between the poles, and the men could move buckets of drink and salt fish from one pole to the next. In Dolley's Nantucket, no man had to go to sea beyond the horizon, and no woman had to stay behind and wonder if she was a widow, and, somehow more painful, at least in Dolley's imagination, wonder how to survive being alone for years at a time.

A face appeared in the serving window, and Dolley started to hand out a plate of hot cakes, but Houston's hand came up flat to stop her.

"I think you're needed down at the beehive," Houston said in a too-loud voice. "Can you come right now?"

"What's wrong? Has Mr. Hart come back?"

"Sam Hart took that knacker's wagon of his up into the hills, and he brought back women just like he said he would, three of them. He's got them all locked in his Smithy with him right now. Temiz is down there with a ring of guns, and Sam's got a gun, too."

"Good Lord, no!" Dolley said. She thought of how she had encouraged Hart to keep up his red eye attitude. "I'll come right now." She began taking off her apron.

"No, Dolley," Jarry said. "That's no place for a woman."

"There are already three women there, Jarry. I helped make that new eye, and I told him it would impress women. I'm part responsible for this terrible thing."

"We only did what he asked, Dolley. We only gave him what he paid for. This isn't your responsibility."

"I think," Houston interrupted, just his eyes and forehead showing over the windowsill, "that Sam Hart is quite taken with your wife, Jarry. If she could come it might help to take him alive in the end."

"I'll come," Dolley said.

"Do you really think they might shoot him?" Jarry asked Houston.

"If you need more pancakes," Dolley said, "that tub there is filled with batter, and you might want to add some cinnamon." She began moving toward the door, talking over her shoulder. "You watch the children close, Jarry. Don't let them out until . . ." The bell on the door cut off her last words.

Dolley and Houston hurried along the walk. "I don't know if I can be of any help," Dolley said. "But I do want to try. Perhaps I can talk those women into coming out."

"Maybe," Houston said. He sounded doubtful. "The men have tried, but they don't understand the women, I don't believe."

"Every man's complaint," Dolley said, in a voice roughened by anger.

"Do you think you understand them enough? Do you understand what kind of need it is that might make a woman—let alone three women—go with a man she hardly knows, just because he gives her a smile and a bright eye?"

Since the first day she had known Houston, Dolley had liked the man, but she had also been on her guard. Many of the things he had said to her seemed to have had a double edge, an innocent—or almost innocent—side, and another quite different side. She tried to gauge the edges of this question. How cold was he? She took a deep breath. "I'll think about that later, Mr. Houston. If an answer comes to me, you'll be the first to know."

"First in line is good enough for me. This way now," Houston said, and he led her into a branching alley. They passed beneath the stairs that led to the Sheriff's office, and down a long unused path through high weeds. Houston led her onto the back porch of a low building and he opened the door. They walked through a dark room where shelves were stacked with spools of thread, cones of rough yarn, and bolts of cloth. Buttons snapped under their feet as they walked. The only light that showed from the sides of their path came from silks that gathered up glimmerings from up ahead. Houston led Dolley through a second door, into a millinery and yard goods store. Two women in leg of mutton sleeved shirtwaists stood with their arms folded, angry looks on their faces, behind the counter. Houston bent an arm around to keep Dolley behind him and led the way to a corner next to one of the store's smaller front windows, where he had her crouch down.

Dolley could see the smithy, see the small opening in the enormous door. A shooting hole, she knew. And then she saw a man's body lying in the dirt near the big door. Outside on the porch, behind rain barrels and a dry trough, four men with guns watched the smithy. The man in the dirt lifted his head and looked back at the millinery store. He smiled, shook his head 'no,' then lowered his face back into the dirt. One of the men on the porch slammed his rifle down and turned to the man next to him. "I wish he'd quit diagnosing," the man said. "He ain't a damn doctor, but he's always diagnosing. All the time. A damn body gets tired of hearing his ills, I can tell you!"

"Best friends," Houston said softly. "Where are you?" he called out to the angry man.

"Except for that fool getting a welcome hole in him, just where we were."

"Where's Temiz?"

"He took a rope and a hook and went that way," the man said, pointing off to his left.

"I would like to try talking to Hart," Dolley said to Houston. "Mr. Hart would never harm me."

"I don't believe so myself," Houston said. "But circumstances are going to make most of the decisions here, not Sam Hart." He lifted a cone of wound yarn off a shelf and looked through it as though the cone were a telescope trained on Dolley. "What each of us might or might not do gets swept away by circumstances." He stood up and, still carrying the cone, walked to the door. He adjusted it so he could see the smithy reflected in the glass then held the cone to his lips. "Sam! Sam, this is Houston!"

Dolley, like the others, expected smoke or a flash would be Houston's answer. But a woman's face appeared around the door. "What do you have to say?" she called over.

"Tell Sam he has to come out. No one's been killed."

"Sam says we're going North, to Utah, where we'll be legal."

"You women will be free to go. Just tell Sam to keep his guns down. If the man in the street dies, then we have a whole new story. He'll have to wait."

"He ain't going to die," the man's friend on the boardwalk said. "He's just diagnosing." Houston ignored him, took an involuntary step through the door, his eyes narrowed.

Temiz was making his way across the domed roof of the smithy. He had one of the glass wig-heads from the millinery shop, carried it upside down as he carefully made his way up the slope. Stoppering the neck of the glass head was one of the cones of yarn. He climbed to the smoke hole and balanced the glass head on his knees. From his pocket he took a silver match carrier and drew out a match. He set fire to the loose end of the yarn. "Houston!" Dolley said, and she tried to force her way past him at the door, but he held her arms. Temiz leaned over and dropped the glass head through the smoke hole. He scooted down the front of the roof, pulled out his pistol, and perched above the door like a barn owl.

No sound had come through the thick bricks of the smithy, and no new smoke was visible through the hole in the dome's cap, but Dolley could imagine the scene inside the smithy when the head struck, burst and spilled fire. Then the door of the smithy opened. At first, only a shivering orange glow showed through the opening, then the long face of a dappled white and gray horse appeared. There was the faint snap of a whip, and the big horse began to pull. The men on the walk flattened themselves to their barrels, to the boards beneath them, became as thin as paper, as still as shadows. Only Houston moved. He pulled Dolley back inside the shop, and took a try-on mirror off the wall. "Wait here," he said. He held the mirror so that Dolley could see the reflection of the street. "You can watch with this." And he hurried out the door. Dolley had to use both hands to keep the mirror steady, but then she could see the horse and wagon emerging from the burning beehive. Houston held up a hand toward Temiz, who looked at him briefly, then back down at the horse.

137

The horse was pulling Hart's inverted buckboard, his blacksmith's knacker's wagon. Most of the wagon was filled with stacked and strapped bags and boxes. Middlemost were lashed three chairs, and in the chairs, sitting in a dignified row, rode the women, their eyes staring straight ahead. Sam Hart held the reins. The horse and wagon made slow progress across Dolley's mirror.

Hart looked down at the man in the dirt. "He'll be fine," Hart shouted across the street. "But you'll probably all get tired of hearing his story!" The men on the porch were dragging themselves into new positions with their boots, placing fingerfuls of spit on their sights.

"Steady," Houston said as he stepped off the porch and into the street. "Sam, the women can go, but you had better get down. Right now, Sam." Dolley saw Temiz take off his hat and set it gently on the edge of the roof.

Hart shook his head. "We're all going to Utah. They've got a higher view of men and women up there." Then there was a roar, and in her surprise, Dolley dropped her mirror. Behind her, the milliners were shouting. Dolley stepped into the broken glass and looked out the window. Hart was no longer on the seat of the wagon. Instead, he was jammed between the right front wagon wheel and the body of the wagon, and his body was acting as a brake. The terrified horse was trying to run, but the wagon would only turn in an erratic circle to the right.

Houston and the other men ran into the street. One of the men ran past the wagon to tend to the wounded man. Houston ran alongside the horse and clapped his hat over the horse's eyes. He covered and uncovered the animal's eyes two more times, more slowly each time, and the animal finally stopped. Dolley could see its muscles twitching, its eyes rolling, as she ran toward the wagon. She ran to where Hart hung between wheel and wagon. Blood covered his face and had run down to the hub of the wheel, and from there down a half dozen spokes. The bullet had entered Hart's left temple and come out through the socket of his lost eye. Splinters clung to his cheek. Houston took a handkerchief and covered Hart's face.

The women still sat in their lashed-down chairs. The foremost of the three woman said, "We're his widows now. We laid with Sam this morning, all three of us. That body is ours."

The woman in the middle added, "He was distracted some by the guns, but he was kind to us." The women looked precariously balanced on their thin-legged chairs. Their belongings, strapped down around them, were like brightly painted rubble, the wagon like a small lifeboat which had fled from a burning ship only to run aground.

Houston looked up at the smithy, but Temiz had gone. Then he said to the men who had gathered around the wagon, "It seems our sheriff is finished with his part in this. Let's respect the widows' wishes."

While the men were freeing Hart's body from the wheel, Dolley stepped up onto the low wagon, and sat on a small box. She reached out and touched the arm of the first woman. "I'm sorry it turned out this way," was all she could think to say.

"We've all had worse, Mrs. But, it may be that none of us has had better. These last twelve hours, with a man willing to die to be our husband if only for one spin of a clock's hands were better than we had expected. Sam had a good idea this might happen, too, Mrs." She smiled, as if Dolley were the one in need of comforting. "We told him how we had come West, in stinking wagons filled with women— prison women, some of us; shamed women, most of us. And we told him all were expecting were paper men, men who would sign the deed and use us in all the ways men do when they have a paper on their side. We'd seen it a few times on the way out. The wagons would circle outside a town, and the men would come buying, getting papers from the wagon master, and the women would be getting their slaps before they were even out of range of the campfire smoke."

The second woman spoke now. "We told him that we all wished that we had stayed East, and how women aren't doing this much any more. Sam thought there would be more and more women coming this way, and he looked real sad when we told him it was stopping now."

139

The third woman added, "We felt a little bad, telling him how we had written letters home telling our friends not to come. But, Sam said he forgave us."

Houston and two other men lifted Hart onto the wagon, laid him across the back on top of a pad of rolled blankets.

The first woman stood up from her chair. She was very tall with blonde hair that was not so much gathered as knotted in a twist. "Women are standing their ground now, back East. It's easier to change your life now, with all the factories. And it's been long enough since the Civil War now that a whole new crop of men has come up, and there's one for almost every woman now—especially if she favors younger men." She smiled. "And who doesn't? But my point is that no one has to settle for a paper man anymore." While she was talking, she moved to the seat of the wagon and took the reins that were handed to her.

Dolley climbed down off the wagon and stood in the street. The woman with the blonde twist shook the reins and the horses began to move. Instead of moving off down the street as Dolley had expected, the woman began steering the horses back into the smithy. The crowd which had gathered began to disperse, and only Dolley and Houston watched as the wagon entered the shadows of the smithy, with the orange glow at its center.

"They must have forgotten something," Houston said.

"I'd like to see if I can comfort them," Dolley said.

"Would you like me to come in with you?"

"I don't think so."

Houston nodded, squeezed her forearm, and started walking back to the millinery shop. When Dolley entered the smithy she found the three women lifting Hart's body off the back of the wagon.

"Is there something we can do for you, Mrs.?" the tall one asked.

"No. I thought I would come and see if there was anything I could do for you."

"If you can help hoist that would be helpful."

"Hoist?"

"Sam. We're going to have to tackle him up if we're going to lower him slowly enough."

"You're going to bury him in the floor?"

The tall woman shook her head. "Sam didn't want to be buried. He wanted cremation. He showed us his tackle lift here, and explained how we could lower him into his own forge, lower him slowly enough that he would burn away little by little."

"My Lord. . . ."

"You had better sit, Mrs. Or maybe you should leave. You're pale as a preacher paying for dinner."

The tall woman held Dolley's arm and led her to a stool. "My name's Nell. Now you just catch your breath for a minute." The woman's upper lip clamped down severely over her top teeth when she spoke, but her smile was reassuring.

"Thank you. Sam told you how to do this?"

"I think he knew that sheriff would find some excuse to kill him. We wanted to surrender, to walk out and spare him, but he talked us into staying. Sam was a great talker. Last night he said this:

> *My blond beehive belle*
> *Know now you're my life knell*
> *So, if you go, you might as well tell*
> *The devil to call, 'cause that would*
> *be my death knell.'*

"Not all his rhymes were jokes, Mrs."

The two other women had fastened a leather strap around Hart's ankles, and now tied it through a loop in a thick rope that disappeared into the gloom at the top of the smithy.

"You should leave now, Mrs.," Nell told her.

Dolley shook her head. "I helped Mr. Hart find the courage to go after you. I want to be here."

Nell looked doubtful, but didn't try to force Dolley to leave. She walked over to the other women and pulled on the rope with them. Hart's body began to lift, to tip up. Dolley sat as still as she could, but her hands trembled. When Hart's head began to drag across the floor,

141

she stood and rushed to lift him by the shoulders. His face was shrouded in a white knit shawl, and his skin was hot from lying near the forge. Dolley felt it at her back as she supported Hart until he was vertical again, hanging upside down. Then Dolley recognized Hart: the tarot deck's Hanged Man. It stood for a crossroads, she thought, and maybe water, but she couldn't remember. But there was precious little water in the beehive. It was all smoke and flame. The only water was sweat, which soaked through the women's clothes as they hauled on the rope. Dolley moved to where they stood and reached for the rope.

"No," big Nell told her. "The fire's too low. Stoke it for us, stoke it."

Dolley hurried to the big bellows. Its wooden handle was so stiff she had to lift with both hands. Pressing down lifted her to her toes. She pumped and pumped again and the light from the forge increased, yellow chasing out the blue shadows. The women tied off the big rope, and Dolley looked at Hart's body, swinging lightly above her. One corner of the shawl that covered his face hung down, like the wick of an inverted taper. A second rope moved the body along some hidden track until it hung directly over the forge. One of the women began turning a crank handle and Hart's body slowly began to descend.

The corner of the shawl caught first, burned quickly and caught Hart's shirt collar as well. Then the shawl fell away and Hart's face was revealed, impassive with his hair afire, his lips blistering. Dolley wondered why she didn't feel sick. But she efficiently pumped the bellows as the women slowly lowered Hart into the fire. His blackened skin twisted as it peeled off, so it looked like it was being unscrewed from his body. No white bones showed, everything blackened as the body was lowered more and more. Dolley found herself watching to see if a splinter from the wooden eye might flare up and she might glimpse it before it was gone. But the skull was already passing into the forge, and she saw nothing. When the body had withered to the point where it slipped through the leather loop and clattered into the forge, Dolley stopped pumping.

Nell came around the forge and hugged her. "Thank you," she said.

"What are you going to do now?"

"Wait for the forge to carbon the bones through. Then we'll be on our way. As Sam's widows I guess we can claim his wagon and horses."

"I'd like to help you."

"Thank you, Mrs., but you've done enough. You just go home now."

Dolley wiped some soot off her face. "I've got a stop to make first," she said.

Chapter 12

THE sky was still storybook blue, but the sun was turning a sailor's-delight red as Dolley approached the sheriff's office. The air in the alley was like the air that escaped when Jarry cut open a freshly killed animal, damp and scraping in her throat. The close buildings and overhanging trees, the rotting smells of wet rain barrels, all soured the open but unmoving air. Directly under the stairs that led to the sheriff's office sat a buckboard. In the bed were two stacked, water-stained mattresses and some damp looking blankets. The floor of the alley would never get any direct sun, but the higher of the white-washed steps and the landing above glowed in the last bright light reflecting off the opposite wall. Dolley took the stairs slowly. A few steps from the top she heard a sound coming from inside the office. It was Morse, the metal shivering of a telegraph key.

When she stepped onto the landing she saw that it wasn't all whitewashed. In the center of the wooden platform was a black square. Secured to one of the posts that supported the high roof was a lever, also black. Looking closer at the black square Dolley saw that it was a cutout, a trapdoor. She slowly tilted her head back until she saw what she had known would be above her: just below the slope of the roof was a stout square timber, and even in the shadow Dolley could see that around it was a dark mark where a rope had been tied. On the same timber, run through a broken bottle that was lashed to it, was the telegraph wire. She also noticed, tucked into one of the corners where the roof met the wall, the shaggy gray bowl of a bird's nest.

Dolley edged around the black square and knocked on the office door. She waited, listening to the nervous rattle of the telegraph, then knocked again. The only sound from inside was that of the code. Dolley opened the door. There was no one in the office. She entered the room slowly, waiting for her eyes to adjust to the dark. She left the door open behind her to let in more light. She followed the knockings of the code across the office. At the far side of the room something was stirring, bobbing. It was the telegraph key, which stood inside a wooden strongbox laid on its side. The box rested on a shelf in a tall pie safe missing its latticed doors. This was behind the large dark desk that sat nearly in the middle of the room, like a wood hut in a small forest clearing.

All around the desk were stacks and boxes of gambling equipment that had lost the smooth ease of movement that made for the excitement of unpredictability. There were splintered wooden bull's eyes, boards with garish numbers slashed by the opened veins of wood grain, jumbled packs of playing cards, chips that something had melted into a mass, and several roulette wheels—one broken through its center so that it looked like a cartwheel. A Sargasso of gambling equipment, tossed up by the busy gaming hall below, surrounding the refuge the Sheriff had taken here.

The telegraph key kept up its drumming. The spool of its coil looked faintly ominous with its layer of oily grease, the dust on it like damp fur. The mantis-body of the key lever dipped its head to the flat slug below it, then snapped up again, like a bird trying to peck open its prey. A message, trivial or life-and-death, was being lost, as indecipherable to Dolley as table-knockings at a séance.

On the desktop were ledger sheets, long as a man's arm, with numbers small as flyspecks, scratched and crossed out in column stacks. An almost sword-length curved knife, and a metal star with no words on it lay next to the ledger. The surface of the star was pockmarked with a fine grain, as if it had been roughly cast in sand. And there was a tiny book. With a glance behind her Dolley picked up the book and riffled its pages. She moved closer to the single window, but the words were in a language she didn't know, an alphabet of scythes and dots. Then, a professional habit, she bowed the book back to look for a fore-edge painting. There was something painted there, but it made no scene. Then she bowed the book back the other way, as if it were meant to be read backward, and a scene appeared: a landscape of sand and rock, but not one of the territory they were in. Buildings inside walls rose to needle points, other roofs were domed and cupolaed, all in the colors of sand and honey. Behind the cityscape was a sunset the shade of rose madder, with a crescent moon and a single pinpoint star just visible.

Dolley heard someone step onto the landing. She laid the book back on the desk, keeping her body between it and the doorway. Then she turned to face the door. The Sheriff's face was pale and craggy, and even in the low light red veins crackled just under the skin of his doughy nose. He had a shaggy black moustache, and gunmetal gray stubble on his chin. He wore a twin of the oddly cast star. His eyes were deeply set in sockets the color of light olives. Dolley was free to study him openly because he was looking past her, at the drumming key.

After a final long chain of rattling, the key stopped, sudden as a slit throat. The Sheriff shook his shaggy head in silent dismissal, then he turned toward Dolley. His voice was a thistly rasp. "Something I can do for you, Mrs.?" The sound was as much raw wind as words, as if half the air pushed from his lungs came straight out, without the shaping of throat or tongue, without the polite shapes of speech. A good match for his expression, which showed none of the signs of human contact, only a raw animal guard.

"Yes, there is" she said, lowering her chin. *Protecting my throat*, she thought. "I want to know why you turned away a wagon train of women earlier this week. And how you could kill Sam Hart when

146

there was no need." She tried to sound firm but, to her ears, there was the sound of fluttering wings in her voice.

Temiz walked to his desk and dropped into his chair heavily, though he was a thin man. When he took off his hat a red flush was visible along the circling line his hat had made. He found and inked a pen, then laid it on the desk and folded his hands. "I turned the women away because I don't want their kind here. I could kill Hart because he broke the law and was trying to escape, and because I decide what is needed here. You have your answers. Now I have a ledger to balance."

If Jarry's French Canadian accent made comic turns inside his words, the sheriff's accent gave each of his a new-whet edge, cast each in some brittle metal older than iron. It must hurt, Dolley thought, to speak in such a torn voice. She couldn't imagine in what strange country this man might have been born. Dolley had come with the intention of delivering a scathing rant, but now she was hesitant. Even two minutes with Temiz told her that a rant would bounce off him like rain off a tin roof.

When she didn't move, Temiz said, "You are the stuffer's wife."

Dolley could hear the sound of piano music through the floor. "The tanner's wife," she said. "Yes."

"And sometimes you make false eyes."

"Yes, I made an eye for Sam Hart."

"So he could be beautiful for the ladies."

"Do you mock cripples, too, Sheriff?"

Some of the gray in his face gave way to a color more alive, and he began rocking his chair on its back legs. "Sometimes I mistake myself for someone clever." He shrugged. "I don't approve," Temiz said. "The only false parts I approve of are the pillow which takes the place of the arm under the tired head; the photograph, which discourages trains and stagecoaches; the wooden bird perch, which spares the living finger . . ."

"And cuttlebone, which spares the toes?" Dolley asked, to break his rhythm.

Temiz smiled. "And alcohol, which substitutes for so many things I can't imagine needing any other falsehoods. Everything else is for hiding behind. And I don't like those who hide. Now, if we are finished, Mrs. . . ." It was another dismissal.

"You haven't explained why you turned those women away."

He looked at her with mild surprise. "I am the sheriff here, Mrs. I do not have to justify myself to you."

"No, you don't. But I live here now, and—"

"I haven't decided if you'll continue to live here."

"You plan to run us out? For what reason?"

"I haven't yet decided that, either. Maybe because I already have Swing T. Or maybe because four of you means four others will have to go. My books have to balance. If I don't have a reason, one will come."

"Then you must be able to explain the women to me. If you refuse to explain the rules, you're not being a sheriff, only a tyrant."

"You are excellent with words, Mrs. Do you know, no one has ever asked me this question before? No one has ever told me why, but I believe it is because everyone has dark spots in their hearts, cold thoughts that make them all want to herd others around just for the power of it, and they assume that my reasons are the same. But, perhaps you are different. Maybe if I answer you, we will both learn something unexpected."

This is already unexpected, Dolley thought. But she said nothing.

"I built the life here, Mrs. I built the life of this town. I know who I want to live in it. This town died once, because it was built by foolish men, men who came here, squatted down and starting digging in the earth with no real thoughts in their heads about what they would do when the digging got too hard. Only a fool starts a life without a plan. I build with a plan. And a front gate. Do you welcome just anyone into your home, Mrs.? Do you let any man enter your heart?"

"Of course not."

"Just so. You make them stand and be recognized before you

open the gate. That's all I am doing, protecting my home. Before anyone comes in, I want to talk to them, to know their mind. Or maybe I'll judge how a horse team has been treated, or what implements a man has brought with him. But you, you snuck in through a back window."

"That's why you're angry with us, you didn't run us through your sieve before we came in? There was no sign, no way for us to know."

"I can't be everywhere. I have those who are with me in spirit and they are my eyes and ears when I am elsewhere, but your Mr. Houston has his own ideas. He might have told you. I have wondered why he didn't do so."

"Told us so we could have lined up, like good little children when Grandpa comes?"

"Just so. Because the final culling is always mine. Just as it was my decision that those women had no place here. These were obviously failed women. I know, because their faces were exhausted faces. Their eyes showed how their spirits were used up." He turned a hand palm up. "They were in need of so much help, they would never have been able to give any. They had no strength left—and there is nothing you could have appointed for them to hide that. And they had no trades, none of them knew how to do anything anyone might want done. All the women in this town—even simple Evie Bonner—help lift. Everyone must help lift, Mrs., everyone. And everyone must respect my decisions, and Sam Hart did not. If I let my decisions be ignored, there will never be harmony here; I will never have a harmony of happy souls."

Startled, Dolley laughed. "All this is because you are worried about the happiness of others?"

"You are skeptical, as all beautiful women learn to be. Do you want to hear, Mrs. Do you want to hear everything? Do you want to hear about celestial copulation and the perfection of happiness? Or are you ready to stop listening, walk away, and believe you know that darkness holds my reasons? I told you I don't have to justify myself."

Dolley had thought the sheriff a simple frontier bully, a small

149

man made large by his star, but Temiz was something else. There was some cracked brilliance behind his cold treatment of his town. "I want to hear you out," she said. "The truth is, I'm not budging until I do."

"A bold answer! You could almost be a woman of my country. Oh, I come from a beautiful country, Mrs., one that looks quite like this one. It is filled with low trees and much sun. It is just as dry but more beautiful, with more goats and more rocks, and a sea that glimmers like blue gold where it passes beneath a bridge that decorates its narrow waist like a gold chain decorates a woman's rippling belly."

"Does it look like this?" Dolley lifted the book from the Sheriff's desk and bent it to reveal the painting.

Temiz looked angry for a moment, but then nodded. "On shore there are so many rocks that you would think that He who was building it ran out of mortar and could not make anything stay together. That is how my whole country was. I fought in a young man's war inside my country, a war that failed." He sat forward in his chair, and reached out for the book. She handed it to him and he slipped it into his shirt pocket.

"Everyone is good at some things, and not so good at others," Temiz went on. "I am brave in battle, but I am lost when I am in defeat. I could find no place in my country where I belonged. So I hid on the first ship that flew a foreign ensign. Have you been to France, Mrs.?"

"No."

"I thought perhaps you had; something in the way your lips surround your words. France is very different from my country, and from this country. Many things grow there. Many thoughts grow there, too. Thoughts about how all men can be brothers. I was young then, Mrs., and I believed that if I could learn how this could be done, I could return to my land and save it. Another time when I made the mistake of thinking I was clever. I listened to the thoughts of all of these men. Most of these ideas were only high clouds, no rain. There was one man who thought that the animal part of us all came from the time when a boy and a girl first go off together and come back a man and a woman. Do you know what I am saying?"

"I know."

"He thought that children below that age were angels on earth. He thought they should lead, and the fallen angels should follow. You have children, do you want to follow them?"

Dolley thought of André, and how he enjoyed so many simple things. "It would be nice to have so simple a life." She knew she sounded wistful.

"It would be nice," Temiz agreed, "but even as young as I was then, I knew it could not be. And it was not just that two handfuls of women had made this boy a man. But I was charmed Mrs., as only a man who believed in revolution can be. This man thought these young angels should lead from the back of quaggas. I had never heard of such things, and I asked, 'What is a quagga?' I was told it was an animal between horse and zebra, half-striped, half not, and that it was not sterile like a mule. I thought that if such an entirely unknown animal could exist, a living animal made of parts of others, then anything might be. If I could have seen one of these quaggas, I might have gone home and tried to make this beautiful, impossible plan work in my country—and died trying, I would guess. But I was fortunate: I learned these animals had all died before I was born. They died because their hides were soft. This is not poetry, Mrs. I was told they became extinct because those who make gloves coveted their hides. So, those in your very trade killed all the animals who were going to carry men into Paradise! Learning such things is what makes us grown animals, not the going off together. The going off together is what makes us angels." He smiled, then shrugged. "So once again I sailed away, again in a direction away from my country.

"The ship I sailed on was a Spanish ship, one carrying rich horse breeders, and a hold filled with fancy dress saddles." Temiz sat up straighter in his chair. "On that voyage, I came to see that the French knew about dreams, but that the Spanish knew about life. During the day I listened to those Spaniards, their fine cuffs fluttering in the sea wind, and I learned about breeding horses, about killing the weak, about saving the mares who had the fine heavy haunches they all wanted, about taking the knife to the stallions when they weren't big enough. These Spaniards had a much better approach to breeding horses than my country had to breeding goats—we just let them roam free among the loose rocks and couple where they could: angels with dirty beards. These were noblemen, and I listened to their stories of how they treated the peasants on their land. It was the same way they treated their horses, and their lands grew ever richer and richer. These Spaniards knew how much of man is an animal. I listened to them and I put their knowledge of breeding in place of some of the dreams in the Frenchman's work. If you don't know the difference between the land of your dreams and where you really live, you are murdering yourself, Mrs."

"So this isn't a town. This is your stockyard. And those women were culls."

"You think you are being cruel, but you are very close to the truth. Still, I would ask you to remember how life is uncertain, Mrs. Even with a plan in mind." He indicated the room around them. "I had an unexpected darkness open under me not so long ago," he said. "And I came to this room. This was to be temporary, but I think I will stay. These toys that surround me, they remind me that chance and gambling are everywhere. They remind me that I must do my best for my town, give it good odds in its gamble to stay alive, because the ground will open again one day and I won't escape. I must choose who lives here as carefully as a gambler chooses which cards to keep, and which cards to throw away. You see that, don't you?"

"Men aren't the same as animals."

"Women usually know best about the animal in man. It was a woman who said, 'The heart is a cage of unclean birds.' She was a wise woman, Mrs."

She thought of the old canary she had bought. "Your cage is just as unclean, isn't it?"

His hands moved again, this time suggesting modesty. "Ah, there's the truth of it. The difference is in whether we listen to those unclean songs our heart sings to us all—and they are beautiful, Mrs., like a dancing and singing woman. But, I don't listen to their songs anymore. I never listen to my heart. I only listen to my plan. That's why I can be sheriff."

"I believe you never listen to your heart, Sheriff. That's what has made you hard and cruel."

Temiz pursed his lips. "You are friends with our Mr. Houston, I believe."

"Hardly friends."

"If Houston could hear you, he might say it is you who are being hard and cruel now." He smiled. "I, too, was once cruel to Houston. Has he told you what I forced him to do so that I would let him live in my territory?"

"No."

"I forced him to keep up his star watching when he wanted to be quit of it."

Dolley was so surprised that she reached out toward Temiz.

"This territory doesn't need another gambler. That is my job. But this Frenchman, part of whose romantic plan I have added to the Spanish sharpness, also knew the stars. Some take the stars to be cold rocks, but," and here Temiz sat forward and raised his hands, as if trying to shape his points in the air, "did you know that planets and stars have passions, that they grow and reproduce? A planet has both sexes, a male at the North Pole and a female at the south. The seeds of new heavenly bodies pass between planets and their sun and are deposited and cared for in the heart of the Milky Way. The skies need their tender, so that we might know their harmonies."

Temiz took brown paper and tobacco out of his desk and began a cigarette. He was smiling as he added, "And it takes only a few minutes of speaking with Mr. Houston to see that stars and reproduction are among his keenest interests. Don't you agree? If he were yours to do anything with, what better job would *you* give him?" After a moment he said, "I may have been wrong. Perhaps you are not so good with words as I thought."

WHEN she closed the door behind her, Dolley stood a moment
on the landing and let the fresh breeze that coursed down the chute
of the alley cool the flush she felt on her skin. It was as if his rough
entry into her had created heat that still lingered. She turned her face
into the wind, and wondered if Temiz were watching her through the
door. But she wasn't going down until she felt cool and steady again.

From where she stood, in the shade on the Sheriff's lynching
tower, Dolley found she could see into the windows of the building
opposite. The mid-morning sun lit the windows of the rooms there,
in even rows like pigeonholes. Then she noticed, level with her own
eyes, a pale shape moving and shifting, shining like the inside of a
shell. It was a woman, and she was nude except for the long blue-
feathered earrings that hung down and brushed her shoulders. She
was facing into the room, and Dolley could see the pale weight of her
flesh shifting on her thick short legs as she danced. She was dancing
slowly, centered in her wide rounded hips. There was no music, or
none that Dolley could hear. The sunlight lit the woman's white skin
and made her curled and wound dark red hair flash and glow as she
moved in and out of the shadows of the window's crossbar. She
seemed to glow even brighter, whiter as she moved across a dark
field, something quilt-sized but dark and heavy-looking that hung on
the deep inside wall, its top half lost in the slate gray of a shadow.
The woman danced without looking around, but seemed to be dancing for the window.

With no calling to nurse, and no sister, Dolley had rarely seen
another woman nude. But she had seen a few, and it wasn't the woman's
skin, her smoothly curved, manila and cream-colored limbs, her behind round and full as a wineskin that held Dolley where she stood. It
was that she was seeing something from across the line, from a man's
world—seeing a naked woman dancing for the man she imagined to
be watching. She had heard that men enjoyed this, had heard that

word of a dancing woman would make men saddle up and ride for miles, but she had never expected to see it herself. She was accidentally being given a view through this window meant for the man behind her, and she didn't know whether to turn away, rush down the whitewashed steps, or stand her ground and see what she might learn about the man from this woman.

Then Dolley noticed what the woman was using as the background for her white skin. The woman danced in front of, and then to the left or right of the big buffalo robe, moved in and out of the slanting light in swaying steps, moved to some precise rhythm of her own (no concentration, only relaxation, showed in her body), then back to where she was centered against the shaggy brown pelt. Then the woman danced to the robe and leaned against it, and her bottom grew magically wider, rounder as her back grew narrower and her hair seemed to weave itself into the pelt. Her thighs opened a little in a new step, the candelabra of lines there growing darker, deeper, then narrowing again as she straightened and backstepped toward the window, her elbows swinging a slow counterpoint to her hips.

And Dolley saw, too, that the dancing was only partly for the man who must routinely watch its progress from where Dolley now stood. Some of the movement—maybe most of it—was for the woman herself, a declaration of powers. However it might look, she was not putting herself "on show" this way, only revealing a secret to someone she wanted to share it with. And the robe was part of this secret, somehow. It was important that its dark and shaggy power in the background, its purpose to supply contrast, and not to be foreground as Jarry would have had it. Mistaking background for foreground was something men were always doing, if Jarry was any measure of men. Maybe this woman meant to remind her man of this, too.

"First you listen to my telegraph, now you watch my heliogram. You are an inquisitive woman." Temiz stood in the doorway behind her. He moved out to stand next to her and looked off across the alley. The naked woman lifted the thick dark robe down from its pegs on the wall and spread it over the bed. Her breasts swung free, thin and flat as melting wax. Where her dance had shown an ease and a power in her muscles, as she prepared to lay back on the bed her body only showed its slackness. Now there was only nakedness there, as unimportant, Dolley thought, as what color ink might be in a pen, and no more messages that Dolley could see. Temiz stood next to Dolley, but he no longer saw her; she had become invisible, background, as he smiled across at his woman going slack on the bed.

"I thought finding a woman to fill her job would be hardest of all. But she found me."

"Slave? Odalisque?"

"Her job is being the someone who loves me. We all need at least one."

"Everyone except Hart, you mean."

Temiz looked surprised.

"And I'll tell you something else. You said everybody has to be able to lift. Those women can lift better than most. They lifted Hart up and held him in the fire until he was ash. They held him until he was coals in his own forge, safe. Could your naked dancing girl do that?"

Temiz's eyes didn't change, but his hand rose, moved toward her own. Dolley spun away and walked down the shallow steps without looking back, leaving Temiz standing on the black gallows square.

CHAPTER 13

THE following morning began with a sound like a repeat of the thunder that had tumbled above them the night of the hard rain. Jarry brought his head up off the table as if it were snapped by a noose. Someone was pounding hard and fast on the front door.

"Mr. Tanner, Mr. Tanner!" The voice was both a grown man's and that of a terrified child. Jarry stood quickly, slipping the doeskin off his shoulders. Instead of moving toward the door he turned toward the back of the store. Dolley had been so upset last night, she asked if she could sleep alone, and Jarry had suffered two nightmares of Dolley being lost in a blinding sand storm. He found her safe, standing just behind him. He saw that she was shivering and pale and he wrapped the doeskin around her. "It's Increase Bonner, the reloader. I know him," Jarry said.

Dolley said, "I know his sister."

"I don't know her."

"I don't know him."

Jarry stood a moment, realizing they must still be half asleep, then he turned and went to the door and unlocked it.

Increase Bonner nearly jumped across the threshold. "Someone's staked," he said. "Just beyond the road head, someone's staked at a

157

rise." His hat was gone, and his hair hung in his face. Lead clattered in his pockets as he shook his hands in the air, trying to shape the story he was telling. "Come," he said. "You've got to come." He nodded again and again, as if trying to coax Jarry into agreement.

Jarry felt himself nodding. Dolley picked up the doeskin Jarry had dropped, and the three of them hurried out.

Some thirty yards west of town, beyond the end of the board-walk, someone lay on a small rise hard along a shallow gully. Increase Bonner pulled up short, like a horse having its reins jerked. Jarry approached slowly. Enough light was coming over the mountains to let him see that she was indeed staked out. She'd been tied around the wrists and ankles, and the ropes were looped around stakes driven into the red sand. There were cuts on each of her cheekbones, with the blood smeared in long curves. The smears were symmetrical. Whoever had cut her had made little half moons on each cheek. Her shirtwaist had been ripped away, and some kind of long needles—their shafts almost black, their tips tan—had been pushed through her breasts, in one side of the nipple, out the other. The blood here was undisturbed, left to run down her ribs as it would. Shorter needles had been pushed through her lips, pinning them together. Her hair was tangled and pulled above her head, and the ropes at her wrists were slack while those at her ankles were tight. The torn sand above her head and at her sides showed that something, perhaps a blanket, had been pulled from beneath her.

"She's dead." Dolley said. "It's the Sheriff's woman, Coulisse."

"You should go back inside," Jarry told her.

"I will. But I've got to cover her first." Dolley lifted the doeskin off her shoulders and draped it over Coulisse's body. "Someone needs to get Temiz," she said.

"I'll do it. I'll do it," Increase Bonner shouted, and he was off at a fast trot.

"Come on, Dolley. We should go inside."

Dolley looked at the mountains, then back at the town. "Do you see, Jarry?"

"See what?" He put his arms around her shoulders, and gently turned her away from the covered body.

"This is the exact spot where that Indian was killed."

Jarry didn't look at the mountains, nor at the dead woman, only at Dolley. "It's going to be alright," he said. "Come on home now."

He led her back inside and sat her in the chair nearest the stove. He stoked the fire and put on tea water. They sat side-by-side, silently staring through the brown lettering on the window, waiting for Temiz to come.

When Sheriff Temiz finally appeared, he wasn't alone. Behind him hurried three women, all dressed in white, all wearing the flowing white headscarves of nurses, moving at a fast walk behind him. It was somehow frightening to see this group pass. Temiz, dressed all in black and riding a black horse, rode just ahead of the women, whose clothes and scarves billowed and flapped in the wind as they trotted behind. Jarry expected Temiz would come to the store to talk to them, but a few minutes later, the woman returned carrying Coulisse in an improvised sling, and there was no sign of Temiz.

"Who are those women?" Jarry asked. "Nurses?"

Dolley pressed her face against the window. Then she said, "Hart's women. Jarry, those are the women Sam Hart brought here."

"The ones Temiz killed him over."

"Yes." She stood quiet for a moment. "I guess he found something they do well enough to keep them."

Increase Bonner appeared at the door again. He spoke in a whisper.

"I wanted to come back to thank you, Mrs., for covering her."

"Certainly. Do you know if the Sheriff has found out anything?"

"No, Ma'am. I know he went to Hackshaw's and bought a sifter, but that's all."

"A sifter?"

"Yes, Ma'am. You know, like Sam Hart used to sing, 'Down by the sea side sifting sand.' That kind."

"Yes, well. Do you know where he's gone since?"

159

"No, I don't know that."

Jarry stepped up to Dolley's side, took her by the arm. "But I can tell you where we're going," Jarry said. "We're going West. We're packing up and we're leaving, that's where we're going. When you see Temiz, you tell him that for me, Increase?"

"Yes, sir," Bonner said.

Dolley pulled her arm free of Jarry's grasp. "Oh, Jarry," Dolley said. "Where do you want to go now?"

"Somewhere Indians don't stake women out to die. Salt Lake, maybe."

"You think the Indians killed her?"

"You said yourself she was staked out right where that Indian was killed. And she owned the robe. It was a revenge raid, that's for sure."

"I don't think the Indians had any way of knowing that. She didn't wear it around town." She put her hands up to make sure Jarry didn't come any closer. "I'm going to feed Gertrude, Jarry. And you go look for André. I want him back here."

"I have to go out," Jarry said to Bonner, and he held the door open until the little man went out.

Out on the boardwalk, Bonner shadowed Jarry. Once they were past the alley, Bonner touched Jarry's sleeve to stop him. The clack of lead in his pockets was almost as loud as his whisper. "Swing T wants to see you," he said.

"He's asking for me? After he left me down a crack out in the desert?"

"He said to tell you that he wants to pay you, and that he has more work, if you want it."

"I'd like to tell him what I want. Where is the bastard?"

Bonner cringed. "He'll be at my cabin tomorrow at dark."

"When all the scavengers come out," Jarry said.

Increase looked confused. "Oh. All I know is that I have something he needs. Maybe you could come, too."

"Oh, I just might. Tell him to keep an eye peeled."

160

Bonner laughed a high gasping laugh, and Jarry flashed with anger.

"What the hell are you laughing about?"

Bonner tried to look sober. "Something Sam Hart told me once. And I can remember it, too.

If you get an eye peeled,
what gets most revealed,
is the way the man feels

"It was funny," Bonner said. "Because Sam had had his eye peeled for him, you see?"

"I see. And it's too bad he's not here to make up a rhyme about Coulisse being killed, isn't it? Maybe he could rhyme Coulisse with 'deceased,'" Jarry said.

"Probably," Increase said, his voice choked with misery.

Jarry turned away. He had no reason to be angry with Increase, he knew. The little man wasn't cruel, just too simple to see that it was the wrong time to laugh. It was just frustration, building up until he needed to release some of his anger somehow. Maybe he could walk it off, looking for the perpetually wandering André.

But he found André easily. He was playing with the children of the sausage maker behind the sunken jail. They were playing a game Jarry had never seen before André had taken up with these children. They always played it there, on the sloping banks and flat winding mound where the railroad once had run. The object was simple enough—to save another player's life. But the ways of the children's imaginations when they played the game were complex, strange. "Saved your life," one of the children would call out as he or she made some small move on the bank of the mound. A challenger would call out "How?" The first child would then explain how, in some mysterious convoluted fashion, the challenger's life had indeed been saved.

"I just moved my left foot three inches forward," Jarry heard one of them say. "*Saved your life!* If I hadn't moved my foot there would have been a clear path for a spider to go past us, and pretty soon a scorpion would have come out to eat it, and would have followed its trail back here in search of more. It would have stung you and you would have died." The other players nodded at the wisdom of this.

"Well," answered the challenger, "I just rubbed my foot: *saved your life!* Because if I hadn't I would have got a cramp in my foot and then later you would have had to stop for me while I worked it out. You would have been grabbed by the bird lady who swoops out of the alleys at night, and she would have slit your tongue to make you talk and then when you couldn't answer her riddles she would have killed you."

The other players looked away from this boy, as if embarrassed for him. Had they already heard that Coulisse had died? Or was the idea of rubbing his foot too active for an honorable move? He stood up and moved a little farther down the bank, looking ashamed, and the game resumed. Jarry had the feeling that the game would continue until no player would slacken his dignity enough to make any move, no matter how small, to save someone else's life. Jarry would have thought this too slow for his 6-year-old son. But he played with as much concentration as the others. His thin shoulders, looking all bone inside his too-wide jacket, were bent like an old man's as he leaned into the ring of all these sausage-making brothers and sisters. The game seemed less cruel than foreign, Jarry thought. The library where he had met Dolley had carried a number of books about a parlor craze for all things Chinese, and Jarry had read a few. (The writing, the characters that had been reproduced made him smile: they looked like brilliantly mounted, tiny exotic animals.) The subtle balances, the blank faces, the point seemingly to always exert just a little less energy than the last child, all re-minded him of what the books had claimed went on in the great courts of the Orient.

Was there something in the abandoned rail bed itself, in its banks, the grade out there just beyond the last fences and pens (even the loose pigs that roamed everywhere else in the small town didn't stray onto the rail bed) that led the children to gather there for this odd game? Listening to the wild imaginings of the children, Jarry let his own imagination run free. He thought about what Houston had told them about his railroad days, how Chinese labor had built the railroads, shoveled the beds and laid down the track. They must have sweated, he thought, even died for every degree of slope, every foot of rail, must have built enough banking to have laid a bridge back to China if they had started the other way from California. Instead, they had been made to criss-cross, dig and honeycomb all the Western lands like ants following elusive trails of promised sugar until, surely, some Oriental spirit was woven over and pounded down into the land itself. Land always had its feel, and that could come from nowhere except from those who had passed and fought over it. What this soaked-in spirit might someday do. . . . All those men who had died so far from their homes, laying endless tracks.

Jarry shook his head. Those books were surely no more reliable than those he had read about the Wild West. He called André. But André didn't respond. Jarry hiked up the mound and touched his son's shoulder. André's head came around slowly, like a snake left too long in the cold.

"Your mother wants you home," Jarry said.

"Père?" André asked. He looked as if he were trying to awaken from a heavy nap. His eyelids looked as though they were heavy enough to drag his forehead down to the ground.

Jarry looked at the other children, their slack arms and unfocused eyes, then lifted André, wrapped his arms tightly around the boy, and carried him home.

ANDRÉ spent the rest of the day in a half sleep, and went to bed before the sun set. After Dolley attended to Gertrude, she sat at the table with Jarry, who had been carefully drawing things on a small square of paper.

"Two people dead in two days," Jarry said, as if the fact were a sum at which he had just arrived, by way of his ink marks. "Terrible things come in threes, yes? So, there may be another."

"Temiz said it needed to be four."

Jarry looked down, as if this new number threw off some important calculation. His papers made Dolley think of Temiz's account books. They probably weren't tax rolls.

"He told me that because the four of us came into his territory that four people had to go. I thought he meant he was going to drive somebody out."

Jarry thought for a moment, then said, "What about those women in white? Does that mean three more will have to die now?"

"I don't know, Jarry. You'd have to ask Temiz. It's his territory."

"I'm not going to wait and be a number in his plan. Because I have a new plan. It seems like nothing from my old plan is working out as planned."

Dolley rubbed her hands over her face. She had scrubbed her hands again and again, but as she pressed them against her face she thought she could still smell the burnt iron of the smoke from the forge that had immolated Hart. She dropped her hands from her face and saw Jarry holding up the paper that he had filled with words and boxes with scribbles and arrows and question marks.

"We need to make a new plan, and stick to it, you see?"

As long as she'd known Jarry he'd done this, taken one idea or even just one word and braided it around and around himself until it seemed to close out everything else. As long as she'd known him conversations would start out normally and then slowly words would begin to drop away until only a precious, obsessive few remained. One sentence would follow the one before, with little to link them except whatever word Jarry had seized on for the moment. Dolley used to think that it was Jarry's limited English vocabulary that caused this, but she had long ago come to see that it was how he focused. She could usually just shrug off these constrictions with a tired smile, but when her nerves were already as tight as the lines of a full fishnet she would feel like they were talking baby talk, babbling themselves into a box. The iron smoke that touched her lungs tightened the winch on her nerves a final notch.

"A *plan?* You think we have to plan to have a *plan?*" She held her arms straight out. "Sticking to a plan got us here, Jarry. Sam Hart stuck to his plan, and see where it got him. Sheriff Temiz has stuck to his plan for this town, and he murders Hart to keep from having any loose ends. A *plan* is the last thing we need Jarry. No more plans."

Jarry turned the piece of paper in his hands around, as if he could find the answer to Dolley's outburst written there. "Well," he said. "What do we need instead?"

Dolley didn't have an answer for Jarry. But she had to get away from him before he could use the word again. "I don't know. Tell you what, I'll go outside and look. Maybe your precious West will jump out of hiding and tell me." As she walked past Jarry she saw that she had hurt his feelings. On a child his expression would have signaled a bout of tears. She hurried out before her hand could betray her and move to touch his cheek.

She hurried outside and down the steps, and kept walking north, out into the desert. When the worst of her anger faded she turned to look back at the town. She shielded her eyes with the flat of her hand, then, with a crooked smile, slowly extended her arm. The town was now the size of her palm. Her crooked smile grew bigger. This was the measure her father had given her when she was small: never stray farther from the house than where it was the size of your palm with your arm extended. She rarely had, then or since. She stood in the low scrub, her arm straight out, until it began to tremble, then dropped it to her side. She started back.

Jarry had once read her a passage from one of his books, a story of two cowboys lost in Death Valley. One cowboy had solemnly warned the other that people lost in the desert tended to walk in circles because one leg was stronger than the other. Then Jarry had told her to remember that whenever lost she should try to find someone left-handed to march out with, so they would straighten one another out. But when Dolley began to veer left as she walked back toward Hugo, she knew it wasn't the strength of her legs, but the focus of her eyes. She was walking toward the painted Nantucket on the big wall, the dream home to which, so she hoped and in some vague way, she had to admit, had planned, she would one day return. From the desert, the painting looked like a doorway, looked like she would only have to step through it and she would be home. She had done a more convincing job than she had realized.

Dolley had had no idea that sand had a nap, a grain to it, but in walking back toward the town she found the sand had changed from a hard wind-packed shell to a toothy grit that dragged at her feet and made it hard to walk. Her shoes were caught fast every time she took a step and she had to pull them up as if they were magnetic and the ground was iron.

She changed her bearing, to see if the sand were easier going along a new bearing. Rather than walking back home, Dolley instead took her sighting on the paint store. The going became an easy glide, and she stayed on that port tack right up the steps and into the paint store. She rested a moment, sitting on the lid of a giant ceramic jar, and then a thought made her shake her head. Here, inside the store with its "Egyptian jars," she was behind the false front of mural, through to the other side of the door she had painted. But this other side was only a dusty room. She had walked up the steps because the walking was easier this way, but this wasn't her room; not at all.

Dolley searched until she found a large potbellied jar labeled zero, and carried it outside. Houston had moved his scaffolding back to its usual place, on the far side of the tanner store, so that its open iron skeleton was the last human sign before the start of the open desert. All that remained to stand on was the set of steps taken from the sunken jail. Dolley put the zero jar on the ground between the steps and the mural, then went back inside. She found a ball of dusty yarn and an old broom. She took them to the top of the steps. She set the yarn down, raised the broom over her head and smashed it against the back of the steps until the head snapped off. Then she used the yarn to tie her widest brush to the broken end.

Dolley began painting out the mural. First to go were the high clouds and spar tops, then the main masts and line of upright logs, then the hulls and the sand. No one came to help her with the erasure, no one came to watch. There was nothing festive about the painting this time around. It was just work. Standing on the small platform at the top of the steps, Dolley felt like an orator, some kind of minister, reaching and stretching, bending and turning, anticly to her flock. But instead of painting a word picture of an ideal heaven, the way ministers did, Dolley was erasing her image. With each bend, each stretch, another part of her ideal Nantucket, its blue sky and green trees, brown ships and black whales, vanished, to be replaced by a blank white space.

By the time Dolley emptied the ceramic jar, she had covered all the mural except the far corners, which were beyond her reach. She didn't mind them: they looked like the paper corners she had used at her aunt's house to help hold clippings and postcards in big album. These corners held no postcard image now, only a wet, brilliantly white oval with edges as indistinct as any cloud's. She started to set the brush down, but then thought she saw something remaining on the wall. With the little bit of paint still loaded in the big brush, Dolley tried to erase it, but then she saw it was only her shadow.

Her arm ached. She dropped the handle and let the brush fall into the dirt and ashes. She wiped her hands on a rag that hung on the step railing, and could see a faint reflection of her movement in the still wet white paint. The now familiar hawk cast a shadow on the white wall, and there was a pool of gathered light that was almost a reflection of the sun above it. Dolley steadied herself by holding on the rail and leaned toward the white wall, only some four feet away. There was so much to almost see there, near-reflections and tilted subtle shadows of things around her. The brilliant, wet white was hypersensitive to light and she could almost see how many people were passing on the opposite walk by the shadows captured, and the floating pool of sunlight told the captain's daughter in her just what time of day it was. In trying to erase the image of her seashore home, Dolley had created a deep white harbor, a docking place for the lights and shadows of the world she lived in now, all faint enough she could please herself in deciding what they were. She wondered now why she had ever painted scenes inside seashells—the pearlescent, shimmering interiors could have captured so many more worlds, taken their owners so many more places without the entombing scene she'd painted in them. She wondered why any painter ever painted anything less than a blank white canvas; everything could be caught there; everything could be seen there. She turned her head to the left, took in the desert. For the first time she didn't think about how much wasn't there, but about how much open space there was, how many opportunities to cast a shadow of one's own. She thought she had an answer now for Jarry.

Calmer now, Dolley walked slowly up the back steps and through the children's room. She stepped into the doorway to the main room and saw that Jarry was still seated at the table. He was carefully writing something on a clean piece of paper. His head was bowed in concentration, and the vertebrae of his neck, the knobs of the bones pushed against the thin skin there, and his skull looked too heavy to be held up by such a precarious stack. From the neck up, he looked like a starving man. The sight slowed her as much as the nap of the sand had. She stopped, quietly pulled off her shoes, and slipped on the soft moccasins Jarry had made her.

She stood looking at Jarry. She didn't know how to tell him what she had seen standing before the blank wall; she had had a pretty good idea of how to shout it at him, but no idea how to tell it. Then the telescoped bones of Jarry's neck reminded her of the way he stacked "plan" after "plan" as he had struggled to tell her his thoughts. She saw then that this was the way Jarry learned things, as if each thought were a stake he had to hammer again and again until it was buried deep enough to keep up a tent.

"Jarry?" she said. "Jarry I have something I want to talk about, talk about with you."

Jarry twisted around to look at her. "Yes?" he asked, softly.

"Nothing," Dolley said.

"But I wish you would."

"No, Jarry, 'Nothing' is what I want to talk to you about." She took a step toward him. "In place of a plan, Jarry. I want 'Nothing' in place of a plan."

"You want us to do nothing."

"Not to do nothing, Jarry, but to put nothing where you want to have a plan, to put nothing in its place." She sat in the chair across from him. "I just whited out my mural, and do you know what I saw?"

Jarry was so startled his hands moved as if to catch something in the air in front of him. "You painted out your beautiful mural? Why, Dolley?" He walked to the stove, leaned over and looked out across the alley. "It was so real. How could you do that to yourself?"

"It's better now. Do you want to know what I saw when I was done painting it out?"

"The Nothing you want us to have." He sat down again.

"No, I didn't. And I don't want us to have nothing, I only want us to use it."

"These are word games. Like you used to do when you went with those bitch witches, like when you used to make fun of a dumb Quebecky who couldn't learn English."

"Oh, Jarry, I never made fun of you. And I'm not now." She tried to take his hand, but he wouldn't let her. "Remember, Jarry, how I told you I was going to walk until I had an answer? When I had walked far enough out into the desert, I turned back to town and I realized that part of our problem was my mural, was that I wanted to go back, to be somewhere else. Temiz told me he didn't approve of false parts, because they fool people, that they're lies. And he was right, Jarry."

"Hart's false eye."

"Not just that. And my mural was a false part, Jarry, false because my Nantucket isn't that perfect, even in my memory. And false because it kept me from seeing what was here."

"Your wonderful 'Nothing.'"

"The nothing I'm trying to tell you about is almost a kind of light, Jarry. A light with no color of its own, so it shows the truth of what it shines on."

"This is just your witch stuff back again."

"No, Jarry. The 'witch stuff,' as you call it, was when I thought I could get beyond my troubles by getting beyond the world I was living in. So the mural was 'witch stuff.' Your yellow back novels are 'witch stuff,' too, Jarry. Do you understand now?"

"This nothing keeps you from fooling yourself."

"I'm so glad you understand. And big plans are 'witch stuff,' too. So many terrible things have happened in the last few days, all because Temiz has a big plan. And we're here to see it crumbling all around him. Doesn't that tell you anything, Jarry?"

"All this talk of yours is romantic, Dolley, but no one can live with no plan."

"We can live with little plans, Jarry. I plan to make Andy breakfast tomorrow. I plan to hold Gertrude. I plan to be happy. I plan to see what's really here. But you're never content with little plans. They just don't fit you. I don't suppose you can help it." She stood up and walked to the window. "We both came out here with pictures in our heads, Jarry. I came with a picture of a memory, and another picture of what I thought my life should be. I want to let go of all those pictures and plans, Jarry. I wish you could, too, but . . ."

"I could try, but there's no work for me here. We've got to move."

"You've got to move, I suppose. But I won't go."

"You're leaving me?" There were tears now; he was struggling to steady his voice.

"No, Jarry. I'm sorry, but I'm staying put. I won't go somewhere where I recognize something, where there might be a familiar peg to hang some old pictures on, a plan to realize. I've found this clear, blank light here. I might not be lucky enough to find it somewhere else."

Jarry held out his paper, but Dolley shook her head. He held it out until his wrist began to shake, then began nervously to roll the paper, to wring it around his fingers.

When Dolley spoke again, her voice was gentle, but it wasn't soft. "I'm staying here. This is the most nowhere and nothing place I can imagine. And I'm not about to lose it to a plan. But, I hope your plan makes you happy. I do."

Jarry smiled. "The same words that started our marriage end it."

Dolley rose from the table and walked to the bedroom. Jarry put his coat on and opened the door, but stood for a long time next to the table, lifting and putting down his paper plan, but never taking his eyes off the bedroom door. He slowly backed out onto the boardwalk, his eyes fixed on the empty bedroom doorway. When he reached out to close it behind him, he found that he had rolled his plan paper around and around his fingers until his two index fingers were locked in opposite ends of the roll. He twisted the paper a little tighter, until it cut off most of the feeling.

Chapter 14

"Hey, Mister, can you spare a fellow a doubloon?"

Jarry turned and found Swing T standing at the corner of the store.

"You abandoned me out there."

"I didn't. I had to protect my negatives. After those bison were gone I circled back, but you had already escaped. You're a resourceful man, Quebecky."

"It was a bison stampede?"

"Of an unnatural sort. It was Indians, hunting them over that same cliff."

"When I climbed down I never saw or heard a thing."

"Even a small mountain makes for pretty good soundproofing. Unlike your walls here." Swing T rapped his knuckles again the store front. "So your wife has cut you loose." He shrugged. "At least you didn't start bawling like a calf with its milk cut off." He smiled. "Or were you just about to get to that?"

"What do you want here, Swing T?"

"One last camera job." He flipped something in the air. Jarry tried to catch it, fumbled it and it fell to the boards of the walk. It was a doubloon. "I have three more of these. A man losing his business, his town and his family all in one night might find that three pieces of gold could come in handy."

Jarry stood looking down at the gold on the worn boards. Swing T walked up and stood with Jarry, looking down, so that the brim of his hat almost touched Jarry's forehead. Without looking up, Swing T softly said, "What else do you have but me, Tanner?"

Jarry bent low and picked up the doubloon. "One more time," Jarry said, and he slipped the coin into his pocket.

"We need to hurry." Swing T took Jarry by the arm to start him moving. He hurried down alleys, past a line of fencing where unseen animals grunted up at them, and on into a low shack with a tipped-back roof. Gaps in the walls were stuffed with wadded paper and rags, the windows were rough-cut squares of oiled paper, and damp sawdust served as sidewalk. The shack flapped like a book being rolled in the wind, and the planks in the door rattled like loose teeth when Swing T opened it. The shack had a split log for a threshold, and the wood felt punky and rotten under Jarry's boot. For a floor there were boards that didn't echo to the step, and furniture with the bark still on. Jarry moved into the single room to allow Swing T room to come in, and saw that the candle on the table was made of ends of older candles waxed together to make the gnarled taper in the tin cup.

"This is Increase Bonner's place," Swing T said. "I gave him four pounds of leads to melt down to let me use his shack for the week. I've got my plates store laid up in here, and I'll being using this as a darkroom. Let me gather up some things and we'll get the hell out of here."

Jarry looked around the shack as Swing T dug under the table, and pulled boxes out of corners. There was a low bed and rough brown blanket, a single blackened pan on a square grate stove. The forge for recasting the lead would be outside—or had he used Hart's forge, the one-eyed giant and the bruised-looking little man united in fire and metal? It would have been like one of those plays with music that Dolley used to take him to. On a rack of fencing hung like a

173

hammock between two nails lay Bonner's bullet molds. They were cast in bars of six each, the halves on fine hinges, with blackened clasps.

"I used to know a man who would pour corn meal into bullet molds like that," Swing T said. "He'd take them for lunch, pop them like pills." He shook his head. "Call me superstitious if you want, but I could never put anything shaped like a bullet into my own stomach."

The walls were lined floor to roof with wooden shelves bowed under the weight of rough-weave sacks. "Bullets," Swing T said. "They're easier made up than used up. There's always the recoil to worry over."

Jarry thought of the Sheriff. "Where are we going to go after this?"

"Where do you want to go?"

Jarry slumped against one of the shelves, and heard the thick click of the bullets shifting away from his spine. "Someplace where things are simpler," Jarry said. "Where you don't wake up finding your whole world changed overnight. Where the spot you were standing a minute ago isn't gone when you come back. Someplace old-fashioned like that."

Swing T tapped his nose with his index finger. "I know where all the ghost towns are, if that's what you're really looking for. Or you could stay right here. This place is as old-fashioned as any. The store up front was built back before the war, by a smudgy little man who campaigned to have this territory enter the union as a slave state. This shack was his toehold. But he didn't have the silver to hire a good lobbying, and when the war broke out he went to Atlanta for breeding stock and Sherman burned him to death. This is genuine antebellum construction you're standing in, Jarry."

The penned animals began grunting again, and Jarry heard the sound of footfalls in the sawdust. Jarry moved back from the door, back where the sloped roof brushed his hat. The door flew open, but no one could be seen. Jarry heard a sound like a flag being whipped in the wind, but that was all.

Swing T took a step toward the empty doorway. "Increase?" But it was Temiz who stepped into the shack. He had a pistol in his hand.

"If you've come looking for Increase Bonner," Swing T said, "he's out."

"As long as I'm here I will have to kill someone else, then" Temiz said, his tone as flat as a poker player requesting a new deck.

"Why?" Jarry's voice squeaked, but he didn't care this time.

Temiz said, "I found these in Coulisse's arm, like a row of porcupine quills." From his vest pocket Temiz brought out a folded paper. He unfolded it with thumb and forefinger. "Cactus needles," he said. "Where do you find cactus needles not on cactuses, Jarry?"

Jarry couldn't help but look at Swing T's hatband, at the cactus needles that lined it.

"Let me see your hat," Temiz told Swing T.

Swing T took off his hat and sat it on the table. "It's yours," he said and stepped back, his hands lifted in mock surrender. Temiz, his pistol pointing vaguely in Swing T's direction, moved closer to the table, his eyes on the four-inch needles in the hatband. Temiz drew the crooked candle toward the hat, his eyes narrowed in a squint.

Swing T's right arm moved in a quick arc, moved again, as he did a quick stuttering dance along the wall of shelves. Temiz lifted his pistol, but it was knocked to the floor as rough sacking parted and bullets—dull gray points, the brass gleams of their shells—poured down over his arm. They crashed against Jarry, too, but only struck against his legs. The bullets rained down on Temiz's arm, then against his chest, leaving tracers of gun oil over his shoulders as they pushed him backward, off balance, and down onto the rough planks. In the last second before the bullets knocked the candle to the floor Jarry saw Swing T grab his hat and step toward the door. Then it was dark.

Jarry hung on to the shelf supports and tried to keep his balance. He took a deep breath and pushed off like a man in a river current, letting the bullets push him toward the door, but something caught his ankles and he fell. The bullets poured over him like dozens of fingers rapping his skull for attention, again and again and again, demanding and painful, and Jarry felt thought slipping away, and prickly dark pouring in to fill the space.

SIGHT registers instantly, but fades just as fast. Conviction is a slippery business, Dolley knew. It can come instantly, and it might stay, but just as often it begins to thin like paint running down glass. So she had expected the moment of panic, the twitching fingers, the old-fashioned uncertainty that swirled around her like a hoop skirt, threatening her balance. When Jarry walked out into the dark, she watched and saw that it was a different kind of nothing, one in which you couldn't see yourself at all—on such a moonless light, not even a hand unless it was held up to the eye.

Dolley stood on the porch and wondered. The white wall, the sand-swept country, were empty enough that she could become anything. But the night was very close here, tight and small. She would need a guide for the nights. It was obvious who that guide should be, and she found she wasn't ashamed of herself for thinking of him. There were no more corners of nothing left in Jarry—she had pried and forced with all her patience, trying to find room inside him she might be able to live in, but he was all planned tight. But maybe Houston still had some empty spaces.

She hadn't taken much away from the churches her mother had marched her in out and out of, but she remembered one kind church woman's practical suggestion: "Just put your hands in place, Dolley, and make the sound of the words. Having your body set out on the way is the surest way to make a path for the heart." The woman had been so kind, had had such deep, dark eyes that Dolley couldn't help but believe her. So she had always made sure never to peak her hands the right way, made sure always to stumble over the words.

Bridge Out, Path Inaccessible. But maybe she could use the scrubbed outline of the plan the way she had used the white wall, as a landing site for shadows of what could be.

DOLLEY closed the door and, joyously and with a pure heart, caved in the crown of the bat wing hat Jarry had sat so carefully on a shelf. She pulled a drawer out of her dresser, and dragged it across the floor of the bedroom and out into the main room. She opened the door of the stove and began throwing in the too clever leather things Jarry had made for her. Shapeless hats, decorative butterflies that shriveled like dead leaves on their pins, odd purses that never kept a trim profile even when empty. It was as if Jarry had managed to copy the outline of something she could use, but then when he colored it in, it was all wrong. It all went into the smokey little stove fire. It wasn't as ravenous as Hart's forge, but in its quaint, homemade way, it consumed the skins she fed it. Finally, from the bottom of the drawer, she lifted out Jarry's strangest creation, something she had never worn. "A doe-skin glove for your body," Jarry had called it. The doeskin was creamy white and soft as Gertrude's belly. It was cut to enclose her front, from where her thighs met to where her breasts swept out toward her underarms. The front had threaded with a black-dyed bootlace, so she could slip in through the top then lace herself in. Handier than corset stays, the lace was in the front, and the loose ends would have dangled to her waist. Where Jarry had seen a model for this, she shuddered to imagine. She thought she should save the black lace as good laces always came in handy, but when she loosened it she saw what Jarry had done to the inside. It was lined with slip material, shiny as far-off water. She felt a little badly that she had never even looked inside, after all the work Jarry had gone through. But she was, unbeknownst to herself, already growing Gertrude inside her when Jarry presented her with this whorey doeskin strutter's glove. And she had turned away with a shudder. Their happy times in bed since would hardly use all a woman's fingers to count. Dolley shrugged, and balled up the body glove. When she turned to the stove her eyes involuntarily moved to the window. There was just enough light for her to see the shadow she cut out of the lantern light that lit the white wall with a dim glow. She didn't know what the future would hold for her, but work would loom large, fashion and primping might be as far off as the Fiji Islands her father had sailed for. She hung the soft glove from the lantern over the stove, telling herself as sure as a new snow fence will call down a blizzard, trying this glove on would call down a visitation she couldn't predict. The last time she had been tempted into wearing a fancy corset, Jarry had come crashing through a window to save her from the unknown. The tales she had heard from her mother and cousins, from widows and bruised women in the wagon train, even what she had seen of poor Coulisse, told her that any time a woman lets down her guard, unwraps parts of her she has always kept wrapped, a quiver is sent into the world, some signal and that signal is always answered, sometimes for the good, most times for the bad. Certainty sometimes comes in a whisper. She had known all along that she would try the doeskin on, had been telling herself all the while, but had pretended she didn't hear.

She slid out of her dress and underthings and took the skin off the hanger. The tanned hide was soft as satin. Her feet chilled when she slipped her stockings off, but the rest of her felt warm, as she stepped into the doeskin. She lifted it and felt the slip-lining slide across her skin as she put her arms through the openings. She pulled the black bootlace tight, and tied it in a bow, looked at how the long free ends swung as she turned. Jarry had certainly made this with relations between the two of them foremost in his mind, but for Dolley it wasn't about what anyone else might see, only about seeing for herself what her muscles and skin could do to the blank cream outline. She felt something she thought might be a memory of the fleetness and grace of the doe who had died, but might just have been a part of herself she hadn't looked for before. She couldn't see any of the stretches or blemishes she had sometimes worried over, couldn't see any of the marks motherhood had given her, she only saw the smooth cream expanse, how her muscles showed, how the curves she made were as long and graceful as a soaring bird's flight on a swift wind.

And there came a sharp slam, like a wagon's hollow body being hammered, but louder, and a terrible, primitive animal sound, something between a scream and a deep wail. Dolley turned to window. She had forgotten to pull the curtain—had someone been watching, there in the dark? But whatever was out there was hurt, thrashing. At the foot of the far wall, hard against the base of Dolley's mural, where the blank white met the dark flatiron of the black ground, something big lay in the ashes and sand. It thrashed like a huge fish thrown onto a bank. The shape thrashed, beat against the ground, and with every blow there was another straining whimper from whatever lay there. Dolley lifted the lantern from the middle of the table and held it to the window. The wedge of yellowish light showed her that it was a horse that thrashed and whimpered and tried to stand. One pair of legs kicked and churned the sand, throwing up a black froth of ashes, while the other legs were rod-straight and unmoving. The head and neck of the horse writhed like snake that had been stuck. The horse was fitted with a blanket and saddle, and as it thrashed in the ashes the body in the saddle rose and struck the ground again and again.

Dolley called, "Help! It's Temiz! He's in the alley. Somebody!" She ran out the back door, feeling the grit of the sand between her toes, the cool wind on her arms and legs. She stopped six feet from the thrashing horse, having no idea how she would get to Temiz without being struck down by the dying animal. She could see Temiz's body, slapping bonelessly like wet laundry against a rock. The horse was trying to look at her, and the terrible crescent moons of his eyes seemed to glow, and the front of his head opened and blood blossomed out and the eyes grew to full moons and then blinked out. The horse's head lay still before Dolley's ears could make her understand that she had heard a gunshot. And then there was a voice, shouting to her from overhead, "Dolley, it's Houston. I'll be right down."

Dolley stood shivering, her hands open near her cheeks, as if expecting her head would roll free and she would have to right it. She felt an odd trickling on her legs and looked down. In the lantern light glowing through her window she could see blood, half circles of it with running streams, a dark jellyfish of blood on each of her legs. She heard running feet on the boardwalk, and saw men without hats coming from all directions, shouting, some of them shirtless, and something touched her shoulder. She jumped and turned, and saw that it was Houston. He made a "shhh" sound and reached for her. She shivered and reached back, but before she could touch him she was yanked backward, and hands were on her arms and legs, and at the back of her neck and she was being lifted above men's heads. She called out but couldn't hear her own words above the shouting of the men who were wrestling Houston to the ground. "Disarm him," they shouted. "Get his cards! Get his cards!" and she was being carried away from him, from the alley, from her home and children and she screamed their names, but the black lacing was so tight she couldn't fill her lungs deeply enough to make herself heard, and with her arms pinned she couldn't untie them, and she felt terrified and light-headed for the lack of air, and she was carried along by this visitation of angry men despite her cries and her kicks and in the midst of it all she felt the back of some man's hand, just the gentlest touch of his knuckles following the curve of her body outlined in the doeskin and she arched her back and gulped for air and for the first time in her life, she fainted.

JARRY awoke with his head lower than his feet. He was rocking gently back and forth, as if in a small boat or a big cradle. A bluish light, with odd cells in it like a fly's or a flea's wing lit the floor and then left it dark, in a rhythm that matched his rocking. The flashes of blue light showed him the shaggy pelt of a huge dark animal just inches from his face. Jarry rolled away quickly but hit his head against something soft. It was the edge of a bed. He saw now that he was lying in the back of Swing T's wagon. He braced himself on the edge of the bed and got to his knees. At his eye level was a small screened window. Through the window he could see the back of Swing T's head. Just above Swing T's shoulder a small lantern swung on a hook. Jarry looked down again at the dark pelt, but already knew what he would find. It was the buffalo robe.

Jarry knee-walked to the screened window and called Swing T's name. Swing T turned to look at him, a smile as big as a country preacher's on his face. "Awake are you? How's the lumps on your head?" He squinted. "And you got lignite streaks down your cheeks, too. Increase heats cheap."

"You killed her," Jarry said.

Swing T bit his lip and nodded his head. "She posed for me a lot. She liked it, and she liked a little adventure in her posing. I've sold pictures of her that would make your eyes steam up. But she was getting a little old for that. And, like I told you, people pay more for pictures of folks failing, for pain and, highest of all, for Western death. She was just supposed to lay there, pretend she was staked out for the Indians, but she couldn't look dead. I coached her and coached her, but she always looked alive still." He shrugged. "I was starting to lose my light."

"How did you do it?"

Swing T grinned. "So, you like the bloody details, too." He held up two fingers in a pinch gesture. "A single quill, forced in through the corner of the eye. That's all. And you want to know what the sad part was? No lens that's been invented focuses fine enough for me to have got a shot of that quill in her eye."

"I . . ." Jarry coughed and tasted vomit at the bottom of his windpipe.

"If you think you've got a problem with this, Tanner, this bit of the past after all, I'll ask you again: What else have you got besides me? I killed her, but I saved you. The Sheriff already thinks you're in on it, and you'd be hanging now for sure. Add to that, the fact that your wife threw you out. And, I hate to break it to you, but out here is where that old saying originated, 'Every man hauls his own hide to the tanner.' Without me, you've got no work. And what's a man without a family or work?" There was a long moment when Jarry could think of nothing to say. "You still back there, Jarry?"

"You know damn well I am."

"Good. Now, you just take that robe that means so much to you, and you pull it up over you and go to sleep. Tomorrow we'll be in a beautiful valley—outside Temiz's territory—and you can forget all those burrs that are worrying you so."

"Let me out of here."

"Not until morning. I need you, Jarry. You help me with one last job, and I'll tell you how to get anywhere you want to go."

"Anywhere?"

"This whole country's wide open to you. In the morning."

Jarry's head still throbbed where the bullets had struck him. He wrapped the robe around his shoulders, wrinkled his nose at the smell of perfume someone had poured over it, and surrendered to the tubby rocking of the wagon, fell asleep listening to the clack of the wagon's flash power teats swaying beneath him.

Dolley awoke to a world which had changed its angle. She lay against a wall, her feet raised, covered with a rough blanket. She threw back the blanket, and swung her legs off the bed. When she couldn't feel the floor she looked down. Below her feet was darkness, an open pit with raw edges and torn roots, which extended down deeper than she could see. She swung her legs back onto the bed. She was a prisoner in the town's half-sunken jail. There were bars on the window, but where the door once had hung there was nothing. There was no need for one, the open mineshaft was enough to keep her frozen to the bunk. How had anyone gotten her into this bed?

She couldn't tell how long she had been unconscious. All the faints she had ever heard of had lasted only a few minutes, but the air that moved over her arms and her legs was cooler than when she had run out into the alley. She saw that the blood had had time to dry on her legs. She shivered at the sight. She propped herself up and looked out the barred window. She saw the cell door then, it was leaning against a tree. The horizon line was an unsteady bar of indigos fighting reds. It must be near morning. She had been out for a long time.

"You're awake, then?"

A scrawny man with a red beard stood on the other side of the gap. He was holding a plank that reached from the dirt floor to a good foot above his head. At the top of the plank, a length of rope was threaded through a knothole. The scrawny man propped the ground end of the plank against his feet and used the rope to slowly lower it across the gap.

"I'm to take you to the hotel," he said. She wrapped the blanket over her shoulders and stood up. "No. Leave the blanket for the next."

Dolley bit her lip, folded the blanket and laid it back on the crooked bed. Barefoot and chilled in the body glove that exposed too much of her to the sharp air and the looks of the bearded man, she stepped onto the plank and slowly moved across. "My children are home alone," she said, walking and not looking down.

"No. That crazy Bonner woman is with them." He reached out a hand to steady her the last two feet of the way. "If you try to run, I'll tie you," he said, and grinned.

The red-bearded man led her through a crowd of more than a dozen men that surrounded the hotel. They all ogled here, a few even laughed. She was led down a short hall, and into a fussily decorated room where men in suits stood against the walls. Their eyes moved up and down, but she was too angry by now to feel any more embarrassment or shame. She sat in the chair they indicated slowly, with dignity, and refused to make any clumsy effort at covering herself. And she refused to let the men be the first to ask questions.

"Why was I locked up?"

One of the men looked at someone behind Dolley, then said, "You probably don't have any experience with these kind of things. Where is your husband?"

"My husband is gone."

"Gone where?"

"I don't know. Why was I locked up? Why was I brought here?"

The man looked over her head again, then said, "Our sheriff was killed and you were there with blood on your knees."

Dolley stood up, swiveled the chair around toward the point the man had glanced toward, and sat back down again. She saw that where her legs met the body glove a line of hair showed, but she refused to resettle herself. She spoke loudly and directly to a mustached man in an emerald green chair, whose cigar froze in mid-sweep toward his mouth.

"I heard him hit the wall and I ran out to see if I could help. This is horse's blood."

The mustached man lowered his cigar but said nothing. "Houston said that he shot the horse. His rifle was still hot," the man behind her answered.

"That's very good," Dolley said to man she faced. "I didn't even see your lips move."

The man came out of his freeze then and smiled at her. "Tell us your version, if you please."

Dolley told the story, leaving out how she had slid into her body glove, feeling at once vulnerable and powerful, expecting something drastic would certainly happen. When she finished telling how the horse's head had opened up and showered her with blood, she stopped.

"That's all you know?"

"Yes."

"I'm glad we got that out of the way. Now tell us what you think."

"I think I need to get back to my children."

"They're being cared for. But we won't keep you long. We would like to hear what you think about how Sheriff Temiz came to break his neck against a blank wall."

"Your guess would be as good as mine."

"No, we don't believe it would."

"Why not?"

"We are told that it was you who blanked out the wall. You painted over a quite beautiful mural, it seems. People who passed while you were painting it out say you had a look on your face like this was a very important task you were doing. What reason would there be for blanking something out being so important?"

"My reason is my business."

"We would like to judge that for ourselves. We took lanterns out into the desert while you were resting, and we followed his tracks backward. He came from a shack that had bullets pouring out of its doors, and he rode his horse from that shack straight into your blank wall. Those who know horses better than me," he smiled as if excusing his ignorance, "tell me there was no sign of him having tried to slow the animal. All the horse hands agree it looks deliberate. So, we thought if making this blank wall meant something important to you, maybe Temiz thought there was something important in that . . . that blankness, as well."

Dolley hadn't thought about that, hadn't yet had time to worry the possibility that it wasn't an accident. Why would he want to kill himself? If so, why her wall? He wouldn't have known that she had painted it over if he had been out trying to find out who had killed Coulisse. He would have thought there was still a seaport scene there, still an anchored ship. Was that it? Or had he known? Would he have had the same thoughts she had about the big blank wall?

"You keep saying 'We,' but you're clearly running the show here. And just who are you?" Dolley asked.

"I'm just an old boomer, Ma'am. That is, I've railroaded some. I just bought up that old spur and I plan to send a lot of rolling stock through here. So, in a way, I'm the new majority stock holder of this territory."

"I see."

"I'm in the business of imagining, you could say. And I'm imagining great things for this territory. I have great plans, but I'd like to clear up the matter of the sheriff's death first. I was hoping you could help me."

"I can. I do know what killed him."

There was a scuffing sound as all the men in the room inched a little closer to Dolley.

"How do you know that?"

"Saz told me."

The mustached man looked surprised. "He was a suicide?"

"According to him, he was. But that doesn't mean it wasn't still an accident. He told me, if you die because you can't tell where you really are from where you're dreaming you are, then nobody's killed you, you've killed yourself."

Out of the corner of her eye Dolley saw one of the standing men raise his eyebrows and nod his head twice, coaxing her to say more.

"That's how much I know. Everything else is a complete blank."

"Convenient for you."

"More than you know."

The moustached man looked irritated now. He put his elbows on his knees, dropped his cigar on the carpet and crushed it in. "You sound like one of the fortune telling gypsies in San Francisco."

"What do you know of fortune tellers, Mr. Boomer?"

"I'm glad you asked, Mrs. What I know of them is what they sounded like when they cursed me for buying up the right of way, and tearing down their shacks for my railroad bed. I don't let anything or anybody stand in the way of my plans." The mustached man leaned even farther forward, and gripped Dolley's bare knees. "Are you sure you've told us all you know?"

"I'm no haruspex, but I know the fortune Temiz told has come through for at least three people. And maybe it'll come true for more. Maybe even for you."

And she swung her knees away.

Chapter 15

THE area of desert Swing T drove them through was more rock than sand. The large stone stretches were like islands, or mile wide griddlecakes poured out to fry on the red dunes. Swing T steered his horse over a miniature open plain that dropped down slowly into a small canyon. And there was the water, just as Swing T had said. The pool was long and narrow, some twenty feet at the waist by ten or eleven score, narrow in the center and more round at the far end than the near: a blue keyhole cut in the bottom of the canyon. They passed through the narrow entrance and moved down a gentle slope into the canyon, which was shaped like a cracked pecan or a great hoof-print driven into the hard floor of the desert. The walls were tumbled red rubble below bare straight shoulders of bleached rock. Jarry had expected any desert water to be brackish, but the water looked clear and clean in the light that bounced and shimmered in the open rocky box.

"This is beautiful," Jarry said. "No one lives here?"

"The only way into this canyon is to travel east from town. Everyone here thinks they need to be traveling west all the time. Few ever find this place. And it's all bare rock, so it heats up like a camp oven on hot afternoons. No one could grow anything here. Well, water lilies maybe. I've been here maybe a dozen times in the past year, and I've never seen a living thing—except those that live in the water."

"There are fish in the pool?"

"Yes, and turtles and frogs."

"How did fish and frogs come to live way out here?"

Swing T shrugged. "Any place on earth any kind of life can get a toehold it appears. How is a mystery, but it never fails. God built a desert here and a camel came, didn't it?" Swing T laughed at his own joke.

"And this wagon train you're going to show me, how did it get here?"

"Greed, stupidity, nothing very mysterious, I'd wager."

At the wasp-waist of the pool Swing T reined in his horse. On the blank rock bank Jarry saw an odd contraption, eight of Swing T's flash powder barrels strapped together on a flat square of old timbers. Tar had been trowled over the holes where they'd been tapped.

"I've been coming here for months, getting this ready one piece at a time, patient as a watchmaker," Swing T said. "And yours are the two hands I need to finish up. Help me lash on the last keg and we're in business." Then Jarry saw that the lashed planks were a raft, some seven-foot square, being built upside down. The empty kegs were its floats. Swing T took an empty keg out of the rope sling beneath the wagon and with Jarry's help lashed it onto the last open corner of the raft. Then together they managed, with the aid of a rope and the horse, to turn the raft upright and slide it into the water. "Now these," Swing T said. And they stood the five remaining powder kegs in a line diagonally across the raft. Swing T had also stockpiled sandbags at the site, and he and Jarry placed a bag between each of the barrels. This seemed an enormous amount of flash powder to take a few pictures, but Jarry rarely questioned a man about his own trade.

"Now, what we're after," Swing T said, "is about eight foot out, right at the end of the pool where it's closest to the cliff. You can't see anything right now, but at midday you can make it out from shore. There are four wagons, and they're only down about nine or ten feet.

It will be simple."

"And I'm supposed to take pictures of what's down there?"

"Yes."

"Why don't you do it?"

Swing T drew himself up like a fancy stump orator, raised his chin high and said, "Because God, in his wisdom, has made me afraid of water. Deathly afraid, morbidly afraid. And I refuse to go against his wishes. He must have his reasons."

"But you've built a fine raft here, it won't sink."

"No. But the man who takes the pictures won't be on the raft."

"Where will I be?"

"Under the water."

"What?"

"Easy now. Let me explain a few things before you start gasping for air." He took Jarry by the arm and led the way back to his wagon. There he opened the back door, and pulled a wooden box out from under his bed. "Did you ever see a square bubble, Jarry? Well, I'm going to show you one."

"I'd rather see the way back to town."

"You don't mean it!" Swing T's surprise seemed genuine. "I thought you were a man after the truth of the Old West, a man about learning all he could about it. Now you're going to let a few feet of water block your way?"

Jarry turned his head to look back the way the had come, but now he was uncertain.

"At least look at my square bubbles. Then I want you to give me your opinion, your true opinion—one craftsman to another."

What Swing T lifted from the old ammunition box was square, but it didn't look like a bubble to Jarry. Swing T had joined together six old glass negatives by sealing the edges together with thick, narrow strips of roofing tar. Inside the bubble was a smaller black square, and on top the glass cube a thumb-shaped sleeve of black Indian rubber had been tar-sealed over a metal rod which was attached to the front of the black inner box.

"One-shots," Swing T said. "You hold your finger on the rubber finger, and when I set off the flash you take the picture, then you drop the whole shebang into a black bag until I can develop it. I thought these up on my own. What do you think?" He took seven more of the glass and tar contraptions out of the big box and lined them up on the low dome of stone.

Jarry crossed his arms tight over his chest. "You expect me to dive down to those wagons, push that rubber button, put the camera in a black bag, then swim back up for the next one—holding my breath the whole time."

"No, no." Swing T touched his chest over his heart. "That would be asking too much of a man. Let me show you the best square bubble of all."

Swing T climbed up into his wagon and crouched down next to his bunk. A brightly colored scarf was tied from one of the legs at the foot of the bed across to the other. Swing T untied the scarf and slid out another glass plate and tar box. This one was three times the size of the cameras. Swing T took off his hat and lowered the box over his head. It came down almost to his shoulders. He lifted two leather laces that were attached to opposite edges of the opening and tied them under his chin.

"What do you think?" Swing T asked, his voice muffled inside the glass. There was something insistently insect-like about his face, the way the glass and tar grid segmented it into sections, and the smeared rainbow shimmers of light bent over his eyes. Jarry could only stare, and tighten his arms over his hands.

Swing T untied the leather laces and lifted the box off his head. "This should give you enough air to take three or four pictures before you start to poison on your own breath. Then you just pop to the surface and the air refreshes itself." He held the box under his arm, and Jarry thought of the Headless Horseman. "I'm as good a scientist as the Indians," Swing T said. "They know the science of gravity, but I know the science of breath." He held out the glass box toward Jarry.

There was a standoff for a long minute, Swing T with his glass box and Jarry with his folded arms. Then a hard look came over Swing T's face and he said, "What else have you got, Jarry? What else aside this box?"

"I'll need some way to sink," Jarry said at last, and Swing T smiled.

"Increase Bonner staked me there." He handed Jarry the glass box, and went again into his wagon. He came out with two stacks of horseshoes, each four shoes high and laid them on the grass. "Increase poured hot lead down through the holes, so they're sealed together. Two horses may be going barefoot in our cause, but we'll be able to afford some extra oats to pay them back."

He sat the horseshoes down at Jarry's feet and Jarry sang, *You're my mule, Even if you don't pull no more.*

"What's that?" Swing T asked, as he began gathering his camera equipment.

"An old French song. A kind of dirty love song, I guess."

"What other kind of love is there, hey? Now, you get shoed up while I load all this on the raft."

Jarry took off his boots and strapped the shoes around his ankle, so the weight rested on his instep. They were heavier on his feet than they had felt in his hands, but he walked to the raft with no pain. Swing T looked nervous as he pushed off from the rock shelf shore. He went white every time the raft tilted to the slightest degree, and tried to paddle without getting close to the edge. Jarry looked down as he paddled. They were skimming over the flared wooden bread pan of a wagon, its rusted hoops bare of any cover. In the wagon were boxes and tools and wheels. At the front of the wagon, the bare bones of horses or mules lay collapsed inside the forks of their yokes.

"It's a damn shame there are no bodies," Swing T said. "The trainers must have escaped somehow. Pictures with bodies in them would have brought a lot more money."

"Who would publish things like that?"

"Publish? No. Such things are too good for the crowds. A few select clients, you know? They pay most for death and sex, all the staples. But, I've never seen a sight like this before, and we should be paid pretty good." He picked up a boot that Increase Bonner had filled with lead, and tied a rope to it. "Here goes anchor," he said. "Get your box on."

Jarry settled the glass box over his head, and tied the rawhide beneath his chin. His breathing sounded raw in his ears. Swing T tied a thin rope around Jarry's waist. "One pull means you're going to push the rubber button on the count of three. When you feel the air going bad in the box, give two pulls and I will bring you up quick."

Jarry nodded, and walked to the edge of the raft. He looked down in the water, at the small wagon train fifteen feet below. He had to walk to the far corner, but he found an open spot, just to the side of the lead wagon. He shook his head to check the tightness of the laces, then stepped off the raft.

Even under the desert sun, the water was cold enough to paralyze Jarry's diaphragm, and stop his breathing. He heard nothing but the pounding of his heart beating against the inside of his ears. He floated slowly downward, his head lagging behind. The buoyancy of the box stretched his spine, like one of the doctors who used to come through Providence now and then, to crack necks and roll hot glass balls in insteps. Half way to the pool floor Jarry managed to force an exhale, and his breathing roared inside the box. He took two more ragged breaths before his stocking feet felt the touch of the coarse sand on the pool bottom. Jarry stood a minute, learning how to balance himself in his horseshoes and looking around him.

Jarry had pushed off hard from the raft and his momentum carried him farther past the wagon than he had planned. Swing T had said that he had to be within a dozen feet of the wagon for the flash to be strong enough to light the shot. Jarry walked toward the wagon. He was surprised at how the underwater landscape looked. It looked no different than the rest of the territory. There were the same rock falls, the same hard pans of bare stone and settlings of gritty sand; the sparse seaweed looked almost identical to the spiky yucca and scraggly cactus of the desert above; the fish, except for a single yellow one that flashed past his face, were the size and color of the flocks of birds that lingered about Hugo. Jarry lifted the first camera box out of the white canvas bag and aimed it at the wagon. He saw that he was still too far away, so began moving again toward it. When he was some ten feet from the wagon he wanted to shoot, he stopped and lifted the camera.

When Jarry held the camera to his eye the view blurred. Except for the surface in front of the lens, the plates Swing T had used to make the camera and breath box were all exposed but spoiled. The smears of chemicals, the stiff costumed townsfolk who looked to be sweeping off to the right like the hands of a fast clock, made it difficult to see detail on the wagon. But he knew he was aimed correctly. And he knew that if he tried to look up, his breath boxes would tip and fill with water, so he had to trust that Swing T would have his flash powder ready. Jarry tugged on the rope then quickly returned his hand to the camera, and began his count of three. Just past two the water was flooded with crisp white starlight and a low boom like the bass drum of a far off marching band. Jarry pushed the rubber button. As he loaded the spent camera into the second bag, metallic ashes, like black snowflakes, drifted down all around him.

Jarry walked toward the front of the wagon, tipping forward against the resistance of the water.

He stopped when he had a clear view of the clutter of bones that had once been a draught animal lying between the forks of the wooden forks. He took out a second camera, and again gave a sharp tug. Again there was the starry flash overhead and the throaty bass noise. Putting the camera away, Jarry made the effort to walk some distance in front of the first wagon, to get a new vista. When he turned and looked back the curve of the wagons, their trough-shaped bodies and bonnet-curve hoops looked like the collapsed body of some animal who had died at the bottom of the pool. He aimed the third camera and pulled the rope. The starlight came again, and the black snow settled over the dead spine.

Or was it dead? Was its tail twitching? It looked to Jarry like something at the rear of the wagon train was switching, waggling like a catfish, and stirring up silt. Squinting, he walked toward the movement, leaning comfortably against the cushion of the water, enjoying himself. *This is how dreams are supposed to be,* Jarry thought as he walked. His own dreams were never calm, he never felt so buoyant in them; they were always swift and dirty and confusing, with people he didn't know always bustling and talking too fast about things he couldn't understand. But plays and books and church women always said that dreams were like this, slow and flowing, the ultimate destination just ahead, always in sight. His dreams had always seemed poor ones. *Maybe I'm having someone else's dream.* Jarry laughed, and the laugh was loud in the glass box. Then he had a short moment of clarity, one just long enough to realize that he was being poisoned by his own breath. He remembered to give the rope two hard yanks, and then laid back as his body began to rise, the bags tied at his waist tipping him backward. Water swirled into the tilted box and the shot of cold on his neck had him struggling to right himself. Then his glass box broke the surface.

Swing T was too frightened to pull him over the edge, so Jarry had to drag himself out. He sat panting on the edge, the glass box again more a block than a bubble, and caught his breath. The raft was littered with ash and burned wood; tiny pieces of burned metal pricked Jarry's hands as he leaned back on them.

"You all right, Jarry?"

"Just needed a flushing of the air, that's all."

"I thought you might get four shots in, but I guess three's going to be about it. So, another long shoot, then a short one, and we're done, on our way to the bank."

Jarry looked around and through the wet glass could make out only a dark shape, shaggy and almost shapeless. He pried the knot out of the laces and lifted the box off his head.

Swing T stood near the center of the raft, taking the used cameras out of the white bag and stowing them in an empty keg. He was wrapped in the buffalo pelt, with a length of rope tied around his waist to keep it from slipping down.

"What?" was all Jarry could manage, and he pointed.

"This? A protection vest. You didn't think I was going to just stand on this raft and let those explosions throw fire and sparks all over me, did you?" He lifted a piece of the pelt from his shoulder and held it across his face so that it was completely covered.

The iron on his feet seemed to be tugging Jarry to slide back in, and he really had no answer to Swing T's question.

"Here's your unused cameras back, now let's go." Swing T had moved close to Jarry, and Jarry knew he could topple the photographer off into the water. If that robe got wet it would carry Swing T straight to the bottom, supply the dead body Swing T missed having in the wagon train. But he wasn't a killer. He lifted the glass box back onto his head and retied the straps. He saw then that he had put it on backward to the way he had worn it the first time. Two inches before his eyes, steady in a sea of smeared emulsion, he could make out the pierced breasts of a woman lying on a bank of sand.

"Good," Swing T said, and he moved back behind the low wall of pans for his flash fires. Jarry rolled his shoulders once against the tightness gripping his neck, and slipped off the raft. This time there was nothing dream-like about the descent, it was just falling.

Jarry worked more quickly this time, and had four more of the cameras used before he felt the warm whirling start at the back of his skull. He gave two tugs on the rope and held his hands close to his side. The rope stayed slack. Jarry gave two more quick tugs, but there was no tightening of the rope. Something had gone wrong. Quickly, Jarry bent and untied the horseshoes from his stockinged feet. With the weight of his soaked clothes, he had to kick toward the sunlight. He began to rise, but too slowly, so he dropped the bag with the unused camera, and kicked toward the surface. Raising his eyes as high as he could without tipping the box, Jarry could make out Swing T's buffalo robe near the edge of the raft. Then there was a flash, an explosion that slapped against Jarry through the yard of water still above him. Jarry tipped backward, and water rose in the box until it covered his lips. He righted himself in the water, and kicked harder this time, again there was the looming buffalo robe and the hard white of the explosion, the boom and the concussion. This one was so strong that it broke one of the panes and water rushed into Jarry's face.

Jarry kicked away from the raft then and surfaced ten feet away. He slid the last pieces of the glass box off his head and looked back at the raft. Swing T cracked some glass plates and began tossing flat shards toward him. They skipped over the water like stones thrown by children, and one of them sliced a long line down Jarry's cheek. Behind Jarry the pool washed up against a sheer rock face. The only open shore where he might climb out was on the other side of Swing T.

Now the photographer was swinging something over his head like a sling. Just as he released it, Jarry saw that it was the lead-filled boot that had been their anchor. The boot sailed through the air trailing the rope behind it, and it came down with a splash and struck Jarry at the base of the throat. The pain spread out like a star, shocking his arms into immobility. He slid backward, turned half around, and slipped under the water.

Jarry didn't know if he was holding his breath or if the blow had crushed his windpipe, but no water flowed into his lungs as he floated slowly downward. He was very close to the rockface and the stripes of the strata were like ties on a railroad track he was following. His heart would begin pounding soon, he knew. Swing T with his deadly lights would still be waiting overhead, but it was better than drowning. He began to kick and moved toward the surface with the scrambling moves of a man climbing a rock face.

As his face broke the surface of pool, a long shadow passed between him and the glaring sun. Another boot, Jarry thought, but he couldn't go back under. His shoulders rose and he covered his head at the sound of a crash and a scream. With water still burning his nose, Jarry jerked his head around to see who had screamed. It was Swing T, his splintered raft swirling away in pieces, as he kicked helplessly, trying to keep his head above water. Then another shadow passed and landed between Jarry and Swing T. A sudden swell rolled over Jarry's head and he held his breath. When he could see again Swing T was gone, and the swell was slapping broken logs against the far edge of the pool.

Then the sky began to fall. Enormous shapes, bulky dark things that bellowed like tortured souls as they wheeled slowly in the air, began crashing into the water, tossing spray a dozen feet in the air, sending more swells washing over Jarry. Bison, falling from above, some landing in the water, some landing on the rocky shore with terrifying cries and yard-wide sprays of blood. And Jarry could hear shouts, the whoops of Indians as they hunted meat in their traditional way.

The animals were falling all around Jarry now, and he watched them as they fell. In motion, in the flying wind of their falls, with the reddened thin light playing over them, they glowed like copper, burnished and beautiful against the big blue sky, the true deep Western smelt running off the cliff in heavy dollops. Jarry's heart was pounding so fast that everything else seemed to have slowed to a lazy crawl. Even gravity seemed to have slowed, seemed to be cushioning the falls of the big animals. The spray and waves from their falls seemed to wash over Jarry's head in slow motion, and the big black-brown shape that cast the dark circle over him moved toward him so slowly that he could see the fear in the big brown eye, could even see his own accepting expression for the space of a single long heartbeat. He felt the stubby horn pierce his throat and wondered if it would pin him to the sandy bottom, but even that long wasn't long enough for him to find out.

Chapter 16

WHEN Dolley walked out the front door of the Royal Hotel, there were no more than a half dozen hands still standing around. Her skin tingled as the cool air moved over her bare arms and legs. She saw the midwife who had dried Hart's eye standing at the bottom of the steps. The woman's mouth moved but no sound came out. Dolley walked down to her.

"I'm innocent, Mrs.," Dolley said.

The midwife found her voice. "You look it. You're dressed almost the way they are when I bring them into the world." The woman blushed, but she smiled.

A black shadow fell across Dolley's bare shoulders. It was Houston's coat, and he settled it around her.

"Good day, Dolley."

"A good day to you, too. But I don't need your coat." She lifted it off her shoulders and held it out to him. "I'm not cold," she said, and she began walking. Houston draped his coat over his arm and fell into step beside her.

"Dolley, I wasn't thinking of the cold so much—"

"So much as the shame? The midwife says I look innocent, Mr. Houston."

"Innocent?"

"Like a babe fresh born."

Houston nodded. "Well, that may be. But, as a less-than-inno-cent man, I'd feel more comfortable if you'd allow me to add a little to your wardrobe."

"If you feel you must." She leaned her head forward, expecting Houston to drape his coat over her shoulders again.

Instead, he took something out of his vest pocket. He reached toward the left side of her face, and slid her long-lost tortoise shell comb into her hair. Her scalp tingled, the tines sliding along the sen-sitive skin on her temple, until he snugged it just above her ear.

"And what else do you think I need?"

Houston looked her up and down, slowly. "Maybe one end of a pair of Chinese handcuffs."

Dolley smiled.

"Other than that, nothing at all."

"And what plans do you have for today, Mr. Houston?"

Houston pushed out his lower lip, shook his head. "None at all," he said.

"Good," Dolley said, and she offered him her arm.

Photo: Aja Bamberger

W.C. Bamberger is the author of five previous books of criticism and fiction, including *Riding Some Kind of Unusual Skull Sleigh: On the Arts of Don Van Vliet* and the short story collection *A Jealousy for Aesop.* He is currently writing a biography of perceptual theorist Adelbert Ames, Jr., and a new novel. He is editor and publisher of Bamberger Books, and lives in Whitmore Lake, Michigan, with his daughter.